A Heiner Müller Reader

PAJ Books

Bonnie Marranca and Gautam Dasgupta

SERIES EDITORS

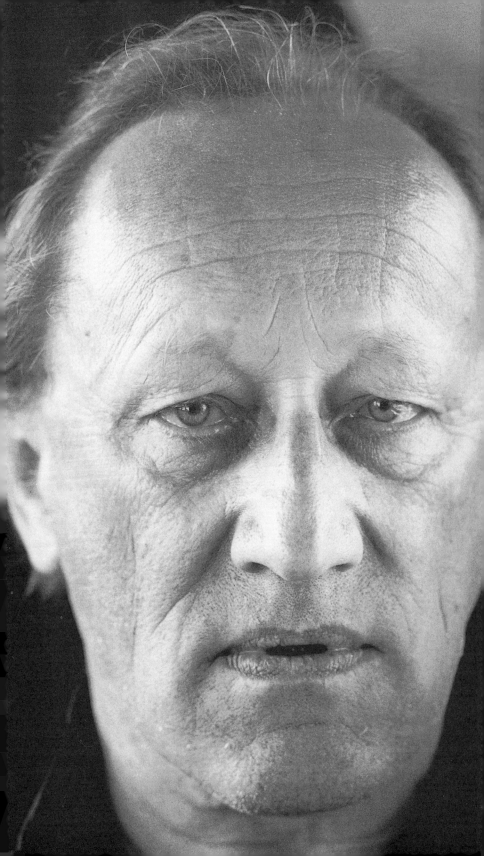

A Heiner Müller Reader

PLAYS | POETRY | PROSE

Edited and Translated by

CARL WEBER

A **PAJ** BOOK

The Johns Hopkins University Press
BALTIMORE AND LONDON

New material ©2001 The Johns Hopkins University Press
All rights reserved. Published 2001
Printed in the United States of America on acid-free paper
2   4   6   8   9   7   5   3   1

The Johns Hopkins University Press
2715 North Charles Street
Baltimore, Maryland 21218-4363
www.press.jhu.edu

To lease performance rights, contact The Marton Agency, 1 Union
Square West, Room 612, New York, New York, 10003-3303.

Library of Congress Cataloging-in-Publication Data will be found
at the end of this book.

A catalog record for this book is available from the British Library.

ISBN 0-8018-6577-8
ISBN 0-8018-6578-6 (pbk.)

Frontispiece photograph of Heiner Müller by Brigitte Maria Mayer,
reprinted by her permission.

CONTENTS

FOREWORD

Love is the great theme of the American theater, love's insufficiencies and betrayals, its dire necessity, its irreconcilability to the present economic and social order, perhaps its irreconcilability to Western concepts of justice. Love is the hiding place of the idea of human connectedness, of communality, of solidarity, of the social and of socialism, of utopia, of whatever you chose to call the antithesis of capitalism. Though we dare not speak of community, we may speak of love between individuals; in human bonds of affection we place all our hope. Our political leaders assure us that human affection will prove sufficient to mitigate against the miseries of life in an unjust, unequal, merciless non-society; our conservative playwrights endorse this dubious assurance, while our more progressive playwrights offer skepticism, and complaint. But we all speak a lot about love, and sing about it, and locate in love the only plausible, attainable shelter from the savagery we expect from life, from other people. Love is what breaches the great fortress of the immured and fetishized and lonely Individual, and so love for us is our hope and our terror and The Problem To Be Addressed.

Heiner Müller says in an interview that love is the perfect metaphor for false consciousness. Müller has the German intellectual's coldness, the mistrust of sentiment, the shrewd suspicion that love is invoked to cover up a variety of appalling crimes. The type of relationship explored most frequently in his work is that of the murderer to the murdered, or that of the murderer to the state; and his treatments of sexual and romantic relationship are usually nakedly about power and terror. These are the crowded, dense, prodigiously eloquent and even prolix plays of a great writer of silence and aloneness. Behind the question mark at the end of a question hides a great dread of isolation, Müller writes; eschew punctuation, he advises, write into the void, learn to embrace isolation, in which we may commence undistractedly our dreadful but all-important dialogue with the dead. Forget about love, writes this most a-social of socialists, and turn your face to History.

Karl Marx made his signal contribution, according to the French Marxist Louis Althusser, as a discoverer: he opened up for further exploration the Continent of History. Marx broke with the long line of grand narrative historians and philosophers of history who preceded him, to treat history not as a single-file line forward-moving towards an end but rather as a space, a spacious albeit bloody place, a topography, a terrain of human consciousness in which human consciousness is resident. History, after Marx, having entered into this new world, traversing this vastness, meanders and corkscrews and loops back on itself. The orderly historical procession disassembles; the pageant figures of Past, Present, and Future drift out of their fixed marching order, crowd in upon one another, lose sight of one another, disappear, reappear, looming out of the hazy air unexpectedly, uncannily, as specters, as nightmares, as uneasy ghosts of the unhappy dead. History is no longer themes and variations ranged sequentially, following reliable laws of cause and effect, no longer the neatly detailed chapters of a magisterially logical book. After Marx, we understand ourselves to be not readers merely but subjects, characters, actors in the text we are reading; after Marx, the book is transformed into a field, a platform: Marx stages the text of history, history becomes a playing space, a stage.

And here are the plays for history's theater: the work of Heiner Müller. They lack everything that makes conventional, American (and for that matter, British) attempts at staging history so delectable and enjoyable, and finally so often useless, or worse. So much of what we stage when we stage history is an elaborately costumed reassurance that we have improved upon that which we now recognize as barbaric; or, from the conservative side, that nothing has changed or can be changed. History in the plays of Heiner Müller is not time gone by but rather frighteningly present, as a sort of hallucination, an ineluctable fever dream from which the present cannot be awakened or rescued. History is the corpse rising out of the hastily dug pit. History lingers as a poison vapor in the present air, we draw it into our lungs with every breath.

Müller's plays frustrate comprehension, following rules and laws of motion of an infinitely expanding complexity and contradiction. Instead of lessons they offer harsh graveside-and-battlefield grief without the relief of lamentation. Instead of catharsis and tears they offer ruthless dissection, investigation, a fearless and unforgiving intelligence. There's no nostalgia here: the past was dreadful, the present is worse, and past and present are engaged in a conspiracy to murder the future. The attentive reader/spectator of these plays is likely to feel miserably complicit, as he or she is meant to feel, though accusations are never leveled. No theater is more difficult, more apparently indifferent to an audience's expectations, than Müller's. From this difficulty and indifference comes some of the richest and deepest pleasure modern theater affords.

There are, scattered throughout the plays of Müller, a number of remarkable stories, or rather incidents and situations; but these are starved of elaborating detail, not shaped into tasty, decodable parables or allegories, offering none of the usual campfire comforts of tales well-told, no brisk, invigorating action. Narrative and sequence are constructed, if they are to be constructed (for some of Müller's plays have an entirely vertical, vertiginous structure, and nothing *happens*) only with hard work from the audience; and nothing blatantly directive, nothing of closure, is provided. Every ending, when there is an ending, feels abrupt, or worse, jerry-rigged, a con.

The plays are mostly situated in a kind of hideous tension between thought and action, in whatever one might call the interstitial place between increments of time, between one second and the next: time, history, stopped, frozen, the sort of drama which does not invite easy breathing, at the conclusion of which one is likely to discover that one has been holding one's breath.

Americans are, famously, hope addicts, frantic for a fix to stave off the despair which, repressed, threatens always an explosive, destructive return. Müller says one must learn to live without hope or despair, and these extraordinary plays seem, as Beckett's do, to accomplish that: despair is made mock of in the vigorous beauty of the poetry, in the great diabolic fun of the dialectics, by means of which the drowning of hope in the blood of the culpable and of the innocent (often indistinguishable) is staged.

Lenin wrote that politics begins with the masses, with the millions—the politics of revolution. I assume that the stern mandate of this politics is one of the sources of Müller's modernist classicism, of the faceless, effaced prototypes and archetypes with which his stage is populated. There's a chilling brutality to this effacement, as well as a bracing rejection of the solace and distraction "personality" provides. On one hand, the largeness of the author's gesture, the size of these characters, their capacity to contain multitudes of misdeeds and tragedies, serve to make the plays civic, political, public: these are the texts of a theater of intensely useful, entirely public political debate. One reads Müller as, for the past half-century, politically engaged people have read Brecht. Müller's work has that immediacy, that wisdom, that imbedded desire to participate fully in the critical arguments of the times—another playwright of the lost republic writing resistance in the age of the Emperors.

On the other hand, that which is classical and classically revolutionary in Müller is also that which seems to express most powerfully a well-earned horror at the very idea of politics, at least of the politics of revolution. Having lived through Hitler and Ulbricht and the tawdry tragicomedy of Honecker and the advent of the New World Order; having lived long enough to write that "THE GREAT OCTOBER OF THE WORKING CLASS . . . was a summer storm in the World Bank's shadow"; having created *Gundling's Life* and *The Task, Mauser* and *Germania 3,* having combed through so much of European literature and philosophy and history to deepen and darken his dialogue with the dead; having made of Benjamin's grieving, backwards-facing but nevertheless forward-moving angel of history the paralyzed victim of a cave-in, ensnared, immobilized by history's rubble, as Müller does at the conclusion of *The God of Happiness*; having shattered the Stalinist left's silence on the matter to become the great poet of The Great Terror, of the human cost of change, of the Janus-facedness of revolution, Müller never abandons the idea of revolution—but he sees no alternatives to the bloodbaths and mass graves, and the spiritual decimation, the automatonization of the human, that are revolution's concomitant (if history is to be believed). That which is implicit in Brecht's *Lehrstück* metaphor, in which death is made to signify human transformation, becomes in Müller explicit: human transformation in history is often a signal for mass slaughter.

That Müller insists upon the bloodiness of historical progress, if progress it is, earns him our admiration. That he does not, as a consequence, advocate that we should endeavor to stop history in its tracks makes him both a progressive and perhaps every progressive's nightmare. That he does not dream of other ways of being revolutionary makes him, as he clearly intends to be, tough and daunting—for some palates, entirely indigestible.

He seems, for example, almost completely uninterested in the movement towards a politics of race or gender or in any liberation movements, nor, it hardly needs be said, in human or civil rights or any rights or liberties at all—I would imagine Müller agreeing with Pasolini that liberalism and its political institutions are merely fascism in slow motion. Those evolutionary/revolutionary movements which have transformed American social and political life—and which seem always to be in danger of being absorbed by America's largely untransformed economic life (which has, in fact, been radically deregulated, a kind of liberation movement for multinational corporations)—these movements have had global impact, inspiring resistance in oppressed peoples around the world, but were apparently felt by the playwright to have been unworthy of his public consideration. Apart from the decimated postindustrial, postnatural landscapes in which his dramas are set and the apocalyptic imagery which runs through all his plays, which bespeak a sharp awareness of the toxification of the planet (unsurprising from a citizen of the ecologically despoiled GDR), green movements—or any current form of political engagement, really—are not Müller's subject. By focusing with such absolute specificity on German and European culture and history, Müller runs the risk of being charged, and indeed *has* been charged, with being Eurocentric and politically irrelevant.

It is incontrovertibly the case that Müller sidesteps the problem of representing effectively on stage successful political movements by addressing almost exclusively the bloody dilemmas of modern German history, which offers almost nothing in the way of redemptive example. But the time has long since passed for a play of exhortatory example like *The Mother,* and dumb Kattrin's martyrdom cannot suffice to account for or offer redemptive possibility to a time so full of holocaust as the twentieth century was and the current one threatens to be. As Schiller and Benjamin and Müller have written, history moves dialectically through tragedy after tragedy. The use of the negative example may be the only recourse for a political dramatist, which I take Müller to be, his protestations to the contrary notwithstanding. Müller's heroism, his engagement, if you will, in movements such as environmentalism, feminism, and Third World anticolonialist insurgencies may be located in his steadfast refusal to strive for an exculpatory relevance for which he was not positioned and is not entitled. He denies himself the mask of the victim, of the oppressed, and ruthlessly identifies himself as speaking from within the crumbling temple of power. His heroism may lie in *not* representing the Other, which would risk transforming the Other into a creature of a condemned, haunted imagination, transforming the future of the Other into that nightmare through which Europe has suffered. Müller's heroism may consist in his writing Europe's deservedly splendid epitaph, in detailing the rituals by which the dead finally, successfully might be buried. "Europe stands surrounded by

Africa and Asia with its back to the hole in the ozone layer." (Like Brecht, Müller is marvelously quotable, a great coiner of epigrams.) In this anthology one may read, as an instance of this sort of heroism, his dream/nightmare, in which he warns his infant daughter to abandon him to drowning. The dream is certainly among the most moving texts in the collection, a rare reference to the existence of children, and to heartbreak.

Certainly the most immediately striking fact of Müller's dramaturgy, of all of his dramatic texts, is that they were written intentionally to resist production, to make of their production an act of appropriation. When one first encounters Müller's plays one worries how they "should" be done, one searches in vain for the key to their staging, assuming that the author has hidden such a key in the text or that it may be uncovered through some sort of anthropological investigation. Research, and learning, is required; but ultimately, familiarity with the plays' referents and antecedents will not reveal *how* they are to be staged. Eventually any theater artists intent on doing Müller's work will find themselves faced with a heady and alarming freedom, for the key to the staging must, to a far greater degree with Müller's plays than with any other major body of dramatic work, be invented upon the occasion—by the historically informed, politically engaged imaginations of those doing the staging. For all of the playwright's formidable erudition and his texts' cultural specificity, for all of their implosive privacy (Müller was revolution's postmodern antipositivist psychoanalyst), these works possess a remarkable openness, they bear witness to a remarkable faith on Müller's part in the collaborative processes of the theater. It is through form as much as content that Müller achieves a universal relevance, and meaning. He has engineered his own ceaseless remaking by everyone who comes after him, by every Other who still has theater, or history, to make.

Carl Weber's heroism consists in forging a presence for this great writer in America, through the translation and publication of Müller's work in American versions of a marvelously generative difficulty and complexity. Mr. Weber deserves our unending gratitude for having made so much of Müller's work available to non-German-speaking readers and audiences, a task to which he has devoted himself for several decades. This is not to say, alas, that many American readers or audiences are familiar with Müller. He remains disgracefully overlooked. This isn't a particularly propitious time in American intellectual, political, or theatrical life for the appearance of an anthology of Müller's writings. Market pressures and a general abandonment of the ideal of theater as a civic, and civically supported, enterprise have pushed our theaters toward the vulgar, the thoughtless, the reactionary, and farther and farther away from intellectual and political engagement, and from serious art. But the dark times only make the publication of this anthology all the more timely, and necessary.

Largely through the medium of interviews, as well as by the example of the plays, Müller continued the Brechtian tradition of theorizing extensively about the practice, meaning, and importance of the theater; and if he failed to synthesize a revolutionary theater praxis, as Brecht almost succeeded in doing, Müller manages to be spectacularly, salutarily provocative. He reminds theater practitioners and their audiences of the productive tensions between the text and the staged event. He exhorts us to recognize the shaping influence of money on our content and our forms. He urges us to "do what we cannot do," to transcend—there is more of utopia in Müller's discussion of theater practice than there is in the inferno of his plays.

In precise parsings of moments of consciousness, Müller locates vast historical events. The beads of sweat on a conqueror's or a murderer's brow he reveals to be distillations of sea changes and oceans of blood. He explores history as it exists in the secret hearts of human beings, wanderers in the continent of history. He sees the excruciating intimacy between the private unconscious life of human beings and their public relationships, psyche and politics constituting a unity in which neither becomes indistinct nor has primacy over the other, reminding us, as we must always be reminded, that we both make and are made by history. In his writings you will find that which is repellant, unfathomable, false, and absurd. You will, in short, find our times, recorded more unflinchingly than almost anywhere else. You will find truth, summoned up out of the ashes and mud, and you will find remarkable wit, intelligence, and beauty: the world, in short, as only the greatest dramatists are capable of describing it.

TONY KUSHNER

ACKNOWLEDGMENTS

I would like to thank Heiner Müller for his suggestions and help in the early phase of working on this book; I'd also like to thank Brigitte Maria Mayer for her support and the photo she graciously made available. Special thanks go to Bonnie Marranca and Gautam Dasgupta who, at PAJ Books, have published five volumes of my translations, those of Müller as well as of other authors, and whose firm belief in the importance of bringing Müller's work to America has never flagged during twenty years. I want to thank Tony Kushner for his longstanding interest in Müller's writings and this project in particular, for his generous advice, and for the splendid essay he contributed. Thanks go also to Matthew Griffin for translating two of the included texts and writing their introductions. Finally, I'd like to thank my wife, Marianne Rossi, whose understanding and admiration for Heiner's work never ceased to encourage my efforts.

HEINER MÜLLER
Writing out of the Past toward the Future

It was in late February of 1995, at Fisherman's Wharf in San Francisco, that Heiner Müller and I talked about a fourth volume of his writings in translation. We discussed texts written during the previous decade, in which we had witnessed the implosion of socialism, the unification of Germany, the disintegration of the Soviet Union, the relapse of Yugoslavia into tribal warfare, and the establishment of a global market. The very last morning of the same year, I got the call from Berlin: Heiner had died the previous night, December 30. It was sudden and a shock. Yet, it was not unexpected. He had been struggling with cancer since 1994 and had just returned to Berlin after receiving chemotherapy treatment at a Munich hospital. His weakened immune system succumbed to an attack of pneumonia. Rushed to a hospital, he died on arrival. He had been appointed the artistic director of the Berliner Ensemble shortly after I had seen him in San Francisco and was planning to stage a new play of his at Brecht's former theater. Rehearsals were to begin in January of 1996. The play's final version—after the revisions he surely would have made during rehearsal—was to be included in the new volume and provide its title, *Germania 3*. (The text was eventually premiered at the Bochum Theater and appeared shortly thereafter on the Ensemble's stage, in May of 1996.) Heiner's exit called for a reassessment of the book's contents.

It appeared to be time now for a survey of Heiner's thought and practice as a writer and man of the theater. And so, this volume will present writings which range from Müller's earliest work to some of the last texts he completed, including most of those we had discussed for the book that would follow the three previous selections, *The Battle, Hamletmachine,* and *Explosion of a Memory,* which were published between 1984 and 1989 by PAJ Books. A few texts from the earlier volumes have been included in revised versions and with updated introductions, texts which represent significant stages in Heiner's thinking and viewing of himself and history.

This anthology traces the multifaceted evolution of Müller the playwright, poet, and eloquent observer of his century's violent trajectory. He watched its progress at close quarters, from the belly of the beast, so to speak—a privilege or a curse, depending on the observer's point of view. He himself considered it a writer's advantage: a life in three political systems, under two dictatorships, and during two wars, the second one a "war without battle," as Müller titled the autobiography he published in the early nineties. During most of his life two mutually hostile sociopolitical systems confronted each other, a global divide that had become manifest in the Berlin Wall. Müller saw this crude edifice also as a symbol of German history, a history marked by fraternal warfare since the first decade of the first millennium, when the nation's legendary forefather, Arminius, fought his brother in the ranks of the Roman invaders.

The Berlin Wall stood for twenty-eight years, almost half of Müller's lifetime. When it was torn down and the Germans became one nation again, he seemed to have lost the basis for his writing, or so he ruminated in his text *Mommsen's Block*. But soon he began to assess the new world order and to take a decidedly dim view of an unfettered global market. He often expressed his observations in a strikingly detached manner, grim and serene at the same time. The awareness of death closing in on him may well have contributed to his stance. Throughout his life, he didn't cease to write about the prospects he perceived when considering the future of humankind and the earth it inhabits, although his vantage point kept changing over the years. In equal measure he was exploring the troubled history of Western civilization, a past where every advance brought new horrors along with its gains. As he liked to remind us, there is a majority of the dead and in their absence they are present and force us to live with their legacy—for better or worse.

Müller did not deviate far from the path he began to pursue in the early 1950s. Although he took many detours and sometimes seemed to reverse his tracks, it is evident that his early views were shaping much of the later work. He first articulated his vision in a text of 1958, *The Hapless Angel,* a re-vision of Walter Benjamin's interpretation of a Paul Klee drawing, *The Angel of History.* In this brief text he expressed a profoundly ambiguous notion of history's progress, a notion which might be defined as joining utopia and dystopia in a dialectical clinch. Müller always maintained that he detested despair as much as mindless hope. "Without hope / without despair / for the next half century," he wrote in 1986.

This volume traces the arc of Heiner Müller's work, from the short stories and the many poems of the early 1950s to his last texts written in 1995, among them *Germania 3*. Included is a sample of the early plays about the arduous forging of an East German socialist society. Several texts explore the violent history of the Germans and the precarious role forced upon artists and intellectuals in their dealing with political power. Other writings dissect the fierce dialectics which impacted the communist revolution as much as any other revolutionary process, or they confront us with the crucible that looms larger with every year that the gap separating the world's rich from its poor increases. There are also examples of Müller's appropriation of Greek mythology, which he mined for metaphors and comments of his own century's history. Aside from the plays, the poetry (whose central role in Müller's oeuvre has only recently been fully recognized), and the prose texts, this selection presents a number of dialogues, the genre Müller increasingly employed during the eighties and nineties to explain his thoughts about contemporary topics. They revive a literary form which originated in classical Greece and had been dear to Diderot and Brecht. Müller articulated here, by way of many examples, his understanding that history represents a perennial pattern of injustice which humans inflict on other humans. Finally, there are "dream texts," recordings of dreams that he either devised as independent prose pieces or inserted into performance texts, where they disrupt and distance the dramatic narrative. They strikingly confirm Müller's conviction that a text knows more than its author did.

The range of topics Müller explored and the multitude of literary models he experimented with have hardly been matched by another author in our postmodern age. Besides and beyond the issues he addressed, the mastery with which he played on genre and form make his writings exemplars for writers to come. Yet, as he once said about Brecht, "to use his works without criticizing them is tantamount to treason." Müller would be the first to agree that this advice also applies to the texts he has left us. We should approach them in this, his own, spirit of critical respect. In using them we will take their measure against the trials the future has in store for us. Time will show which of his texts will stand the test and continue to speak to readers and spectators in years to come. Many may do so in the immediate future; others, like Müller *Hapless Angel*, may be buried and gain force again when the times are ready to listen to their voice.

Müller regarded the writer's task as one which must separate the work from the author's personal life, even as it is forged from that life's experience. Inasmuch as he explored the predicament of the individual in the turmoil of history, he clearly articulated his recognition of the individual's evanescence during the century he witnessed. And so he elected to preface his autobiography with a haiku-like poem:

Shall I talk of me I who
of whom do they talk when
they talk of me I who is that

C.W.

A Heiner Müller Reader

ABC

A Collage of Poetry and Prose

ABC is a collection of poetry and prose mostly written during the early fifties. *The Father* was written in 1958. *Alone with These Bodies, Yesterday on a Sunny Afternoon,* and *Obituary* in 1975–76. Several of them had been printed in literary journals or books between 1956 and 1977, the year Müller combined these texts with hitherto unpublished poems, prose, and a short play for the collected works edition published by Rotbuch Verlag. *ABC* appeared in *Germania Tod in Berlin,* Rotbuch Verlag, Berlin, 1977.

In their carefully composed sequence, the texts may be read in many ways, for instance, as a free rendering of Heiner Müller's biography from 1933 to 1976, which reflects on historical and personal events, as well as the author's spontaneous or studied responses to them. They also may be viewed as a "catalogue of gestures," representing many of the recurrent topics in Müller's writing. Some pieces eventually were made into stage texts: *The Iron Cross* became Scene 3 of *The Battle; Schotterbeck* reappeared in the scene "The Brothers 2" in *Germania Death in Berlin;* the text "The peasants stood with their backs . . ." contains the core of *Mauser.* Aspects of *The Father* and *Obituary* surface again in many of his later writings. Pervading all these texts are the themes of treason and violence-in-service-of-ideology, both central to Müller's work.

ABC provides occasion to study Müller's casting of his topics in a variety of literary forms. Experimentation with structure and genre is done not merely to discover the most appropriate form for a given content, a rather traditional approach, but to capture various angles from which the content might be approached and thus evoke the multiple and often contradictory insights such re-visioning entails.

Most of the texts reflect on history, from the Thirty Years War (*Grobianus*) to the "Real Existing Socialism," as the ruling Socialist Unity Party (SED) of the former East German Republic used to define her socioeconomic system. Others deal with traumatic personal experiences. The brief paragraph "The peasants stood with their backs . . . " refers to an incident in the Russian Civil War of 1919–20. The poem *A Hundred Steps* retells an episode from Daniel Defoe's *A Journal of the Plague Year. Schotterbeck* describes an incident in an East German penitentiary during the uprising of June 1953. *Philoctetes 1950* revisits Homer's tale; during the sixties Müller wrote a free adaptation of the Sophocles drama and also a ballet scenario of the same title. *The Voyage* is the only adaptation from the Japanese No theater Müller has published; he studied the ancient tradition during the fifties when he was evolving his own model of the *Lehrstück,* in the footsteps of Brecht who had been influenced by the Japanese form some twenty years earlier. In its entirety *ABC* might be viewed as a collage, a sample of the "synthetic fragment" as Müller called the new theatrical model he explored during the seventies.

C.W.

DON'T LAUGH BUT IF A TOWN HAS PERISHED
(Grobianus)
I WANT TO BE A GERMAN
(Entry in the exercise book of an eleven-year-old Jewish boy in
the Warsaw Ghetto)
THE TERROR OF WHICH I WRITE ISN'T FROM GERMANY
IT IS A TERROR OF THE SOUL
(Edgar Allan Poe)
THE TERROR I WRITE OF IS FROM GERMANY

AND BETWEEN ABC AND TWO TIMES TWO
We pissed whistling at the school house wall
The teacher whispered through his teeth
DON'T YOU FEEL ANY SHAME We didn't.

When night did fall we climbed the tree
From which at dawn they cut the dead. Empty
Stood his tree now. We said: THAT WAS HIM.
WHERE ARE THE OTHERS? BETWEEN BRANCH AND GROUND IS
    SPACE.

The Iron Cross

In April 1945, a stationer at Stargard in Mecklenburg decided to shoot his wife, his fourteen-year-old daughter, and himself. He had heard from customers about Hitler's wedding and suicide.

A reserve corps officer in World War One, he still owned a revolver and two rounds of ammunition.

When his wife brought in the dinner from the kitchen, he stood at the table and cleaned his gun. He had pinned the Iron Cross to his lapel, as he usually did only on national holidays.

The Führer had chosen suicide, he stated in reply to her question, and he'd be loyal to him. If she, his wedded wife, would be ready to follow him in this, too? He wouldn't doubt that his daughter preferred an honorable death from her father's hand to a life without honor.

He called her. She didn't disappoint him.

Without waiting for his wife's answer, he asked both to put on their coats, since he was going to lead them to a suitable place outside of town, to avoid drawing any attention. They obeyed. He then loaded the revolver, had the daughter help him into his coat, locked the apartment, and threw the key through the slit of the mailbox.

It was raining as they walked through the blacked-out streets and out of town, the man in front, without ever looking back at the women who followed at some distance. He heard their steps on the pavement.

After he had left the road and taken the path to the beech grove, he turned to them and urged them to hurry. Because of the night wind that blew with increasing force across the treeless plain, their steps made no noise on the rain-drenched ground.

He yelled to them that they should walk ahead. Following them, he didn't know: was he afraid they could run away or did he himself wish to run. It didn't take long and they were far ahead. When he couldn't see them any longer, he realized that he was much too afraid to simply run away and he very much wished they would do so. He stopped and passed his water. He carried the revolver in the pocket of his pants, he felt it cold through the thin fabric. As he walked faster to catch up with the women, the weapon bumped against his leg with each step. He walked more slowly. But when he reached into the pocket to throw the revolver away, he saw his wife and daughter. They stood in the middle of the path and waited for him.

He had intended to do it in the grove but the danger that the shots would be heard wasn't any greater here. When he took the revolver in his hand and released the safety catch, the wife embraced him, sobbing. She was heavy and he had difficulty in shaking her off. He stepped up to the daughter, who stared at him, pressed the revolver against her temple and pulled the trigger with his eyes closed. He had hoped the gun wouldn't fire but he heard the shot and saw how the girl reeled and fell.

The wife trembled and screamed. He had to hold her. Only after the third shot was she still.

He was alone.

There was no one who ordered him to put the revolver's muzzle against his own temple. The dead didn't see him; no one saw him.

He pocketed the revolver and bent down to his daughter. Then he began to run.

He ran all the way back to the road and then down the road, though not in the direction of the town but westward. Then he sat down at the roadside, his back against a tree, and considered his situation, breathing heavily. He discovered there was some hope.

He had only to keep running, always to the west, and avoid the nearest villages. Somewhere he could then disappear, more so in a larger city, under another name, an unknown refugee, ordinary and hard-working.

He threw the revolver in the roadside ditch and got up.

As he was walking he remembered that he had forgotten to throw away the Iron Cross. He did it.

The peasants stood with their backs to the quarry. He looked at the peasants, the peasants looked at him. Their eyes were wide with fear, then narrow with hate, then wide again, then narrow again. He looked at their hands: they were worn-out, then at his own worn-out hand that was sweating. He said the often said phrase louder than usual: FIRE AT THE ENEMIES OF THE REVOLUTION and he fired first. The volley scattered the three bodies down the grassy slope into the quarry.

A Hundred Steps
(After Defoe)

In the century of the Plague
A man lived in Bow, north of London
A boatman, without means nor distinction, but
Loyal to his family. Prudent too
In his loyalty.
From the towns downriver
Where the Plague was
He hauled food upriver
To the well-to-do, fearful
On their ships
Midstream.
Thus the pestilence nourished him.
But in the hut
With his wife and the four-year-old
The Plague was too.
And every night he hauled a sack with provisions
Fruit of a day's work, up from the river to a stone a hundred steps
　　from the hut.
Then, retreating, he called the wife. Watching
How she picked up the sack, observing closely each of her movements
He stood for a while
In the safe distance
And returned her greeting.

SCHOTTERBECK when he, on a June morning in 1953, collapsed with a sigh of relief under the blows of those who were in prison with him, heard in the noise of the approaching tanks outside, muffled by the thick Prussian walls of his prison, the tune of the International, never to be forgotten.

Philoctetes 1950

Philoctetes, in his hands the bow of Heracles,
    sick with
Leprosy, marooned on Lemnos island, empty
    without him,
By the princes with few provisions, he didn't
    show any
Pride but screamed till the boat disappeared, not held back by
    his scream.
And got accustomed, the island's ruler but also
    its slave
Chained to it with the chains of the waters around it,
    of weeds
He lived and of game, sufficient to him for more than
    nine years.
But in the tenth ineffectual year of the war
    the princes
Remembered the man they abandoned. How he handled the bow,
    from afar
Deadly. And boats they sent forth that should carry home
    the hero
That he'd adorn them with glory. But he showed himself then
    from his
Proudest side. With violence they had to drag him aboard
To satisfy his pride. Thus he made up for
    past failure.

The Voyage
(After Motekiyo)

KAGEKIYO. HITOMARU. WOODCUTTER. CHORUS.

1

HITOMARU: Kagekiyo went to battle for Heike. Heike sent him into exile after the battle. He lives in Myazaki. I am not used to travel but I want to go to him. He is my father.

He is old.

(*Sings.*)

The voyage
Is hard.
I pass through the province of Sagami.
Totomi I leave behind me.
I cross the bay in a narrow rented boat.
When will I be in Myazaki?

2

KAGEKIYO: Here in Myazaki I spend my life, under the thatched roof. I, Kagekiyo, the exile who went to battle for Heike. Blind, not knowing the passing of time. My property: one coat for summer and winter. My body: a bundle of bones.

CHORUS:

See the feared one
See the bundle of bones!
His sword is broken.
His sword
Has broken him.

HITOMARU: Here in Myazaki I will ask for my father. (*To Kagekiyo.*) Where is Kagekiyo living, the exile who went to battle for Heike?

KAGEKIYO: (*Remains silent.*)

HITOMARU: (*Walks on.*)

KAGEKIYO: This woman is my daughter. I loved her mother in Atsuta. I found the child of no use and gave her away.

3

HITOMARU: Where is Kagekiyo living, the exile who went to battle for Heike?

WOODCUTTER: Under the thatched roof.

HITOMARU: The beggar?

WOODCUTTER: Yes.

4

WOODCUTTER: Hey, Kagekiyo!

KAGEKIYO: I am an old piece of iron, of no use. Who is Kagekiyo?

CHORUS:
  The exile
  Ponders the time when he was famous and bloody.
  The blood is still on his hand.
  Where is his fame?

KAGEKIYO: Wind is coming from the mountain. Snow is coming behind the wind. I hear how high tide is assaulting the beach. I heard it when I went into battle for Heike and after the battle. Who is asking for Kagekiyo?

WOODCUTTER: Who are you?

HITOMARU: Hitomaru, daughter of Kagekiyo, who for Heike . . .

WOODCUTTER: Your daughter is asking for you.

KAGEKIYO: I am covered with scurf and shame. She is young.

HITOMARU: The voyage was hard. Rain in Sagami, in Totomi snow. Across the bay in a rented boat.

KAGEKIYO: (*Sings.*)
  In the boats of the men from Heike's crew
  Loudly acclaimed above others was Kagekiyo.
  Courageous were his men, fast when sailing.
  Now the leader himself is
  worn out.

WOODCUTTER: (*Sits on the ground, eats.*) Tell her the story.

5

KAGEKIYO: Heike's crew came on boats. The foe stood at the shore. He had beaten us in the mountains of Harima. He was smart and fast. Kagekiyo went ashore with Heike's men and the enemy fell upon them. Kagekiyo drove them before him, friend and foe alike. He sang:
  Our general doesn't like the other general's nose.
  But he likes his rice paddies well. Run, you dogs!

WOODCUTTER: (*To Hitomaru.*) They were dogs before him. Now he can't lift a leg anymore.

KAGEKIYO: Kagekiyo brandished the spear. Terrible is your arm, Myonoya
    screamed. Tough is your neck, Kagekiyo shouted. They laughed after
    the battle. That was Kagekiyo.

WOODCUTTER: The brandisher of spears.

CHORUS:
    The exile has told his story. The daughter
    Is silent.
    Shall she leave him whom no one helps at the end
    of his career?
    Shall she stay with him whose cheeks won't be
    filled by the blood he once shed?

The Father

A dead father would perhaps
Have been a better father. Best
Is a stillborn father.
Always anew grass grows over the border.
The grass must be torn up
Again and again as it grows over the border.

1

In 1933, January 31 at 4 a.m., my father, a functionary of the Social Democratic Party of Germany, was arrested from his bed. I woke up, the sky outside the window black, noise of voices and footsteps. In the next room, books were thrown to the floor. I heard my father's voice, higher than the other voices. I climbed out of bed and went to the door. Through a crack I saw how a man was hitting my father in the face. Freezing, the cover pulled up to the chin, I lay in bed when the door to my room opened. My father stood in the door, behind him the strangers, big, in brown uniforms. There were three of them. One held the door open with his hand. The light was in my father's back, I couldn't see his face. I heard him softly call my name. I didn't answer and lay very still. Then my father said: He's asleep. The door was closed. I heard how they led him away, then the short step of my mother who came back alone.

2

My friends, sons of a low-ranking official, explained to me after my father's arrest that they weren't allowed to play with me anymore. It was on a morning, snow was lying in the roadside ditches, there was a cold wind. I found my friends inside the tool shed in the backyard, sitting on wood blocks. They played with tin soldiers. Outside the door I had heard how they imitated the roar of cannons. When I entered they became silent and looked at each other. Then they continued playing. They placed the tin soldiers in battle arrays facing each other and took turns rolling marbles toward the enemy front. While doing so, they imitated the roar of cannon. They addressed each other as Herr General and called out triumphantly the casualties after each charge. The soldiers were dying like flies. The war was fought for a pudding. Eventually, one of the generals had no soldiers left, all his army was flat on the floor. This decided the contest. The soldiers killed in action, friend and foe pell mell, were thrown into the cardboard box, along with the one survivor. The generals got up. They would have breakfast now, said the winner and, passing me, he added that I couldn't come along, they weren't allowed to play with me anymore, my father being a criminal. My mother had told me who the criminals were. But also, that it wasn't good to name them. So I didn't tell my friends. They learned it twelve years later, sent into the fire by great generals, under the roar of countless real cannons during the terrible last battles of World War II, killing and being killed.

3

One year after my father's arrest, my mother received permission to visit him in the camp. We took a narrow gauge railway to its last station. The road climbed uphill in curves, it passed a sawmill with the smell of freshly cut timber. On the flat top of the mountain the path to the camp branched off. The fields alongside the path were fallow. Then we stood in front of the wide gate with its meshed wire until they brought my father. Looking through the wire mesh, I saw him approaching on the camp road covered with gravel. The closer he came the slower he walked. The convict's garb was too large for him, consequently he looked very small. The gate wasn't opened. He couldn't touch our hands through the narrow wire mesh. I had to step very close to the gate to see his thin face completely. He was very pale. I can't remember what was said. Behind my father stood the armed guard with a round, rosy face.

I wish my father were a shark
Who tore to pieces forty whalers
(And in their blood I had learned to swim)
My mother a blue whale my name Lautréamont
Died in Paris 1871 unknown

4

Because she was a woman, my mother didn't get work. She accepted the offer of a manufacturer who had been a member of the Social Democratic Party until 1932. I was allowed to share lunch at his table. So every noon I pushed my weight against the iron gate in front of my benefactor's house, walked up the wide stone stairs to the first floor, pressed with some hesitation the white bell button, was led by a maid in a white apron to the dining room and placed by the manufacturer's wife at the large table, beneath a painting that depicted a collapsing stag and the dogs which were falling upon him. Surrounded by the massive figures of my hosts, I ate without looking up. They were kind to me, asked about my father, presented me with sweets, and permitted me to stroke their dog: he was fat and stank. Only once I had to eat in the kitchen when guests who resented my presence were coming. When I pushed my weight for the last time against the iron gate until it gave way with creaking hinges, it was raining. I heard the rain coming down as I climbed the stone stairs. The husband wasn't sitting at the table. He had gone hunting. They served potato dumplings with boiled beef and horseradish. While I was eating I heard the rain. The last piece of the potato dumplings fell in two halves off my fork on the carpet. The wife noticed it and looked at me. In the same moment I heard the noise of a car on the street, then, in front of the house, braking and a scream. I saw how the wife went to the window and rushed from the room. I ran to the window. In the street, next to his car, stood the manufacturer in front of the woman he had run over. As I stepped from the room into the hall, two workers carried her in and laid her on the floor; I could see her face, the distorted mouth, the blood running from it. Then another worker entered with the hunter's booty, hares and partridges, which he also laid on the floor with enough distance from the bleeding woman. I felt how the horseradish was coming up from my stomach. There was blood on the stone stairs. I hadn't even reached the iron gate when I threw up.

5

My father was released with the stipulation never to show himself again in his home county. That was in winter 1934. A two-hour walk outside our village, we waited for him on the open road that was covered with snow. My mother carried a bundle under her arm, his overcoat. He came, kissed me and my mother, put on the overcoat and walked the road back through the snow, hunched as if the coat were too heavy for him. We stood on the road and looked at his back. One could see vary far in the cold air. I was five years old.

6

Since my father was without employment, my mother worked again as a seamstress. The factory was two walking hours away from the village where we had a room and an attic. The house belonged to my father's parents. Once, my mother took me along into town, to the savings bank. At a window she paid three marks. The man at the window smiled down at me and said now I would be a rich man. Then he gave the savings book to my mother. She showed me my name on the first page. As we left I saw how a man next to us stuffed into his coat pocket a fat wad of banknotes. My grandmother stood at the stove in the kitchen when I showed her the savings book. She read the amount and laughed. Three marks, she said, and threw a big piece of butter into the frying pan. She put the pan on the stove. Yes, I said, and watched the butter melt. She cut off a second, smaller piece of butter and added it. Since my father was against Hitler, I'd have to eat margarine. She took potatoes from a pot, sliced them and dropped them into the sizzling fat. A squirt got onto the savings book I held in my hand. She wouldn't eat margarine, she said and: Hitler is giving us butter. She had five sons. The three younger ones were killed at the Volga River, in Hitler's war for oil and wheat. I was present when she received the first death notice. I heard her scream.

7

When Hitler ordered the autobahn system to be constructed, compositions about the great project had to be written in German schools. Prizes were offered for the best ones. I told this to my father when I returned from school. He said: You don't need a prize, but two hours later: You should make an effort. He stood at the stove, threw an egg into the pan, then, already with some hesitation, a second one, and finally, after looking at it and holding it in his hand for quite a while, the third one. This will make a good meal, he said. We ate and my father said: You must write you are glad Hitler is building the autobahn. Then my father, too, will surely get work again, he who was unemployed for such a long time. You must write that. After our meal, he helped me to write the composition in this manner. Then I went to play.

8

Thirteen years later, we were living in a market town in Mecklenburg; a baroness was sitting at our table, widow of a general who had been executed after the abortive assassination attempt on Hitler July 20, 1944, and she implored my father, the functionary of the newly founded Social Democratic party, to help her against the land reform. He promised to help.

9

In 1951, my father crossed Potsdam Square into the American sector of Berlin to disengage himself from the war of the classes. My mother had accompanied him to Berlin, I was alone in the apartment. I was sitting next to the bookshelf reading poetry. It rained outside; while I was reading I heard the rain. I put the poetry volume down, put on a jacket and overcoat, locked the apartment door and walked through the rain to the other end of town. I discovered a tavern with a dance hall. I heard the noise from afar. When I stood at the door of the dance hall, a break was announced. So I stepped into the bar. At one of the smaller tables a woman was sitting alone, drinking beer. I sat down with her and ordered booze. We drank. After the fourth drink I touched her breast and said she had beautiful hair. Since she smiled obligingly, I ordered more booze. Next door in the dance hall the music started again, the percussion was booming, saxophones bawling, violins squealing. I pressed teeth and lips on the woman's mouth. Then I paid the check. When we stepped into the street, the rain had stopped. The moon stood white in the sky and diffused a cold light. We walked all the way in silence. A rigid smile was on the woman's face while she undressed without further ado beside the double bed in my parents' bedroom. After intercourse, I gave her cigarettes or chocolate as a present. My merely polite question: When shall we meet again? she answered with: If you please, and nearly bowed to me, or rather to the position she believed my father still to be in. He found his peace years later, in a small town in Badenia where he paid out pensions to murderers of workers and to widows of murderers of workers.

10

I saw him for the last time in the isolation ward of a hospital in Charlottenburg. I took the el train to Charlottenburg, walked down a wide street, passing ruins and tree trunks, was led at the hospital through a long bright hallway to the glass door of the isolation ward. A bell was rung. Behind the glass a nurse appeared, nodded silently when I asked for my father, walked down a long corridor and disappeared in one of the last rooms. Then my father came. He looked small in his striped pajamas which were too large for him. His slippers were dragging on the floor tiles. We stood there, the glass between us, and looked at each other. His thin face was pale. We had to raise our voices when we talked. He rattled at the locked door and called the nurse. She came, shook her head and went again. He let his arms drop, looked at me through the glass, and was silent. I heard a child screaming in one of the sickrooms. When I left, I saw him standing behind the glass door and waving. He looked old in the light that came through the large window at the end of the hallway. The train moved fast, passing rubble and construction sites. Outside was the iron gray light of a day in October.

ALONE WITH THESE BODIES
States Utopias
Grass grows
On the railway tracks
The words putrefy
On the paper
The eyes of women
Grow colder
Goodbye from tomorrow
STATUS QUO

E. L.

You came like a princess across the sea
Blown to Denmark on your flight from Danzig
On a transport, by submarines chased and visited by bombers.
It was like a sacrilege when you
Put on glasses next to me at the movies.

Trees growing wild Roots in the riverbank's mud
Rushes green

HIS LORDSHIP
BEGS TO BE EXCUSED he'll take the early train
With Schiller you know at least when it's over

TILL SOON both know it will be never

EXCUSE ME MADAM*

*In English in the original.

YESTERDAY ON A SUNNY AFTERNOON
When I drove through the dead city of Berlin
Returned from some foreign country
I felt for the first time the desire
To exhume my wife from her graveyard
Two shovels full I threw on her myself
And to look for what is left of her
Bones which I have never seen
To hold her skull in my hand
And to imagine what her face was like
Behind the masks she had worn
Through the dead city of Berlin and other cities
When it was clothed with her flesh.

I didn't yield to my desire
Afraid of the police and the gossip of my friends.

Obituary

She was dead when I came home. She lay in the kitchen on the tile floor, half on her belly, half on the side, one leg bent as if asleep, the head close to the door. I stooped, lifted her face out of its profile position and uttered the word I called her when we were alone. I had the feeling that I was playacting. I saw myself leaning against the door frame, partly bored, partly amused, watching a man who at three in the morning was crouched on the tile floor in his kitchen, bent over his perhaps unconscious, perhaps dead wife, who held her head in his hands and talked to her as if she was a doll for no other audience but myself. Her face was a grimace, the upper row of teeth crooked in the gaping mouth as if the jaw had been dislocated. As I lifted her up, I heard something like a groan that seemed to come rather from her guts than from her mouth, in any case from afar. I had already seen her frequently lying there as if dead when I came home and lifted her up with fear (hope) that she was dead, and the horrible sound was reassuring, an answer. Later the physician enlightened me: a kind of belch, caused by shifting her position, a remnant of breathing air, of gas squeezed from the lungs. Or something like that. I carried her to the bedroom, she was heavier than usual, naked under the housecoat. When I lowered my burden on the couch, dentures fell from her mouth. They must have come loose during the agony. Now I knew what had distorted her face. I hadn't known that she wore dentures. I went back to the kitchen and switched off the gas stove, then after a look at her empty face I picked up the telephone, thinking, receiver in hand, about my life with the dead woman, viz., about the various deaths she had sought and missed for thirteen years until today's successful night. She had tried it with a razor blade: when she was finished with one of her arteries, she called me, showed me the blood. With a rope after she locked the door but, out of hope or absent-mindedness, left open a window that could be reached from the roof. With mercury from a thermometer that she had broken for this purpose. With pills. With gas. She wanted to jump from the window or the balcony only when I was in the apartment. I called a friend, I still didn't want to acknowledge that she was dead and a matter for the authorities, then the emergency number. ARE YOU OUT OF YOUR MIND EXTINGUISH IMMEDIATELY YOUR CIGARETTE DEAD ARE YOU SURE YES FOR TWO HOURS AT LEAST ALCOHOL THE HEART DIDN'T YOU NOTICE THAT YOUR WIFE WHERE IS THE LETTER WHAT LETTER DIDN'T SHE LEAVE A LETTER WHERE WERE YOU FROM WHEN TO

WHEN TOMORROW NINE A.M. ROOM TWENTY-THREE A SUMMONS THE CORPSE WILL BE PICKED UP AUTOPSY DON'T WORRY YOU WON'T SEE A THING. Waiting for the ambulance, a dead woman in the next room. The irreversibility of time. Time of the murderer: the present erased within the brackets of past and future. Going into the next room (three times), looking at the dead woman ONE LAST TIME (three times), she is naked under the blanket. Growing indifference to ThatThere with which my feelings (Pain Grief Desire) have nothing to do any more. Pulling the blanket again over the body (three times) that will be cut open tomorrow, over the empty face. At the third time, the first traces of poisoning: blue. Back to the waiting room (three times). My first thought of my own death (there is no other), at the small house in Saxony, in the tiny attic I slept in, three low floors up, I five or six years old, alone around midnight on the inevitable chamber pot, moon in the window.
HE WHO HELD THE CAT UNDER THE KNIVES OF HIS PLAYMATES
    WAS I
I THREW THE SEVENTH STONE AT THE SWALLOW'S NEST AND THE
    SEVENTH
STONE WAS THE ONE THAT HIT IT
I HEARD THE DOGS BARK IN THE VILLAGE WHEN THE MOON
    STOOD
WHITE IN THE ATTIC WINDOW ASLEEP
I WAS A HUNTER HUNTED BY WOLVES WITH WOLVES ALONE
BEFORE FALLING ASLEEP SOMETIMES IN THEIR STABLES I HEARD
    THE HORSES SCREAM.
The feeling of the universe during the night march on a railway embankment in Mecklenburg, in boots too tight and uniform too large: the resounding emptiness. CHICKENFACE. Somewhere on the way through the postwar world he had attached himself to me, a skinny figure in a flapping army coat that dragged on the ground after him, an oversize fatigue cap on the much too small bird's head, the haversack dangling at his knees, a child in field gray. He trotted at my side, silent, I can't remember that he said one single word, only when I walked faster, even ran to get rid of him, he uttered small plaintive sounds between wheezing gasps. A couple of times I believed that I had lost him once and for all, he was merely a dot in the plains far behind me, then even that no more; but during the dark hours he gained on me and at the latest when I woke up, in a barn or in the open, he was lying next to me, muffled in his torn coat, the bird's head near to my knees, and when I succeeded in getting up and leaving before

he was awake, I soon heard behind me his plaintive panting. I reviled him. He stood before me, looked gratefully at me with watery dog's eyes. I don't remember any more if I spit into his face. I couldn't hit him: you don't hit a chicken. Never had I felt such a fervent desire to kill a human being. I stabbed him with the bayonet that he had dug from the recesses of his army coat to share his last tin of corned beef with me, I was the first to eat so I didn't have to taste his spittle, thrust the bayonet between his pointed shoulder blades before it was his turn, saw without regrets his blood glisten on the grass. That was at a railway embankment after I had kicked him so he would take another direction. I slew him with his infantry spade as he just had heaped a mound to protect us against the wind that blew across the plain where we had to spend the night. He didn't resist when I snatched the spade from his hand, even when he saw the blade coming down at him he didn't manage a scream. He must have expected it. He only raised his hands above his head. With relief I watched in the quickly falling darkness how a mask of black blood blotted out the chickenface. On a sunny Mayday, I pushed him off a bridge that had been blown up. I had let him walk first, he didn't look back, one push at his back was enough; the blasted gap was sixty feet wide, the bridge high enough for a fatal fall, below there was concrete. I watched his trajectory, the coat bulging like a sail, the rudder of the empty haversack, the deadly landing. Then I traversed the blasted gap: I only needed to spread my arms, borne by the air like an angel. He doesn't have a place in my dreams any more since I have killed him (three times). DREAM I walk in an old house overgrown with trees, the walls busted and held by trees, up a staircase, above which a giant woman naked with huge breasts, arms and legs spread wide apart, is suspended with ropes. (Perhaps she sustains herself in this position without any fastening: levitating.) Above me the enormous thighs, open like a pair of scissors, which I enter further with each step, the black wild bushy pubic hair, the rawness of the labia.

Report on Grandfather
A Short Story

Report on Grandfather (*Bericht vom Grossvater*) was written in 1950 and first published in the playbill for the production of Heiner Müller's play *The Resettled Woman, or Life in the Country* (*Die Umsiedlerin, oder Das Leben auf dem Lande*) at the student theater of the College of Economy, Berlin-Karlshorst, in 1961. The production was canceled after one performance for reason of "grave ideological errors." Heiner Müller was consequently expelled from the East German Writers Association. When the West Berlin Rotbuch Verlag began to publish his works, the text appeared in the first volume, *Geschichten aus der Produktion I,* Rotbuch Verlag, Berlin, 1974.

This short story is among the earliest literary texts Müller put on paper. The narrative encapsulates within one lifetime the history of a large part of the German working class during the first half of the twentieth century. Their political choices contributed to the failure of the German revolution of 1918, to the rise and twelve-year reign of Hitler and, after World War II, to the end of the Germany they grew up in. Left behind in the wake of the century's violent history, many failed to comprehend the social upheavals that kept changing the political landscape of Europe throughout their lives. The text reveals the attitude that shaped Müller's thinking and writing during the early years of his career. Forty years later, in his autobiography, *War without Battle,* the author took a more compassionate view of his grandfather. "These generations were cheated of their life . . . For a goal that was an illusion . . . I would like to talk with him now, to apologize for the story."

C.W.

In July nights when gravity is weak
And his graveyard overflows its walls
The dead cobbler comes to visit me
The grandfather, the much beaten old man

My grandfather died when I was seventeen. My mother said of him: he was never ill, but his brains weren't quite right anymore at the end. Today, five years later, I know what wasn't right there.

His father died early. For the funeral of the dead breadwinner—the place beneath the ground doesn't come free—a cabinet had to be sold, an heirloom. The mother, alone with the child, spent a decade at the sewing machine, sewing shirts in poor light, so by the tenth year she at first couldn't see the eye of the needle, then the half-finished shirt and, finally, not even the light. The doctor recommended an operation but didn't bring along the money for it. So the operation couldn't be done. My grandfather took care of the blind woman, as of a child, until his fourteenth year. Then she died.

During his apprenticeship with a shoemaker he worked for a pittance, suffered hunger which he was used to, and was beaten: his master, turned into stone by an apprenticeship of a similar kind, handed down his experience. The beaten boy learned how to put up with the beatings, at best how to beat also, but not how to beat in the right direction. He wasn't a capable person. He didn't even become a master since you had to pay a fee for the examination. He became a worker in a shoe factory.

Twenty years old, he married. His wife was the daughter of a rich farmer, yet she didn't bring any dowry since the farmer was against the marriage beneath her class. He who had learned early the art of hunger was a good instructor for his wife, and she learned well. They had ten children. Two died early, eight they could bring up. My mother, when conversation turns to her childhood, likes to tell the parable of the salt herring. It's hanging at a long string way down from the ceiling. It always has to last for a week. Only on pay day is it renewed. Three times a day the procession of eaters—"one bite for each one"—marches by.

After the shoe factory went bankrupt during World War I, my grandfather found work with a bridge construction company. After an accident at work, a fall from the scaffolding onto the stony, nearly parched river bed, he was fired. Three more workers fell from the same scaffolding, one after another. Two were fired, the third one died on the spot. The two went to sue: the construction company had saved on the wood for the scaffolding and was sentenced to pay. As for the dead man, he was shown to have been negligent. My grandfather, invited also to sue, said: I don't want trouble. Even twenty years after the accident his back pain increased when the weather changed. He then used to say: there is a good side to everything. For him, everything had its good side. Forced to eat dry bread, you learned to appreciate it; out of work you had time to go for mushrooms in the forest; doing piece work, you had no time for thoughts which only made you restless; when there was war, everybody had less. (Those tables that were more richly laid weren't shown to him, he wouldn't have seen them anyway, even had they been shown to him.)

He was on friendly terms with his "betters." Better—that meant: not a worker. The employers of the town, all of them popular, liked to show themselves in the streets talking to the common people, especially to the elder ones.

During the troubled times after 1918 when in Saxony the workers were also fighting for a better life, he repaired the shoes of those on strike as well as those of the scabs, of the traitors along with the fighters, cheaper than anyone else. His shop was a corner of the kitchen. At that time he also started to go along to church when his wife asked him to, though he didn't care for it.

After the children were on their own, he drank on Saturdays. It was cheap for him since he couldn't tolerate it.

He wasn't for Hitler. When it became dangerous not to be for Hitler, he said if something went against his grain: Hitler doesn't know it; and when my father went to jail the second time because he couldn't put up with the new order: why didn't he shut up, you need to shut up, that's what they demand. I still remember that I, eight years old, one day during my vacation with him, hammered a good dozen nails into the floor. When my grandfather came in, he pulled them out, tried to hammer them straight again but didn't say a word. At that time iron was in demand again for the bigger flying nails, meant to strike through living hide, not the tanned one; plain nails were scarce.

After World War II, during the first months of hardship, the inconceivable happened; my grandfather, all his life a patient beast of burden, lost his patience as his life ran out. His wife's letters to my mother voiced the fear of God who might punish the man. She wrote that he was sinning against Him. She renounced him so that she wouldn't be punished with him. There was nothing contemptible in this: to her hell was real. My mother's siblings thought the incident was rather funny. The oldest one wrote: Father—it has to be said—isn't quite together anymore. Therefore he thinks only of himself. As if he is alone in this world. For instance, he took it into his head that he wants butter. But when butter was available, he only ate margarine. It's ludicrous. He's like a child. He simply doesn't believe her that she can't get butter for her money, he says she doesn't want to, she's stingy, she begrudges him everything. Mother suffers from it. He scolds her, he never used to do that. And he used to be so modest.

I always was a good worker, he often said at that time, so I ought to be well-off today, in the worker's state. He didn't understand that patience was needed to eliminate the consequences of patience. Too many had endured too much for too long a time.

I still see him with his crinkled child's face, mindlessly content, later when his time was running out hardening into the sullen grimace of a clown who's taken off his make-up, him, my grandfather, a worker from Saxony, who died in 1946, seventy-five years old—impatient—of the consequences of patience.

The Correction
A Play

The Correction (*Die Korrektur*) was written in close collaboration with Inge Müller, the playwright's wife. Originally conceived as a radio play, in 1957, it was published in the literary journal *Neue Deutsche Literatur, #5,* 1958. The authors wrote it after having spent time at the construction site of the Black Pump, a large industrial complex for the mining and processing of lignite. As in the earlier play *The Scab (Der Lohndrücker),* the authors explore issues of the difficult reconstruction period in postwar East Germany. A preview of the stage version caused massive criticism of its "negative and depressive aspects." Müller published in reply a statement: "The author's self-critique has entered an executive phase: The Correction will be corrected." A revised version was staged in a double bill with *The Scab,* in September 1958, at the Maxim Gorki Theater, Berlin. For this production Müller added a prologue introducing the characters of the play. The conflicts of the protagonist, Bremer, are less foregrounded, and the positive role of the party is emphasized. The play ended with an "uplifting" epilogue spoken by the young Heinz B., who joins the party in the last scene. Altogether the dramaturgy follows a more conventional pattern.

Heiner Müller insisted that the original radio version be used for the translation. He told me that while writing it he worked on a play to be called *Death of a Foreman.* The title alludes, of course, to Arthur Miller's

Death of a Salesman, an indication that Müller had been thinking of a tragic ending.

The Correction, like *The Scab,* is representative of Müller's early work for the stage. It shows the strong influence Brecht's model had on the young playwright but also first signs of an effort to re-vision the model.

C.W.

A report on the building of the industrial combine "Black Pump."

A Foreman

BREMER: Are you the secretary?

PARTY SECRETARY: Yes. What is it?

BREMER: My name is Bremer, I've been in the party since 1918, was in a concentration camp until '45, functionary until a week ago. The party ordered me to go into the field because I hit a Nazi in the face; he had a position with the National Front.[1] And now I am here at the combine.

PARTY SECRETARY: Good, Comrade Bremer. You'll work in section 6 as foreman. (*Pause.*) You're going to have problems. Socialism isn't built with socialists only, not here and not elsewhere, and here least of all. The combine is a construction site, not a model plant, and we have to build fast. Our industry needs electricity and coal, and it needs both fast. You won't make it if you don't stick with the party.

BREMER: You are the party here, right?

PARTY SECRETARY: The party has placed me here. You can criticize me when I make mistakes. That's what meetings are for. For that too.

Story of the Worker Franz K.

FRANZ K.: I am a construction worker, red since 1918, not as red anymore since '46. I've turned the Erzgebirge mountains upside down for Wismut.[2] Eight hours a day, in uninspected pits that could flood any day. Whoever didn't drown in the pit drowned in vodka. Whoever wasn't wiped out by the vodka was finished off by the women. It was hard to stay clear of them: of the pits, of the women, of the vodka. Now, things have improved: the pits are inspected and the women are married. I didn't break my back here at the combine. If management thinks it's going too slow why doesn't management visit us at the building site? Sometimes they send a dispatcher on a motorcycle. He arrives in a cloud of dust, makes a lot of noise, and disappears again in a cloud of dust before we can get a word in edgeways. But in the meetings they address us as "the working class." At least they could make sure that we have no waiting periods. We're waiting for blue prints. We're waiting for material. That pushes down wages. We know what we're worth

---

1. A coalition of several parties in the former GDR.
2. Soviet-owned company for the mining of uranium ore.

and do nothing without pay. Before we let them cheat us, we take care of our own ass first: wages rise faster than the walls, the wage curve faster than production. The foremen write the time sheets the way we need them and the supervisor closes both his eyes. It isn't his loss. Bremer was the first who didn't play ball. He kept repeating: That's fraud. Fraud is out of the question. He didn't play ball, not for the beatings he got, and not for the beer we offered him. He is red to the marrow.

The Swing of Norms

THE MAJOR: Get on the swing, foreman. On the swing of norms.

FRANZ K.: He is new. He knows from nothing. Show him the light, Major.

MAJOR: Now listen, foreman. You're new here and know from nothing. Here, this is the norm, established by one pushy bastard with six assistants, he got a bonus for it: a blatant injustice. It has to be adjusted. Corrected. What we don't make on the job we'll make on paper. The pencil is yours. You need only to compute, that's all.

HEINZ B.: That's the swing of norms.

(Laughter.)

FRANZ K.: The waiting periods push the wages down, we're pushing back. And the norm remains where it is.

FOREMAN: Fraud is out of the question.

MAJOR: I wouldn't call it fraud.

FOREMAN: What sort of a guy are you? Why do you call him Major?

FRANZ K.: He was a captain. We promoted him to major. He is a rat. But he is right about the norm.

FOREMAN: Actually, what are you working for?

HEINZ B.: For money.

(Laughter.)

FOREMAN: I know what I am working for.

FRANZ K.: So? You know that? (Sings.) The Pole gets the coal, the Czech gets the light . . . (Continues talking.) For that, right?

MAJOR: Write two hundred percent. We won't do it for less. We have our fixed price.

FOREMAN: On my sheet is written: hundred and twenty. Hundred and twenty is what we've done.

FRANZ K.: Right. And that's not enough. Therefore, we round it off and write two hundred.

FOREMAN: If you want to earn more, work more.

MAJOR: A proposal, foreman. One case of beer for an arithmetical error. Premium beer.

FOREMAN: I'll get you to Waldheim,[1] you rat.

MAJOR: What do you mean, Waldheim? We're deaf on that ear. But we do need the two hundred. If the beer won't do it, we'll talk plain language. Whoever isn't with us is against us.

FOREMAN: Fraud is out of the question. As long as I am foreman here.

MAJOR: Then go and apply for another job right away.

Story of the Engineer Martin E.

MARTIN E.: The combine is a construction site. When it's completed, the largest lignite combine in the world will be completed. Then we won't lack anymore the bituminous coal the Ruhr barons are sitting on. Whatever can be made from lignite we will make here: in briquet factories, power plants and carbonization plants. In the meantime, we're building, with new methods and with old ones. Here, a man sits at an instrument panel and controls a machine that replaces a hundred workers. Within a stone's throw, three men, sweating and badly paid, dig a trench with tools like the old Romans used them. Many a plant is administered by the method: My friend, the plan. That looks like this: The plant is in debt so we rename the plant; gone it is and so are the debts. After all, the plant is owned by the people, after all, it belongs to nobody, you can do with it as you please, the state will foot the bill. There are other stories the newspapers won't print. The one about the union boss in the women's dorm won't be printed either. That was in the early days: he had been assigned to watch so nothing happened to the women. Every night the colleagues climbed through the windows and that didn't help their job performance. Yet, he couldn't stay up all night. So he laid down to sleep among the women. When the secretary appointed another man to watch the watchman, he slept there too. That's class consciousness for you. Or the story of working in the forest with the girls from the Spremberg spinning mill. We had female help from a spinning mill to clear the site and, since it was midsummer, we called the HO[2] to deliver soda. The HO shipped us wine. The wine was swilled like soda. The girls were chased through the woods. The trees were not cut down. Those were the wild

---

1. Well-known penitentiary.
2. Handels Organisation: state-owned trade organization.

days. The forest is cleared now, the site is leveled. The first buildings are up: smokestacks, cooling towers, the steel frame of the assembly shops, foundations, and the satellite town for the workers is going up at Hoyerswerda. The landscape doesn't look like itself anymore. To rebuild humans takes more time. I know what's going on in the bars at night: The "gold diggers" who are always on the move hang out there. They always follow their nose. They smell money from a hundred miles. They "subscribe" to big building sites. Hardships only make them smirk. They earn a lot and drink even more, they go home and cuss as they pass the posters proclaiming Socialism, and in the morning they are at their job and build Socialism with a hangover. During meetings they abuse the front office engineers. The engineers listen. To rebuild humans takes time.

Regulations

ENGINEER C.: (*On the telephone.*) Construction office, engineer C, section 6, please, building management.—Listen, you've got to suspend work on the foundations immediately.—Until further notice.—Three days, two weeks, what do I know.—Pay attention, I'll tell you precisely what's happened. We received the blueprints for the bunker from central planning, as usual. There's been a mistake in one of the drawings.—No, nothing complicated, as far as we could determine. Easy to correct. But we can't do anything without talking to Berlin.—The blueprint has to go back, to be checked, discussed, and redrawn. We have to wait.—That's normal.—You need to deal with the workers.—Those guys have to wait too.—The plan? The plan has to wait too.—Won't work? How do you know what's going to work. (*Puts the receiver down.*)

ENGINEER E.: That won't do.

ENGINEER C.: What do you mean?

ENGINEER E.: I say it won't do. The plan cannot wait.

ENGINEER C.: (*Thinks it over.*) All right. Tell the project director the blueprints will be with the brigades by tomorrow at noon. We'll get them ready.

ENGINEER E.: It's against regulations.

ENGINEER C.: Yes. We have to take the risk.

ENGINEER E.: We won't be ready by noon.

ENGINEER C.: We still have the night. Tomorrow at noon the blueprints will be with the brigades.

ENGINEER R.: (*At the telephone.*) Construction office. Please, section 6, building management.

Story of the Worker Heinz B.

HEINZ B.: My father croaked in the coal pits of the Ruhr. My mother froze to death at the Ruhr, in the winter of '47, because I was in jail for stealing coal and couldn't filch coal anymore. Later I met a girl from East Germany. She told me there were jobs and so I went. We planned to marry, that takes money. That's how we came to the combine. She was a mechanic. She made a good salary, more than I did, and she got bonuses for outstanding work. After three months I noticed she was doing overtime at night too. Two bricklayers were beating each other up on the site. That's when it all came out. One of them had offered her twelve marks. He was a foreman, and she had told him: Fritz isn't a foreman and is paying thirteen; I won't let a foreman have it for less than fifteen. I asked her: What do I owe you, and can I pay in installments. I won't be able to make it in one installment, what with her scale. Now she is where I came from, in the West. She can't score there as a mechanic; as a whore yes. We had already picked an apartment, with bath and incinerator, at Hoyerswerda in those new developments. The building was ready, they had only forgotten the sewers. Else we would have moved in and I'd have thrown her down the incinerator chute. Shortly after, I quit at the VEB[1] because our foreman was an asshole. I said that too loudly and management got me by the tail. I got a job with a private firm. The workers were married to the company. I had sworn to myself I'd never marry. But the work clicked along: they didn't waste materials, the deadlines were kept. I asked myself: Why can't it be like that at the VEB? The boss said: We are one big family. That meant: overtime and no pay. I wasn't used to that. As he pats my back and says: I won't ask you what party you belong to, I ask him: Which one do you prefer, boss? He took that amiss. I left because of the overtime, back to the VEB. The new foreman was an eager beaver. The ditty "The foreman's pencil likes to hear / the clinking of a case of beer" didn't apply to him. We beat him up since we thought maybe he'd listen to that tune. He didn't hit back. He got up and wiped the blood off. He didn't play ball for anything. He said: "Fraud is out of the question. If you want to earn more, work more." Then, the major set him up in the tavern. He took Franz K.'s slide rule away and planted it in the foreman's pocket. It was supposed to look as if he had stolen it. A slide rule comes to about two marks, but the colleagues believed

---

1. Volks Eigener Betrieb: People-Owned Enterprise.

it, K. first of all. That really shook the foreman. Then the scandal with the foundation happened. It cracked because we didn't remix the concrete. You know what the problem is with the concrete: We get it from the mixing tower. That runs automatically and is the hottest new gimmick. But management lent the special trucks for transporting the concrete to another plant when we had a waiting period. We haven't seen them again. So, the concrete dries up during transport and we have to remix it. That takes time and our money. I said: It's too dry. It'll settle all right, said the major. The foreman doesn't let us earn what we need. We've got to look after our own ass. Time is money. Franz K. said: We already had to wait for the blueprints, and it's not the first time. Shall we lose money because the intelligentsia is late? Are we sitting on featherbeds? It doesn't have to go wrong, he said. That business about the blueprints is correct. Normally it's like this: everything is built in one piece, but only after the project is completely designed. The combine is delivered by the slice: One slice designing, one slice building. But we didn't remix the concrete. The foreman wasn't present. He controlled the casings in the adjoining section. After it happened he asked: What have you done? The major said: The same as usual. The foreman was responsible for our work. He got stuck with it.

Foundations

THE CHAIRMAN: The corner foundation of site 6 is cracking. It has to be ripped out and poured anew. Bremer's brigade was working there. They did poor work. It needs to be investigated.

A FEMALE WORKER: We demand that the accident on the railway tracks be investigated. A lines woman was run over at the intersection of tracks and main road. The truck didn't brake when she gave the stop signal, she had to jump aside onto the track and the train engine ran her over. She has four children and she's in the hospital now, both legs gone, she's dying because the truck driver was in a hurry.

A YOUNG WORKER: He's paid by the number of runs.

THE WOMAN: He kills by the number.

THE YOUNG WORKER: He sounded his horn.

THE WOMAN: He didn't stop.

A HOARSE MAN: If we always wait for you womenfolk we'll never manage.

THE WOMAN: I know you. We're the fifth wheel when your pennies are at stake. When you want to hump us you'll pay any price.

THE HOARSE MAN: I won't make you a child anymore, Prohaska.

THE WOMAN: I can make my children myself. I don't need you for it, you old goat. We demand that the accident be investigated.

FIRST WORKER: First the foundation.

THE WOMAN: We demand a hearing. We work like you do. That's a foundation too.

CHAIRMAN: We don't deny that. Your demand is justified, the accident will be investigated, the truck driver punished if it's clear that he is guilty. But one thing at a time, the most important first. You've got to understand that.

THE WOMAN: We're not important, are we? Why don't you pour us into your foundation with the concrete?

CHAIRMAN: Because we don't build this combine for the heck of it. We can't help your injured colleague if the doctors can't help her. We'll help her children if we build better and faster. So, first the foundation.

SECOND WORKER: Where are the children?

THE WOMAN: In the maternity home.

SECOND WORKER: Does she have a family?

THE WOMAN: No.

SECOND WORKER: So we've got to see what happens to the children now.

THIRD WORKER: We have another complaint here. A Sorbian[1] farmer complains that a truck carrying lumber took a shortcut across his beet field.

CHAIRMAN: Call him in. But he ought to make it brief.

(*A farmer enters.*)

THE FARMER: A truck from the combine drove across my beet field. I want damages. I have already lost three fields to your combine. The Russians gave them to me. You want them for your Socialism now, and your Socialism is driving trucks across my only beet field.

FIRST WORKER: Our Socialism listens to the name of Fritz Erpen. We've warned him twice before. His last job was with a circus. Fire eater. He's drinking his gas away. Then, he hasn't enough of it and needs to take short cuts.

CHAIRMAN: Is he here?

THE WORKER: No.

THE FARMER: I want damages.

THE HOARSE MAN: Don't steal our time. We've got more to do than to listen to your whining, Polack.

---

1. A Slavic minority in eastern Saxony.

THE FARMER: I am a Sorb.

THE HOARSE MAN: That's the same.

THE FARMER: Polack is what the SS used to call me. Now the word is Sorb.

THE HOARSE MAN: Two of your people are working with as at the bunker, Sorb. Who will pay us damages if they push up the norm for us because they want to butter up management? I know what's going on.

CHAIRMAN: We'd be ahead if you'd work half as much as your Sorbian colleagues.

THE FARMER: I'll be short of beets. I didn't set the quota.

CHAIRMAN: Get your damages from the main office. Whoever drives through your field will be fired. Anything else?

THE FARMER: I'll ram the pitchfork into his tires the next time. (*Exits.*)

CHAIRMAN: Now the foundation, Bremer, you are the foreman. You've poured the foundation. What do you have to say?

BREMER: We worked as usual. There must be a mistake in the drawing. That's what happens if the eggheads don't show their face on the site. If something goes wrong because they don't care, they blame the workers.

ENGINEER: I am the engineer who is responsible. I did the drawing. It is correct. You bet your life. It has been double-checked. I am not responsible for the execution. Who are you anyway? You are new here, aren't you?

BREMER: I did eight years in a concentration camp. You filled your bellies during those years and designed war planes for Hitler, as armament specialists. You've ruined everything and made a healthy bundle doing it. And now you're profiting from it. We have to rebuild what you have destroyed.

CHAIRMAN: Enough, Comrade Bremer. Stick to the facts: The foundation. The engineer is right. The drawing is correct. You are responsible for the execution.

BREMER: I don't trust anyone who worked for Hitler. And that's a fact.

ENGINEER: That is a defamation. Cooperation is impossible on this basis. I demand that this man be fired. (*Leaving.*) I won't put up with this.

VOICE: That's the last we saw of him.

CHAIRMAN: Comrade Bremer, you will apologize to the engineer. He can't leap out of his skin. He is giving us everything he has in his head. You have no right to insult him.

BREMER: I'd tear myself to pieces for Socialism. But I won't crawl into an engineer's behind.

CHAIRMAN: Not even for Socialism? Think about it, but fast. What is the matter with the foundation? (*Pause. Agitation.*)

HEINZ B.: Foreman, we didn't remix the concrete. That could have done it. The concrete dried up during transport because we've got no special trucks. We wanted to save time.

FRANZ K.: We already had to wait for the drawing.

CHAIRMAN: I see: Three weeks time was lost because you fought for the minute. Not to mention the expense. Bremer, what do you say now? You blame the engineer that he is costing money and doesn't care for the brigades. Your brigade committed sabotage and you were in charge. The foundation costs more than an engineer.

BREMER: That's no brigade, that's a bunch of crooks.

VOICE: You're a good foreman, only the brigade is good for nothing, right?

BREMER: In the concentration camp I knew why I was doing time. Now I know nothing anymore.

Story of the Party Secretary

PARTY SECRETARY: I came back to Germany from the Soviet Union late in '44, dropped by parachute into Pomerania on a party assignment. What I saw was worse than we had expected. Middle class women decked out with their husbands' conquests: dresses from Paris, furs from the East. Mothers who pushed their children into the army. Widows in proud mourning. And our comrades on death row. At that time I thought: we ought to hack off every hand that stirred for Hitler. Today I see how this combine is built, with such hands too. I read the transcript of the production meeting in which Bremer insulted an engineer. The engineer threatened to quit. Bremer refused to apologize. All his life he put his head on the line for the party but he couldn't get this into his head. I had to summon him. It wasn't easy for me. I could understand that he didn't understand what the party asked of him.

The Correction

PARTY SECRETARY: Bremer, the engineer is threatening to quit. We have to settle this mess. You've blamed him without justification. So, you have to apologize to him. I understand it's hard on you but it has to be done.

BREMER: So that's where we are now. I am wrong. Maybe the engineer did time in the concentration camp for the party, and I designed war planes for Hitler?

PARTY SECRETARY: You did time in the concentration camp for the party, the engineer designed war planes for Hitler. No one is questioning that. But we are building the combine. We need the engineer. You've failed as a foreman, you have offended him without reason, and the party demands that you settle this mess.

BREMER: So that's where we are now.

PARTY SECRETARY: We can afford to build Socialism even with people who don't care for Socialism. That's where we are now. We cannot do without them. We are not there yet. And when we get there it won't be necessary anymore because they will care for Socialism.

BREMER: Do you still know where is right and where is left? I fought on the barricades in 1918, on the right side: on the left. I still know where the enemy is.

PARTY SECRETARY: We don't need any barricades, Comrade Bremer, we need industrial combines. We have to work Capitalism to the wall. If you don't understand that you have understood nothing. We demand that you apologize.

BREMER: I won't make a fool of myself. The eggheads are laughing at us.

PARTY SECRETARY: They are working for us.

BREMER: They're paid for it, and more than enough.

PARTY SECRETARY: There aren't enough of them yet.

BREMER: So the party demands that I crawl on my belly before a bourgeois engineer.

PARTY SECRETARY: To correct your mistake.

Story of the Engineer Herbert C.

ENGINEER C.: It never happened to me before that a worker dared to challenge me like that. I always delivered clean work, correct even under trying circumstances like these. What happens on the building site is not my concern. I am an engineer. Two days after the production meeting about the botched foundation in section 6, I led a delegation through the building site—students, journalists, technical experts from Czechoslovakia. Bremer approached me near the cooling towers. He had a slip of paper in his hand. He looked tired. I nearly felt pity for him. He handed me the slip and walked on. He'd written on the paper: I take back the accusation I've made against engineer C. during the production meeting. It doesn't correspond to the facts. Bremer. One of the journalists asked me about the rapport between workers and intellectuals at the combine. Good, I said.

The Agreement

HEINZ B.: I want to join the party, foreman.

BREMER: I'm not a foreman anymore.

HEINZ B.: But you're in the party. I smashed the major's nasal bone. Will that be favorably counted for my application period?

BREMER: It isn't our job to smash nasal bones. We are the ruling class. Our weapon is the state. You want to join the party. Do you know what you're bargaining for? A lot will be asked of you. Less beer, more work. Up to the navel in mud if need be. Getting up when you've fallen and getting up again when you've fallen again. And don't believe there will be a position in the bargain. The party is no social service. How many women do you have? Count carefully. Two are too many.

HEINZ B.: None.

BREMER: That may be too few. But you've got time. So: You know what you're doing?

HEINZ B.: Yes.

BREMER: Good. Then talk to the secretary. And what'll happen with the foundation?

HEINZ B.: We'll do the foundation again.

BREMER: I'll break your skull if it cracks again. Agreed?

HEINZ B.: Agreed.

Poems

1949–1992

Poems is a selection from poetry Müller wrote between 1949 and 1992. Many of the poems appeared in various books and journals during the decades in which they were written, and all of them were included in the comprehensive collection of Müller's poetry *Heiner Müller Die Gedichte,* Frankfurt am Main, 1998. Frank Hörnigk, editor of *Die Gedichte,* reminds us in his epilogue that "Müller wrote for nearly ten years exclusively poetry before he made his first mark as a playwright in the late fifties."

The poems represent more or less spontaneous responses to events which were shaping German history as well as the personal life of the author. They often place those events in the larger context of a world divided by hostile social systems and ideologies. Included is a set of adaptations from Chinese and Japanese poetry, written during a period when Müller became deeply interested in Asian literature and drama. (The playlet *The Voyage,* in the collection *ABC,* is another result of his exploration of classic Japanese literature.) A number of poems reflect on the life of writers who, at some time or another, provided models for Müller's work, such as Georg Büchner, Vladimir Mayakovsky, Bertolt Brecht, and Anna Seghers.

Read in sequence, these poems show the arc of Müller's thinking in its many changes: from 1949, the year the (East) German Democratic Republic was founded, when the author was a committed communist, to

1992, when socialism in Europe had collapsed and the East German state had been absorbed by the West German Federal Republic.

Leading figures of Central and East European socialism are topical to several poems: the Hungarians Laszlo Rajk and Imre Nagy, who both were accused of being traitors to their party and then executed, during the fifties, and Janos Kadar, who tried to save Hungary for socialism by calling in the Red Army to suppress the uprising of 1956 but later began to dismantle its socialist system. The East German head of state and party, Erich Honecker, was deposed in November 1989. Gregor Gysi became the chairperson of the Socialist Unity Party during the GDR's final year, 1989–90, when it was renamed Party of Democratic Socialism. One prose poem is devoted to the West German artist Gunther Rambow, who designed a number of posters for plays by Müller that were performed at the Frankfurt theater during the seventies.

The poems offer something like a record of the often controversial positions Heiner Müller took during his life as a writer and *zoon politikon.* They trace his increasing disenchantment with the self-destructive course followed by the so-called "Real Existing Socialism" of the GDR. They also betray the growing pessimism he felt when considering the future at the end of the millennium. He once succinctly defined his stance in an interview: "I am neither a hope nor a dope dealer."*

C.W.

---

*This statement, and lines and phrases marked with an asterisk in the poems, were in English in the original.

Images

Images mean everything in the beginning. Are durable. Spacious.
But the dreams curdle, assume a shape and frustration.   .
Even the sky will no longer contain an image. The cloud from the
     airplane's
Window: a vapor obstructing the sight. The crane merely a bird.
Communism even, the ultimate image, always refreshed
Since washed with blood again and again, the daily routine
Pays it out in small coin, not shining, tarnished from sweat
The great poems: ruins, like bodies loved a long time and now
Of no use anymore, by the wayside of a species that's finite but
     using up plenty
Between the lines: lamentation
                              on the bones of the stone carriers: happy

Since the beautiful means the possible end of the horrors.

Missouri 1951

The states had denied
Funds to enforce the dam
Since they didn't provide
The river called their sham.

He rapidly rose to full size
He found the dam too old.
The townspeople were to realize
The water was very cold.

The cut down forests do not rot
They go on growing below the ground.
Dresden in Saxony is a burnt spot
The dead will have the last word

Question and Answer

1 (japanese)
Comrade do you see the cloud above the mainland
Comes wind Comes snow
Comrade where will our bodies lie

Where we will fall our bodies will lie

2 (chinese)
The cup of rice wine before you and
Paradise Old man what else do you want
I'd want my cup to fill itself
I'd like my friends to visit me
Instead of the official who collects the tax
I'd also like to see my children well off
Then I'd want to live another hundred years

And give up paradise

A Wide View from Foreign Hills

(after Poo Sung-Ling)

Better die here, a stranger, than
Live where the taxes
Keep us down.
He who is
Farming the rice, won't eat it.
When the meal has been cooked
It isn't yours anymore.
When, great heavens above, will you give us a good year, and
Better rulers?

No rain all year long! Two feet down
The soil was like dust, without water. Then
As the harvest was ripe, vermin fell upon it.
The taxes took the rest.

Looking about
From hills far from home
Toward heaven we face
Ever hopeful. But
From there will come probably nothing.

On the way to the country with
Rice where he will not arrive
The hungry man sold his son
For a morsel to eat on the way.

The emperor needs soldiers, father
Stop up your ears, son
So you cannot hear the drum
And cover yourself with manure up to above your eyes
So you won't be blinded by the weapons' splendor.
(after Poo Sung Ling)

I was a hero, my fame enormous
In my banners the four winds were roaring
When my drums were rumbling the people went silent
I have wasted my life.
(after Po Chue-I)

Heroic Landscape
Variation on a Theme
by Mao Tse-tung

The hill of seven colors
Plowed with bullets with corpses covered
Is beautiful as it was before battle

In the wars that will come
Shall blanch the seven colored hill

Mayakovsky

Mayakovsky, why
The leaden full stop?
Heartache, Vladimir?
"Has
A lady
Closed herself to him
Or
Opened
For another?"
Take
My bayonet
From your teeth
Comrades!
Blood, curdled
Into medals' tin
The walls stand
Speechless and cold
In the wind
The banners are clanking.

or Buechner who died in Zurich
100 years before your birth
Age 23, from want of hope.

Brecht

Truly, he lived in dark times.
The times have become brighter
The times have become darker.
If brightness says, I am darkness
It spoke the truth.
If darkness says, I am
Brightness, it doesn't lie.

Old Poem

At night while swimming across the lake the moment
That puts yourself in question There is no other one anymore
At last the truth That you are merely a quote
From a book that you didn't write
Against this you can type for a long time onto your
Worn out ribbon The text will come through

1959 . . .

Self-Portrait Two A.M.
August 20, 1959

Sitting at the typewriter. Leafing
Through a detective story. Going to know
At the final page what you already know:
The smooth-faced aide with the vigorous stubble
Is the senator's killer
And the love of the young sergeant from Homicide
For the admiral's daughter will be returned.
But you won't skip a single page.
Sometimes while turning the page a quick glance
At the blank sheet in the typewriter.
We will be spared that, now. That's at least something.
The paper reported: somewhere a village
Has been razed to the ground by bombs.
It's regrettable but why should it concern you.
The sergeant is just preventing the second murder
Though the admiral's daughter (for the first time!)
Offers him her lips, duty is duty.
You don't know how many died, the paper is gone.
Next door your wife dreams of her first love.
Yesterday she tried to hang herself. Tomorrow
She'll cut open her arteries or whatdoIknow.
At least she has a goal to look for.
That she'll attain, one way or another

And the heart is a spacious graveyard.
The story of Fatima in *Neues Deutschland*
Was written so badly that you had to laugh.
To torture is easier learned than describing the torture.
The killer has walked into the trap
The sergeant is embracing his prize.
You can sleep now. Tomorrow is another day.

Babelsberg Elegy 1960

It is a long way to the cashier's office
Especially in the rain
Dry in their brand-new cars are passing me
The writers of bad movies.

Film

45 years after the Great
Revolution I see on the screen
In a new film from the land of the Soviets the transformation
Of a tardy waiter into a sprinter
Due to the false report that the hundred-and-first
Waiting customer is a State Prize Winner.
The spectators, more or less dressed alike
In the small movie house in the split capital
Of my split fatherland, laugh at
The everyday occurrence, not everyday
On the screen. Why are these people laughing.
Oh tardiness of those who aren't driven any longer
It can't be praised enough! Beautiful lack of kindness
Of those who can't be forced to smile any more!

1969 . . .

Projection 1975

Where is the morning we saw yesterday
The early bird is singing through the night
The morning in his red coat's walking through
The dew which glistens in his tracks like blood
I am reading what I have written three, five, twenty years ago, like the text
of a dead author, from an age when a death still could be fitted into verse.
The killers have ceased to scan their victims. I recall my first effort to write
a play. The text has been lost in the confusion of the post-war period. It
began with the (youthful) hero standing in front of the mirror and trying
to learn which roads the worms would be walking through his flesh. At
the end he stood in the basement and cut open his father. In the century
of Orestes and Electra that is rising, Oedipus will be a comedy.

1979 . . .

Driving by the park of Charlottenburg Palace
    suddenly the grieving
GREEN IS THE COLOR OF MISFORTUNE The trees
    belong to the dead

Caries in Paris

Something is eating away at me

I smoke too much
I drink too much

I'm dying too slowly

Letter to A.S.

. . .
Now you are dead Anna Seghers
Whatever that may mean
Your place where Penelope sleeps
In the arm of suitors who can't be rejected
But the dead girls are strung up on the clothesline on Ithaca
Blackened by the sky in their eyes the beaks
While Odysseus is plowing the surf
In his back laughter
At the bow of Atlantis

Cultural Policy According to Boris Djacenko

Boris Djacenko told me After they had banned
My novel HEART AND ASHES Part Two
Where for the first time had been described
The horrors of the liberation by the RED ARMY
My censor invited me to a private chat
And the official reader proudly showed me the banned
Typescript bound in expensive leather SO MUCH
I LOVE YOUR BOOK THAT I HAD TO BAN IT
IN THE INTEREST YOU KNOW IT OF OUR COMMON CAUSE
In the future said Boris Djacenko
The banned books will be bound
IN THE INTEREST YOU KNOW IT OF OUR COMMON CAUSE
In leather tanned from the hides of their writers
Let's keep our hides in good shape said Boris Djacenko
So that our books in their durable binding
Will outlive the time of official readers

Meeting the Wicked Cousin Again

Who broke my toy behind her back
SHOW ME and I showed it to her and she took it
And I heard it crack between her sausage fingers
Saw her smile never to be forgotten   Even today
In my ear the cracking in my eye the never forgotten smile
I still badmouth the things I love as a precaution
Now she sits opposite me and knows from nothing
The terror has turned cold   Flesh and fat
The daily routine   Children screaming
Garbage of the species

1989 . . .

Light rain on light dust
The willows at the pub
Will turn green and green
But you Master should drink wine before you take leave
Since you will have no friends
When you arrive at the gates of Go
(for Erich Honecker after Ezra Pound and Rihaku)

Television

Margarita says my father*
Was Howard Hughes a member*
of the next generation*
       last
Which doesn't move its ass*
From the tv-chair because*
Outside lives man the beast*
On the screen at least*
It is flat and doesn't watch you*

1 Geography

Facing the GREAT HALL OF THE PEOPLE
The monument of the dead Indians
On the SQUARE OF HEAVENLY PEACE
The track of tanks

2 Daily News* after Brecht 1989

The torn-off fingernails of Janos Kadar
Who called out the tanks against his own people when they began
To string up his Comrades the torturers by their feet
His dying when the betrayed Imre Nagy
Was dug up again or what was left of him
BONES AND SHOES* the television was there
WE WHO WANTED TO PREPARE THE GROUND
FOR KINDNESS
How much earth shall we have to eat
Tasting of our victims' blood
On the way to a better future
Or to none if we spit it out

3 Self-Critique

My editors rummage through the old texts
Sometimes when I read them I shudder That's
What I wrote OWNING THE TRUTH
Sixty years before my probable death
On the tv screen I see my compatriots
With hands and feet vote against the truth
That forty years ago was mine own
What grave will protect me from my youth

4 for Gunter Rambow 1990

On television, the arrest of Erich Honecker at the entrance to Charité hospital following his cancer operation. An old man marked by sixteen years in power that had demanded far too much of his intellect and crushed his character, already undermined by ten years' confinement in Brandenburg penitentiary—sad proof of Jünger's thesis of a growing discrepancy between the agents' stature and the scope of their agency in recent history—now offered up by his creatures as a scapegoat to the people's fury. (Meantime the church has taken him in, an ancient power nowadays grasping only for souls and no longer for bodies.) I see the images and think of Rambow's theater posters in Frankfurt, the capital of banking and prostitution and, for a brief moment, political theater in the Federal Republic. *Antigone*: Hölderlin's republican chair, ablaze at the stake of Restoration. *Gundling*: the torn figure of the bisexual plunging Icarus LessingKleist FriedrichtheGreat; fluttering in its left upper corner *Neues Deutschland*, a paper without readers, lost topgallant of socialist still-birth. *Hamletmachine*: the Hamlet actor without a face, a wall at his back, his face a prison wall. Images no production could match. Markers across the swamp that already had begun to close above the temporary grave of a utopia which, maybe, will shine again once the phantom of the Market that has displaced the specter of Communism shows its cold shoulder to the new customers, the iron face of its liberty to the liberated.

Heart of Darkness after Joseph Conrad

For Gregor Gysi

Frightful world Capitalist world
(Gottfried Benn in a radio discussion
with Johannes R. Becher, 1930)

In the hard currency bar of the METROPOL Hotel
At Berlin Capital of the GDR tries
A Polish hooker a guest worker to take care of
An old man with a head cold
Between the chapters of his presentation
On liberty in the USA
He blows his nose into his handkerchief shouts for a trash can
Still gripped by pity for her tough vocation
I hear two salesmen
Bavarians according to the sounds
Divide Asia: WELL THEN MALAYSIA'S FINE WITH ME
THAILAND TOO KOREA'S PART OF IT
WELL THE CROSSRAIL SYSTEM FOR YEMEN
I'D STILL DEVELOP IT THEN

I'D CALL IT QUITS
            CHINA'S PART OF IT TOO
CHINA'S THE ONLY PROJECT THAT'S BEEN SOLD
On the el train ZOO STATION—FRIEDRICHSTRASSE
I have met two GDR citizens
One of them told me My son three weeks old
Was born with a sign on his breast
ON THE NINTH OF NOVEMBER I WAS IN THE WEST
My daughter same age I have twins
Wears the words ME TOO
THE HORROR THE HORROR THE HORROR*

Self-Critique 2   A Broken Key

> The uprising broke out on the twenty-third of October but it
> began already on the sixth of October with the solemn funeral
> of Rajk and his Comrades when 200,000 people paid their re-
> spect to the murdered men but most of all were demonstrat-
> ing for the overthrow of a murderous regime. Only a few still
> remembered the Stalinist Rajk, as one of the demonstrators did
> who muttered under his breath: Had he lived to see this, he'd
> given orders to shoot at the crowd.
>
> (Hodos: Show Trials, p. 250)

Blackbeard's forbidden door Forbidden dream
Dead women in the room that has been danced to shreds
Blood on the key that no rain will wash off
The death on your retina that no grave will hide
No angel with his wings will burst your room
The dead women will eat your dream
The last coitus is the execution
In the year of wolf's milk you will see your face

Hapless Angel 2

Between city and city
After the wall the abyss
Wind at the shoulders The alien
Hand at the lonely flesh
The angel I still hear him
Yet he has no face anymore but
Yours that I don't know

Love Story
A Short Story

Love Story (Liebesgeschichte) was written in 1953 and published in Heiner Müller Geschichten aus der Produktion 2, Rotbuch Verlag, Berlin, 1974. It is another example of Müller's early narrative writing and might well reflect aspects of his own life: He had married, at the age of 23, a young nurse who was pregnant with his first child. They never actually lived together, due to the housing shortage in postwar Berlin, and they divorced a short time later. They remarried, however, and then divorced a second time after he had met Inge, a young writer who became his second wife and a collaborator on several literary projects. (Inge's eventual suicide is described in Obituary; it is also the subject of several poems and is referred to in Hamletmachine and in the final segment of Quartet.) Several incidents in Love Story surface again in Müller's stage texts: the two men in the street bickering over a cigarette reappear in the opening scene of The Scab; the lakeside where the student's clumsy seduction of the girl takes place can be found in a more detailed description in Despoiled Shore.

The story offers vivid impressions of daily life in the East Berlin of the early fifties, with its subway and tramways, its uninviting restaurants, its cityscape still pockmarked by the war's bombing raids and artillery shelling. It was a place where people were intent on enjoying whatever little pleasures were available to them. The young woman's living alone implies that her family may have been killed during the bombing raids, as Inge Müller's parents were. She is working in a factory, as a great number of women did, since the male workforce had been depleted by the war. Her insistence on attending a meeting suggests that she is either a member of the Socialist Unity party (SED) or of an affiliated organization, such as the Youth League (FDJ) or a trade union (FDGB). The student is clearly one of the new breed who studied at a so-called Workers and Farmers College (*Arbeiter und Bauern Fakultät*) where young people, who had never had a chance to enter Germany's expensive secondary education system of the prewar years, could prepare now for graduate studies. In the new East German republic, higher education had been made generally available. Of course, education was marked by the Marxist ideology on which the state's ruling party based its legitimation. What appears most important from today's vantage point is that the story portrays a woman who takes a stance which only decades later became generally accepted. The quote preceding the text is from Friedrich Hebbel's play *Maria Magdalena* (1844), whose protagonist drowns herself when she becomes pregnant and the father of her child refuses to marry her.

C.W.

Love Story

KLARA: *Marry me!*   (Hebbel, *Maria Magdalena*)

1

The student Hans P. met a girl one summer night in Berlin on the over-crowded subway. Walking back and forth on the station platform, brief-case stuck under his arm, he was thinking about his new assignment, "equal rights for women." The girl stood next to the newspaper stand and looked in the direction from which the train had to appear. She's got nice legs, he thought, walked past her and glanced sideways at her face. He kept walking back and forth in ways that enabled him to see her but raised his eyes only when he was sure she couldn't see him. Whenever he caught her eye, he made an effort to assume an imposing expression. At the same time he tried to look bored so the people around him wouldn't notice any-thing. That was exhausting. When a train entered the station—he was just passing her for the seventh time—he looked the first time into her eyes. She stopped in her tracks and looked at him. She didn't get on the train. Then another train arrived and this time she got on. In the crowded com-partment he succeeded in positioning himself next to her.

2

They met the next evening in front of the station. Fifteen minutes before the appointed time, he stood below the clock at the south entrance and was afraid she wouldn't come. He hastily smoked two cigarettes in a row, walked to and fro, turning sharply when one of the swinging doors was pushed open. He felt himself being observed. What if someone who had watched him waiting for so long saw him leave all alone! He lit the third cigarette, a stale taste in his mouth. That was when he saw her. Wearing a light summer dress, she walked toward him across the large square that bordered on the park's lawn. Now he was amazed that she was on time. He threw the cigarette away and walked in her direction, slowly, with an effort to smile: he suddenly had remembered that he had no money, not enough, in any case, to invite her for a drink. Only when she asked what they were going to do, where they would go, did he notice that he was holding her hand. He lit a new cigarette and said he would leave this to her. It's a beautiful evening, she said, while they walked down the street. Yes, he said, and pondered what he could do so that she wouldn't feel thirsty. On no account was she to notice that he had no money. In the same moment she said: It's warm. We could have a drink. It's really a beautiful evening, he said quickly and looked at the dove-colored sky. At the horizon behind the high buildings there was a trace of red. You could see it wherever ruins opened up the view. He told her that he had no money, in any case not enough. They needn't run up a big tab, she said, and yesterday had been her payday. They went to a restaurant. It was a large rectangular space with bare walls, bright under the fluorescent lights. Everything was new and clean. The metal fittings at the bar were gleaming. They sat down at one of the small round tables with only two chairs; a waiter approached, the student looked nervously at the blank face, then at the girl. We could have wine, she said. Yes, of course: Wine. He lit a cigarette, smoked, and looked past the waiter at the wall. He offered a cigarette to the girl when the waiter had brought the wine. They smoked. He looked at her arms, at her half-opened mouth with only a trace of lipstick that was moist from the wine, drank hastily and pushed the glass back and forth on the cold marble top. Then he began to ask questions. What, for instance, was she doing at night. She leaned forward and he saw the upper part of her breast, white below the tanned neck. She has small breasts, he thought and asked her if she knew *The Young Guards,* the book by Fadeyev. She knew it. He didn't like it when she began asking questions now, and he answered in monosyllables. Meanwhile new customers had entered the restaurant, they were sitting at the round marble-topped tables, talking and laughing, the louder the more they drank. A ventilator was humming. At one of the adjacent tables a young man was sitting with a skinny girl who looked down at her hands in her lap. He sat facing her, his upper body leaning forward, his hands enclosed the stem of his wine glass. Now he began to talk intensely to her and looked from narrow eyes stealthily at her. Several times he urged her to drink. She drank. When she was putting down the glass, he quickly snatched her hand, held it tight and whispered something to her. She blushed but didn't pull back the hand, raised her head and looked with swimming eyes at him, gratefully. When she raised her head, he smiled. When she stopped looking at him, his eyes narrowed again, the smile disappeared, he continued to watch her. The student had looked on. Now he looked at the girl who sat at his table. She laughed. Isn't that funny, she asked, Yes, he said and gazed at the spot where the tip of her left breast was visible under the thin dress. The skinny girl at the adjacent table had gotten up and went to the rest room. The young man, who just now had been looking radiantly at her and had fondled her hand, wiped his brow, put his hands in his pockets, and stared with a pinched face at the table top. It has drained him, the girl said to the student. When the skinny one returned to the table, the young man continued to act his role. He moved his chair closer to her and took her hand again. He lifted the glass to her lips, she drank, he put an arm around her: mission accomplished. He paid the bill. When standing behind her he held her coat, he was grinning. But he went ahead and held the door open for her. The student looked at the girl who was sitting opposite him. She looked past him at the wall.

3

One Sunday they took the subway to its final stop. On the way they had quarreled. To his question if she had time for him the next day, she answered: No, she'd have to attend a meeting. Whereupon he said that to him she'd be more important than any meetings. She didn't answer. It was already getting dark when they arrived at the spot for bathing, right behind the Beach Hotel, at the north end of the lake. The trees at the water's edge formed a roof above the sandy strip in front of the reeds. While he was undressing, he looked across the lake to the other shore. It isn't far, he said, you can swim across. It's misleading, said she, at night all things look different, closer. She stood in her bathing suit at the water's edge and played with her toes in the moist sand. Then they swam, next to each other. There was nothing between them save the water that carried them. When they waded out of the water, he was cold. He forgot it as he pressed his mouth on her cold lips. He felt how she trembled and her body became heavy. Then she freed herself and pushed him back. She ran to the tree where her clothes were lying, laughed and shouted: We've got to get dressed. He followed her. She put the bathrobe around her shoulders and asked: Don't you want to get dressed? When she pulled down the wet bathing suit, he saw her breasts. A light wind had started, and it smelled of mud and mussels. He tried to do everything the way he had read in books and seen in the movies, kissed her mouth, then her neck, the shoulders, groped for her breast, and so forth. He was glad he didn't need to undress her. Now he had to swoop her up in his arms and put her down. He stumbled while trying and they fell on top of each other. He was afraid she might laugh at him. In haste, pressing his face against her shoulder, he pushed himself into the right position. Later they walked down the street to the Beach Hotel, entered the pub with its low ceiling, sat down at a table and he ordered beer. They drank. At the next table an elderly man was telling dirty jokes in a loud voice. They heard the hoarse laughter of approval. It was hard for him not to join in the laughter, and he put his hand on top of hers. She looked up at him. Then it became too hard for him and he laughed along with the others. Then he asked the second time if she had time for him the next day, and she replied, no, she'd have to attend a meeting. I thought you loved me, he said. No, said she, I don't love you, and got up and left. When he caught up with her, in front of the station, he saw that she had cried. He kissed her, and she leaned against him. While they were waiting for the tramway, they noticed two men who took leave of each other in the middle of the street and walked away in opposite directions, both of them drunk. On the sidewalk across the street the younger one stopped and shouted, Want another cigarette? Yes, the other one replied. Then come over here! The younger one, in a light-colored suit, took one cigarette from a full pack and held it out for the other one. Fine, he said, each of us half the distance. He walked two steps, the younger one didn't move. All the way for one cigarette? No. The other one laughed and said again: Come on over! I'll take two steps more, said the man in the street. See. Now come here, give me the cigarette. I said half the distance. Come, said the younger man grinning. And so they stood, maybe for a minute, slightly tottering. Then the man in the street said: No. Not one step further. The other one grinned again and held out the cigarette. But his partner wouldn't play anymore. Don't be inhuman, Willi! The student burst into laughter. The girl first looked at him, then at the man who was standing in the street looking at the man on the sidewalk. The one in the light-colored suit pulled two cigarettes from the full pack. Two, he said. Then the tramway came.

4

In the time that followed they saw each other nearly every day. He had told her he was thinking of her all day, it would be enough for him if he could only look at her. It was, of course, not enough for him, and she didn't want that either. Once he threw a fit when he had been waiting for her in front of her workplace and had seen her come through the factory gate with a young worker at whom she had looked too friendly during their leave-taking, or so he felt. For a long time she couldn't forget the way his face had changed as he was screaming at her. In October she knew she was pregnant. She didn't know if she should be glad about it. A day later she asked him what he would say if they had a child. They were sitting on the edge of the bed in her room, a spacious attic, and were eating oranges. He lit a cigarette and smoked hastily. But you're not going to have one? No, she said. He offered her a cigarette. I am a student, he said, I can't afford a child. After that evening he occasionally didn't keep their appointments. When he did come, he talked a lot, as if to avoid saying anything. Later he became taciturn, standing in her room at the small window and smoking one cigarette after another in silence. Or he watched her putting the room in order while he was sitting on the edge of the bed. One day he told her he had to go on a trip, for two weeks probably. He promised to write her. He didn't write. Three weeks later he stood one night in front of her door. She had decided to conceal from him that she was pregnant and to tell him that she didn't want to see him again. She didn't say it; she suffered his kissing her in silence and kissed him back. He saw that she was pregnant. He said he would find a doctor. I want you, he said, but the child has to go. I don't want to see you again, she said.

5

At the factory during lunch break she was asked by another woman: When are you two going to marry? I won't marry, she said. The woman, with beady eyes set in pink wads of fat, looked triumphantly in her face. Really? You won't marry? I hope he is going to pay. Is he making good money? She got up from the table and went to the machine she operated.

6

The student Hans P. was preparing for his exams. He sat in the room he had rented, surrounded by heavy bourgeois oak furniture, and leafed listlessly through the *Communist Manifesto*. At the same time he thought with a slight ache of the girl and, with apprehension, of the child she was carrying. He read: . . . In your society as it exists private property has been abolished for nine-tenths of its members. It exists exactly because of the fact that it doesn't exist for nine-tenths . . . and so you accuse us for wanting to abolish property that has as its necessary condition the absence of property for the vast majority of society. . . . He tried to visualize her face but he saw only her body. He decided to marry the girl. I want to have her, he thought. She must stay with me.

7

During the night, P. dreamed: He had spent the evening with four men, there was some kind of celebration, women attended the event. In the house of one of the men he climbed a ladder to the attic. In the attic—which resembled the one in his grandparents' house, where he had played

Father and Mother with his female cousin and had been surprised by an uncle while they were playing—the owner of the house, a short old man with a tough gray-white stubble, was carving up one of the women (when P. woke up he didn't know what made him recognize her) with an axe; he stuffed the body parts into a barrel for salting meat. P. watched it from his place on the ladder, his head and shoulders above the trapdoor's opening, and quickly proceeded to climb down again. Not quick enough: the butcher noticed him from the corner of his eye and beckoned to him with the axe, not interrupting his work for one moment. At the entrance to the house stood the twelve-year-old daughter of the old man. We won't let them make us poor again, she said, and: I'll tell the blind men all about it. P. ran down the dirt path to the road, then along the winding road; when he looked back while running he saw in the far distance himself, running along the same road and looking back while running, in flight from the blind men.

8

The next day he stood across the street from the factory gate in the shadow of buildings and waited for her. As he was smoking the second cigarette, she came and walked without looking back down the long street to the station. He followed her slowly on the other side of the street. Then he crossed the street and walked faster until he had caught up with her. I have passed my exam, he said. She was silent. He said he had thought only of her, even during the exam. And she belonged to him after all. He reached for her hand. She pulled her hand back and pushed it into the coat pocket. I would marry you, too, he said. She stopped, looked at him and said coldly: You don't need to walk with me any further. I can't help it, he said, I can't live without you. You know that you can, she said. He continued to walk at her side and kept talking to her. She mustn't belong to anyone else, he thought, pulled her with a sudden movement close and tried to kiss her. She turned her head away, with a tense face. He felt her bulging belly. On the station platform they were standing next to the newspaper stand, she looked in the direction the train had to come from, he looked into the crowd. Close by a well-dressed middle-aged man was standing with his wife and child. The wife carried a shopping bag, under the other arm a lampstand wrapped in paper. The man didn't hold anything in his hands. The child stood pressing itself against her hips and looked up to the man. The man and the woman were quarrelling without looking at each other. The child said something. He pulled it by the hand to his side.

The wife pulled it behind her back and swung the shopping bag against the man. Why don't they split it between themselves, the student thought. He had to laugh at the idea of man and wife walking in opposite directions, the man with the right, the wife with the left half. The child ran into the crowd. The man made the woman aware of it but didn't budge from his spot. The woman was scared and ran after the child. Why don't you want to marry me? asked the student. The girl didn't answer, shook his hand when the train came, and got onto it. He saw, as he was trying to follow her, the sign that stated "No Smoking" and went to the next car. It felt like he had failed an exam and had to learn once again what he already had learned.

The God of Happiness
Fragment of an Opera

The God of Happiness (Der Glücksgott) was written in 1958 and first published in *Heiner Müller Theater-Arbeit,* Rotbuch Verlag, Berlin, 1989.

Heiner Müller explains the reasons for its writing, and also his eventual
abandoning of the project, in his introductory note. It was the first collaboration with the composer Paul Dessau (1894–1979) who was to become one of Müller's closest friends. In the late 1960s, he completed a
libretto for Dessau's opera *Lanzelot,* which premiered at the Berlin State
Opera in 1969; this text, written in collaboration with Ginka Tscholakova
and based on the play *The Dragon,* by Jevgenij Schwarz, was published
as *Drachenoper* in the same volume.

The fragment's scenes range from the battlefields of World War I to the
harsh realities of the young (East) German Democratic Republic. While
traveling, or, rather, tumbling through the world like a football, the God
of Happiness encounters mutilated soldiers, functionaries of the East German Socialist Unity Party (SED), their disgruntled subjects, a deposed former emperor or king, and all sorts of people who simply feel scorned
when the god admonishes them to be happy. The fragment ends with a set
of poems which evoke the long history of humankind's lack of happiness
that neither so-called miracles nor revolutions were able to repair.

The text's last segment is the by now often quoted paraphrase of Walter Benjamin's interpretation of a drawing by Paul Klee, *The Angel of History*. It reveals Müller's skepticism about a simplistic idea of progress as it was embraced by the East German Socialist establishment. In the early nineties, Müller wrote another, even bleaker, paraphrase; *Hapless Angel 2*.

C.W.

It was in 1958, I think, that Paul Dessau asked me if I could create a libretto from Brecht's fragment *Voyages of the God of Happiness*. I didn't know anything about the fragment beyond what Brecht had told us in his late preface to the early plays—in a strangely sensuous prose written with the view of his graveyard—and I agreed. Then I read the fragment. I remember little more of it than a general impression. The sensuousness appeared to be more of an assertion than an experience: He who drinks water is preaching about wine. This is less a criticism of the author than of the place where he had been writing, Hollywood, the Weimar of the German antifascist emigration, and of the era or, rather, his concept of it according to which he fashioned his work (= his attitude toward the era's contradictions). The fashioning constituted a reduction, the price that had to be paid for discipline.

The first difficulty (impossibility) was the figure of the God of Happiness [GOH]. Fixed figures (gods, monuments, types) are useful as catalysts when human experience has left history behind in its tracks. Petrifactions that can serve as depositories for a wisdom that will be available again as an explosive when called upon by history's progress. If an inverted movement is beginning, they won't serve anymore. This goes as well for their playing space, the parable. It becomes marginal. It has a (sinister) future: when the opportunities have been squandered, what used to be the design for a new world will begin anew in a different way, as a dialogue with the dead. In science fiction, which shrinks catastrophes to mere punch lines, it appears in its trivial incarnation. Positively stated: Against the background of a world history that has as its condition Communism (the equality of opportunity), this dialogue stands for the liberation of the past. Anticipation produces what is merely arty, which compares to true art the way cosmetics compare to surgery.

Dessau, as a contribution to the development of a new kind of "Hausmusik," had set to music a few of the *Songs of the God of Happiness* written by Brecht during the forties, texts of a beauty that had been dismissed by history. (If it will again be summoned, it will dress itself in a different way or go naked.) I could find neither a place for them nor any reason at all for songs during the tests of endurance the GOH was exposed to after his expulsion from the parable's shattered model of a sound world. The houses the war left standing are destroyed by the reconstruction, as far as they might serve as sites for Hausmusik. The duel between industry and the future won't be conducted with songs which make you settle down happily. Its music is the scream of Marsyas, a scream that tore the strings from his divine torturer's lyre.

The failure of the experiment to complete an outline by Brecht may be instructive about the change of function imposed on literature during a period of transition. Ruins, like monuments, are building material that comes from quarries.

The project revealed itself quickly as one that wasn't doable (by me). Brecht's poetic way of entry—an angel with scorched wings, who has come from an earth that is devastated by wars, perturbs the God of Happiness—an entry which investigates the problem on the given playing field, is based on a concept of the world as a sound affair. It appeared to me that my own reality of 1958 couldn't be described anymore in such conclusive fashion, or not yet. My globe was composed of battling segments that at best a clinch might unite. I could bring the well-rounded (i.e., impermeable for reality) figure of the GOH (he can't be destroyed = he can't learn) into play only as a ball which, being thrown back and forth, permits through its passive movement conclusions concerning the dimensions of the playing field and the ever-changing positions of the players: he can't put a foot on the ground. Three efforts to bring him into play.

The Football Introduces Himself

GOH: I am the God of Happiness. I have slept for ten thousand years. Where? That doesn't matter. I was awakened by a din that arose from the earth, a kind of thunder, only louder and lasting longer. Since it didn't stop, I cast a glance down. There I saw huge fires running all over the planet. I decided to take a look . . .

The Ball Enters the Game out of Nowhere

FARMER: We are farmers. We had a very bad harvest, and so on. We have ten children. This is my wife. We are now taking our seats. Music.

(*Music.*)

FARMER, WIFE, CHILDREN: We're eating our last piece of bread.

(*They eat during the overture. Enter the* GOH.)

GOH: I am the God of Happiness. I shall give you this basket for a present since you are poor. Whatever you take from it, you won't lack ever after.
FARMER: There is nothing in there.
GOH: Because you put nothing in.

FARMER: We have nothing. Maybe we should put him into the basket. He is fat.

(*The* GOH *flees.*)

The Kickoff

The heavens. The GOH *on a cloud. He is asleep. The cloud is torn apart by an explosion. The* GOH *tumbles down to earth.*

Battlefield

GOH: I am finding this star greatly changed. Seven days already I have been on my way and haven't seen one single tree, for instance.
(*He stumbles over a tree stump.*)
No trace of human beings.
(*He falls into a bomb crater. When he climbs out again, he is holding a steel helmet in his hand. He doesn't know what to do with it, tries it as a hat, a piss pot, a football, a drum.*)
Not one human being.

(*A* DEAD SOLDIER WITH A WOODEN LEG [S1] *climbs from the bomb crater.*)

GOH: Who are you, flesh, through which the sun in shining
Where do you come from with your wooden leg?
S1: Have you been drumming?
GOH: Yes.
S1:   What for?
GOH: For nothing.
S1: Then stop it.
GOH: As you wish.
S1:   I want it stopped.
GOH: Why be a foe, my friend?

(*A* SECOND DEAD SOLDIER, *wearing a gas mask, climbs from the bomb crater.*)

S2:   Foe, why so friendly?
GOH: I am no foe of yours. Look at me, brother.
S2: If you lend me your eyesight.
GOH: Blind?

(*The* SECOND SOLDIER *takes off his gas mask. He has no face.*)

S2:   You see?

(*The* GOH *covers his eyes with his hand and turns his face away. The* SOLDIER WITH WOODEN LEG *laughs.*)

S1: (*Still laughing.*) Go on and shake his hand. It's made of iron.

(*The* BLIND SOLDIER *holds out his iron hand and walks up to the* GOH, *who shrinks back.*)

GOH: I do believe you and I won't need proof.
   (*From a distance.*)
   Who, One Leg, took your other leg?
S1: (*Points at the* BLIND SOLDIER.)   He did.
GOH: And who has blinded you?
S2:   He did it.
GOH: (*To both.*)   Why?

(*The* SOLDIERS *laugh.*)

S1: He's mocking us?
S2:   I think that guy is stupid.
S1 + S2: Because there was a war.
GOH: A war? What's that?
S2: You've got a bullet in your brain, brother?
GOH: I am a god, I don't know what a war is.
S1 + S2: He is a god and doesn't know what war is.
   (*They laugh raucously. Laughing they demonstrate to the* GOH *what war is like, by hitting him on the head, kicking his butt, throwing him back and forth between themselves, and so forth.*)
S1: When fire drops from heaven,
S2:   and the earth.
   Spits fire.
S1:   and fire faces you
S2:   And fire
   Flares behind you.
S1 + S2:   Then it's war, God.
GOH: Why?
S1 + S2: I am a soldier. How should I know why.
GOH: How did you know you're enemies in war?
S2: If you've got eyes you see it.
S1:   It's the coat.
GOH: If you took off your coats, what made you different?

s1 + s2: Nothing.

GOH: And why then did you put them on?

s1 + s2: I was defending what is mine against him.

GOH: I see you've defended it well.

s2:   That one
     Will step onto my land no more.

s1:   Indeed,
     It's been destroyed.

s2:   Like you are.

s1:   And you've got
     No eyes to see my land and its green forests.

s2: Do you need eyes to see what is no more?

The GOH Puts His Hope in the Children and
Receives a Stony Rejection

The GOH, *who is the only being standing upright and not suffering hunger (all the trees have been burned, all the other dogs been eaten), is pissed on by a (the last) dog, whom the* GOH *tries to protect from a bunch of marauding* CHILDREN. *The* CHILDREN *chase the* GOH *away with three songs and catch the dog.*

1

Once upon a time there was a child
A lot of beer it drunk
The teacher smelled it on the child
And quickly he got drunk.

2

A guy on crutches stood at the wall
Has got no work nor can he steal
Got time to watch the children all
Who played cut-off-a-leg for real.

3

Said the teacher to the child
Take your hands out of your pants
But I didn't wash my hands
Said to the teacher the child

The teacher quickly ran to the king
The child has his hands in the pants
And he didn't wash his hands
Arrest the child said the king.

Said the king to the child
Take your hands out of your pants
But I didn't wash my hands
Said to the king the child

Then wash them right away he said
Or I'll give orders to hack them off
Well said the child *hack them off*
And the king turned white and shook his head
Turned white in his face as if he were dead.

The GOH and the Street

1

GOH: Where could I find my pupils, tell me, please?
CROWD: Hang him. It's he who's sent us this disease.

(*The GOH escapes into the government building.*)

2

GOH: What are you drinking, brothers?
FAT MAN: (*Grunts.*)   Water.
THIN MAN: (*Proudly.*)   Right.
GOH: I'm here and you do that? Drink water like cattle?
    When on the rack, it's wine for which I cried.
    I thought you're free for happiness at last.
THIN MAN: We are, old man, and thank you for it, too.
    No other road to happiness . . .
FAT MAN: For us.
GOH: Vineyards I see all over. Where's the wine?
THIN MAN: It's been exported, paying for machines.
GOH: Machines are noisy.
THIN MAN: And are feeding people.
GOH: For a grim yesterday you've got a grim today?

(*Points at a poster.*)

I didn't teach you that.

YOUNG MAN: Who is this clown?

GOH: Alas, my pupils they are mocking me.

YOUNG MAN: Who are you, fatso?

GOH: Watch your language, friend.

I am the God who knows all your desires.

And I have never asked how steep their price.

FAT MAN: The fat guy is all right. I think he's cool.

YOUNG MAN: God or no god, he surely is no fool.

FAT MAN: He doesn't fuck according to some rule.

YOUNG MAN: Won't break his back, work like a stupid mule.

BOTH: (*To the* THIN MAN.) We shit on your machines.

(*To the* GOH.) Now get us wine!

THIN MAN: Back to your work. Tomorrow wine for all.

Go, beat it, God. Or you'll be taught a lesson.

GOH: And so I'll go, unhurried yet afar

To be my own god where no humans are.

The GOH and the Beggar

GOH: Who are you, bones, owning neither rags nor hair.

BEGGAR: Once I was called an emperor, king, or czar.

Now I am scum. The dogs are shitting on me

GOH: I am a god. Which no one likes to be.

BEGGAR: You're not that golden head the songs are praising?

GOH: I am. But I'd rather be of iron.

BEGGAR: I had you hanged once while I was on top.

The show was paid for by me, you the star

Danced hanging from the rope.

GOH: Those were the days.

BEGGAR: Let's not indulge ourselves, they're over now.

When I had your head chopped off—by the best

Executioner my money could buy—

You played football with your noggin.

GOH: That was a time one felt alive and kicking.

BEGGAR: And then you put it back onto your shoulders.

The crowd was cheering.

GOH: And what am I now?

An offside ball the players shit on.

BEGGAR: I thought by now they'd be crazy for you.

GOH: I thought so, too.

BEGGAR: If you'd like to essay
The old game once again, why don't we play?
You are a god, man, you simply shout: Boo!
And new grows old and all the dreams come true.
When I'm on top, there's honey in your pot.

GOH: I'd rather be a fly atop you while you rot.

(*Kicks the* BEGGAR *down and dances on top of his body.*)

**The GOH's Address to a Dead Rat, in Praise of Its Happy Final Chore
as a Fertilizer and a Building Site's Dirt**

Friend and foe he vanquished, Sulla, the unhurried Roman
Alexander the Greek reached with his hand for India.
He was devoured by lice, the other one killed by a fly sting.
Disastrous for humans the vermin sharing the star they call home
Rats and lice, capitalists, generals, and microbes . . .
Children now born in Chungking will never see in Chungking
Any more rats, no rat in China as long as they'll live.
Not without curiosity they'll view the picture
Of the extinguished rodents, hardly believing they were
For their elders a horror, and they'll learn all the dates
Of that final ten-hour battle which killed the
Plague, ten thousand years old . . .

[*At this point, the author inserted a report about* The Battle against the Rats
of Chungking, *by Bruno Frei, published in the weekly* Weltbuehne, *July
16, 1958.*]

The Roles of the GOH
(Singer, Rabble-rouser,
Model Worker, Statesman)

1

There was a town called DAN DEE
There lived all sorts of people
They were praying and made loot
Until a singer arrived who cried:
With the mighty power of songs

Let us forge eternal bonds
In Dan Dee

And through the power of song
All the people became brothers
Both the strangled and the stranglers.
It lasted only one night long.
With the mighty power of songs
You cannot forge eternal bonds
In Dan Dee

When again the sun in Dan Dee
Separated light from shadow
Shame was felt about the night now.
And the singer was knighted/hanged
In Dan Dee.

Orpheus Plowed Under

Orpheus the singer was a man who could not wait. After he had lost his
wife, due to copulation too soon after childbed or the forbidden gaze during their ascent from the nether world after she had been liberated from
death through his song, so that she slipped back into dust before being
renewed in the flesh, he invented pedophilia, which spares the childbed
and is closer to death than the love of women. The rejected ones hunted
him: with the weapons of their bodies branches stones. But his song pro-
tected the singer: whatever he sang about couldn't pierce his skin. Peasants, frightened by the clamor of the hunt, ran away from their ploughs,
which hadn't gained a place in his song. So his place was under the
ploughs.

2
The Happiness of Productivity: A Soldier's Bride
(after Urs Graf)

Armless girl with the wooden leg
Before a landscape with lake, pregnant.
Cheap: she can't pull the money from your pants.
Comfortable: she can't hold on to you
ARMLESS IS HARMLESS. Run after you
She can't either: when you're going

You're going.
Perhaps you wave to her once more.
After all, she still has eyes in her head (two).
Four thousand armless girls embrace you
Four thousand pregnant girls with a wooden leg
Come marching in your tracks.

3

HE WAS THE FIRST AND BEST ONE: When the others
Combed the countryside for generous farmers
He was digging coal with old tools and new methods
In his pocket a crust of dry bread.
They kept beating him up, freezing. They stood
At the slowly starting drive wheels
Cursed him and followed his example.

4

NAPOLEON FOR EXAMPLE wept when
At Wagram his guardsmen took flight
Across the bodies of their own wounded
And the wounded cried, VIVE L'EMPEREUR.
The monument was moved: his mortar cried.

One Sunday after his work he, LENIN,
Went to hunt rabbits, driven by
His chauffeur, no other companions.
This was his time off. Into the forest
He walked alone, since the chauffeur had to
Stay with the car which was irreplaceable.
Lenin met a peasant who searched the forest
For mushrooms. His hunt was cancelled.
The old man cursed the Soviet power
In his village, still some on top and most below
Much talk, no flour. The mushrooms, too, are scarce.
He laughed when Lenin wrote down his complaints
The village, the names and mistakes of the Comrades.
He had once before complained. Not again.
Who are we. If you were Lenin, for example,
And Lenin were a man like you who listens

You might believe that things would change for better
But you're not Lenin and it will stay the same.
Why didn't Lenin tell the old man in the
Forest near Moscow that he was Lenin . . .

The Cheerful Corpse

GOH: Why so cheerful, corpse?

CORPSE: Should I be dead
    And not be cheerful?

(*The* GOH *weeps.*)

The Hapless Angel. In his back the past is piling up, it pours detritus on his wings and shoulders with a din like the sound of buried drums, while in front of him the future is damming up, it grinds his eyes into their sockets, explodes the eyeballs like a star, turns the word around into a resonant muzzle, chokes him with his own breath. For a while you still see his wings flapping, hear in their whir the rock slides crash down before, above, behind him, the louder the more violent his futile movement, more singular when it slows down. Then the moment closes itself on top of him: at his rapidly buried standing room the hapless angel comes to rest, waiting for history in the petrifaction of flight vision breath. Until the renewed whirring of powerful wings will move in waves through the stone and signify his flight.

Heracles 5; Tales of Homer; Oedipus Commentary
A Comedy and Two Poems

Heracles 5 was written in 1964–66 and published in the volume *Philok-tet/Herakles 5* (Edition Suhrkamp), Frankfurt, 1966. It premiered in June 1974, at the Berlin Schiller Theater. *Heracles 5* is one of the two plays Müller labeled comedies, the other one being *Women's Comedy* (*Weiberkomödie*), 1971, which was based on a radio play by his wife Inge, *Die Weiberbrigade*. However, Müller has stated that many of his texts should be considered comedies.

Heracles 5 satirizes the need—or, rather, the craving—for heroes which has marked human thinking throughout history. It also reflects on the hero's ambiguous position: while lip service is payed to his "greatness," he is snickered at and often maligned by those who profit from his glorious pursuits. Müller's satire directs its barbs at Heracles and his gargantuan appetites as much as at the Thebans who are clamoring for his fifth deed.

At the time of its writing, the play would have been understood as a critique of the "personality cult" which was ubiquitous in the East European communist states. Today it might be read in the context of a popular culture which idolizes, devours, and quickly discards its heroes/stars at an ever increasing rate. The text also ridiculed a stance taken by the East German authorities during the fifties and sixties, when even the least attractive menial labor was glamorized as a heroic achievement in the service of socialism. Müller's text calls for the elimination of degrading labor by new technologies—not necessarily an ecologically "correct" position, as might be argued from today's point of view.

Müller was evolving his own version of Brecht's *Lehrstück* model at the time the play was written, and the model is distinctly visible in the light-hearted piece. In its bold imagery and cheerful neglect of the stage technology available at the time, *Heracles 5* anticipated a theater of images and fragmentation which Müller did not fully explore until the mid-seventies. In his 1972 play *Zement*, a dramatization of Fyodor Gladkov's Soviet novel about the Russian civil war of 1919–20, one of several interludes deals with another of our hero's labors: *Heracles 2 or the Hydra*, possibly reiterating a dream/nightmare the author experienced. And in 1991, he published a poem *Heracles 13, after Euripides* which begins: "The thirteenth labor of Heracles was the liberation of Thebes from the Thebans," and continues to retell the story of Heracles' death as it is presented in the Euripides play.

All these texts reflect Müller's lifelong discourse with Greek mythology and drama. He adapted works by Aeschylus and Sophocles during the 1960s, among them *Prometheus, The Persians, Oedipus Tyrant,* and *Philoctetes,* while also writing poetry about figures of classic myth and literature, such as Oedipus, Electra, Homer, and Horace. I have included here two poems which reinterpret the classic tradition, *Tales of Homer* and *Oedipus Commentary.* The first text was written in the fifties and published in *Rotbuch 134, Die Umsiedlerin oder Das Leben auf dem Lande,* Berlin, 1975. *Oedipus Commentary* was written in 1966, as a prologue to Müller's adaptation of the Sophocles drama *Oedipus Tyrant,* when it was staged at Berlin's Deutsches Theater. It was published in the production's playbill, although not used in the performance.

C.W.

Heracles 5

CHARACTERS: Heracles, Augias, Zeus, two Thebans

1

HERACLES *asleep in the midst of cattle skeletons; he's holding one in his hand; snores.* VOICES *call:* "Heracles." TWO THEBANS *enter. They're holding their noses.*

FIRST: Again. He's gorged up to his gullet.

SECOND: Softly.

FIRST: (*More softly with increased anger.*)

    After each labor it is one ox more!

SECOND: Would you then like to do the job?

FIRST: Would you?

SECOND: The paean.

FIRST: (*Terrified.*)   All its stanzas?

SECOND: (*Indignant.*)   Without nose?

BOTH:

    He who strangled the Hydra

    (*Both shake their heads.*)

    Beheaded

    (*Both nod.*)

        the Nemean Lion

    (*Both shake their heads.*)

    He who has strangled the Nemean Lion and beheaded the Hydra

    He who has captured the hind and the boar, destroyer of harvests

    (HERACLES *yawns.*)

    Heracles, son of Alcmene, sired in Amphitryon's bed

    (*They grin.*)

    Not by Amphitryon—

    (*Thunder. The Thebans spit into each other's face.*)

    Swine, you're insulting the Gods!

    (*Louder.*) Heracles, son of Amphitryon, lend us,

    You doer of four great deeds, your arm for the fifth one

    And deign to cleanse the stables of Augias. Oh, liberator,

    Liberate us from the stench of this fleshpot, we regrettably need.

    (HERACLES *holds his nose.*)

FIRST: We count your oxen as we count your labors.

SECOND: It will be the fifth labor.

FIRST: Makes five oxen.

HERACLES: Liberate yourselves. (*Snores.*)

BOTH: You're Heracles.

HERACLES: (*Gets up, vainglorious.*)

I'll liberate your Thebes then from its stench.

And my advance . . .

(*Roaring of an ox who's being butchered.*)

THEBANS: You hear it roaring, don't you.

(*The ox is brought in.*)

HERACLES: (*Sits down.*)

You're dismissed.

THEBANS: And rush the job, please. Thebes

Needs our arm.

(*Backdrop: Thebes in ruins, the populace in rags.*)

HERACLES: And me. Get off my table.

(THEBANS *exit;* HERACLES *eats the ox.*)

2

Augias's stable, right and left a river. Enter HERACLES. *He holds his nose.*

HERACLES: Augias! (*Enter* AUGIAS.)

AUGIAS: Heracles. What do you want?

HERACLES: Clean your stable.

AUGIAS: With one hand?

(HERACLES *takes his hand off his nose, collapses.* AUGIAS *laughs.* HERACLES *holds his nose again, gets up.*)

My beef is good for your bellies, your noses are too fine for its muck. And even if the plague is stinking from my stable: are you immortal without the plague? The end lives in the beginning, the dead in the loins. What do you have against manure? How long does it stink? Open your nostrils. Three days and you can't breathe without the stench that burst your nose on the first day. The muck is rising, the stench increasing. Not for you, you live in it. Your fifth labor?

(HERACLES *counts his fingers, nods.*)

Did you know Sisyphus? Do you hear my cows shitting?

(*Music.*)

And no end to it. Number six is canceled. Feces are the other condition of the flesh. And its last shape. No exit from the shitting community but to the democracy of the dead. Two rivers. Take your pick. A river swallows it all, flesh or manure makes no difference, and out to sea. A bucket, a shovel.

(*From the flies: a bucket, a shovel.*)

You can have two shovels. You won't be able to handle more than one, with two hands at a time. Two shovels aren't more than one, two thousand won't be more, with all that muck. And my cows are shitting fast, you hear it.

(*Music.*)

You won't finish it one way or another: you can use the handle for dredging. And don't you hope that the wood will sprout leaves and cover itself with foliage, flip-flop back into the tree against the root, muck turns into grass on its way back through the flesh, and so forth, because your father lives one heaven above us. Or use your hands, if you like: ten prongs. How did you slaughter the sea-wolf at Crete? A dive from the cliff through its jaws into its belly and back through its flesh with the knife. Here's your towering cliff, your gleaming knife, your stinking fish.

(AUGIAS *exits.* HERACLES *shovels and hauls manure, first with one hand, the other holding his nose, then with both hands.*)

HERACLES: Oh, envied Sisyphus, his stone rolls without odor.

Oh, happy water, it has no nose. Father, thou maker of all flesh, why does your flesh shit?

(*Throws bucket and shovel down, takes his bow.*)

Stench, where are you? Come out of your monstrous shape, show your ugly mug. Is your dwelling the void of nothingness? I will lard it with arrows. And if you're everywhere, I'll hit you everywhere.

(*Shoots wildly in all directions, throws the bow down and takes his club.*)

We're enemies, dung. Go voluntarily into the river of your choice. The river or the club.

(*Waits for the effect. No effect.*)

You've made your choice.

(*Slams the club into the muck, howls in pain, blinded by the muck. Laughter of* AUGIAS.)

I'll laugh after you.

(*To the cattle.*)

Out of your stable.

Come and wash your feces from my face.
You ate the grass. Now also eat what you
Have made from grass. The earth sustains you and
You shit on it in gratitude. Now eat or
I'm your stable and your grave my belly.
(*Protest from Thebes.*)
You're lucky, beef. Thebes doesn't want to eat grass.
(*He picks up the shovel again.*)
And I won't eat manure!
(*He throws the shovel down again.*)
Hear me, Thebans! See my weakness and release me from your labor
which was too great for me. Look at my arms, not strong enough to lift
this tool.
(*He demonstrates that he cannot lift the shovel.*)
Look at my legs which barely are supporting me.
(*He falls down. Applause and laughter from Thebes.*)
VOICES: Bravo. What an act. Hurrah for Heracles. Da Capo.
HERACLES: Who's Heracles? I, body without a name. I, dunghill without a face.
(*Increasing applause.*)
VOICES: Look at his mask! That's what I call style!
HERACLES: (*On his hands and knees, hides under his lion's skin, roars.*) I've
eaten him, your Heracles. He's lost his way in the maze of my guts.
Through the fence of my teeth his last word was uttered. I'm the Ne-
mean Lion. There is room for three Thebes in my belly.
(*Increasing applause.*)
VOICES: He doesn't act the lion, he *is* the lion. I can't stop laughing. My
husband laughed till he dropped dead. That's the art of acting. Nice art:
I have four children. Stop it. Go on. Murderer. Enough. Da Capo. Stop
it. Go on. Enough. Da Capo.
HERACLES: Yeaaaaaaaaaaaaaaaaaaaaaaaaaaaaaaaaaaaaaaaaaaaaaaaaaaaaaah!
The dunghill, that's me; the voice from the feces is my voice, under that
mask of feces, that's my face. That's what his fifth labor made of Heracles, the doer of your deeds. Would I hadn't done the first one! I
wouldn't stand in this my fifth one, stinking, my fame my prison, with
each deed snared into the next one, with each freedom harnessed to
a new yoke, a victor conquered by his victories, Heracles forced into
Heracles. Willingly you've fed women to the Hydra, deaf to their last
screams while you expected your own last scream when the lion was
devouring the men. I've strangled the lion, I returned, more a wound

than flesh, in its bloody skin, and you wanted to keep your women. I've cut off the Hydra's heads for nine long days, sealed the necks with fire, the remains to the dogs, I returned on my hands and knees, breathless, to your Thebes that breathed a sigh of relief, and the small evils were colossal. They're gone, now you want your beef without the muck. I reduced your death by four of its shapes, now you want life without its last one, the murder of the new tomorrow: Immortality. I'll take back all my deeds. Time shall stop. Roll backwards, Time. Crawl back into your skin, Nemean Lion. Hydra, grow your heads back again. And so forth. (*Applause from Thebes.*)

VOICES: Hear, hear how he thinks. That's what I call dialectics. Heracles the thinker.

(HERACLES *hurls muck into the audience. Frenetic applause.*)

Look how he's working. Heracles the working man. Go back to your houses; don't disturb his work.

HERACLES: Watch, Thebans, what I'm going to do now

With Heracles, the doer of your deeds:

I'll throw him in the muck, the muck his grave

And rising it will bury you and Thebes.

(*Goes into position to jump into the muck, vomiting.*)

What's Thebes to me, and who are you then? I

Am nobody, nobody's son who hasn't

Done a thing.

(ZEUS *on a cloud. He holds his nose.*)

ZEUS: Do your job now, Heracles, my son.

HERACLES: Why me, father?

ZEUS: Here is your reward.

(*He beckons. On another cloud,* HEBE *sails by. She is nude and also holding her nose.*)

HERACLES: Stay! Those breasts! And what a pair of thighs!

Surrender, muck, Heracles is himself again.

Did I say you stink, burden who supports me?

See my fist, it hits the slanderer.

(*Hits himself on the nose.*)

Beauty of labor, fragrance of the muck

I am anticipating blissful luck!

(*Enter a jealous bull.*)

Welcome in heat! What do you want? It's not
Your cows my third leg's getting up for.
My heaven grazes on another meadow.
You've got one horn too many?
(*The bull attacks.*)

                              Sure.
(*Bullfight.* HERACLES *is victorious and harnesses the bull to the bucket.*)
                              Pull!
(*The bull does so and falls into the river.*)
                              Halt!
(HERACLES *pulls the bucket and with it the bull from the river.*)
You've got to earn your death, now do your job.
Pull, Heracles!
(*The bull doesn't move.*)
                    Your pay: five pecks of grass.
(*The bull pulls.*)
And a cow your heaven.
(*The bull pulls faster.*)
                              That quickens him.—
Fill the bucket, too, and empty it.
Do all the work if you want all your pay.
(*The bull tries dredging the muck, the muck spills on* HERACLES *instead
of into the bucket.*)
Oh mirror most imperfect! Half-baked toy!
If you won't be complete, be nothing then.
(HERACLES *hurls the bull into the river. With the bull goes the bucket.*)
AUGIAS: My bull! You'll pay for him.
HERACLES: River, my bull!
Keep the bull but spit back the bucket. Would you like to wash the sta-
ble? You can forget the ocean. Your banks will devour you. My cows
will fill you with shit. Your banks will devour you with the assholes of
my cows. My cows will shit you full with the jaws of your banks.
AUGIAS: Did I hear you say: my cows?
HERACLES: And your muck.
(*Throws the shovel down. Protest from Thebes.*)
I shit on Thebes.
(*Hear! Hear! and jeers from Thebes.* HEBE *sails by on her cloud.* HERA-
CLES *picks up the shovel again.*)
                    For Thebes. River, the bucket!

Augias. A bucket.

AUGIAS: First my bull.

HERACLES: My father on your cloud, step forward here
And tell your river: Lend my son an ear.
(*Silence.*)
Who's more to you, your river or your son?
Hear what I want, tell him what's to be done.
(*Silence.*)
Your silence, dad, is smacking of my pain.

(ZEUS *on his cloud, in his arms a nude woman, etc.*)

ZEUS: Do your work. Without pain no gain.
(*He's gone.*)
HERACLES: Did you say work? Gulp down the shovel, too.
(*Throws the shovel into the river.*)
Be what you robbed me of, river: my bucket
River: my shovel and my bull. You on the
Left there, too. Two will wash more than one.
If you won't hear me, listen to my fist
I'll tame you and I'll change your course and tame
You too, your course will change if my fist speaks.
(*To the above.*)
Watch out, what I'll do with your water, dad.
You didn't help me, now observe how I
Will help myself and what your river can do
When he must do it since he's yoked by me.
(*Struggles with the river.*)
River, have you no body then but none?
River, have you no other weight but mine?
Who are you, foe and battleground in one
Who armed with myself is now wrestling me?
There's no neck I didn't harness, but
Your river has no neck to throw my yoke on.
(*A cow steps to the riverbank, drinks and pisses.*)
Thanks for your model. How to steer a river.
(*Drinks.*)
I am your mouth.
(*Pisses.*)
                          I am your source as well.

Now do my work and wash the stable.
You're getting lost in the intestine's maze?
Where is your stride that in its torrent canceled
My strength with your strength of a thousand bulls?
And now you're mocking me with this your weakness
That won't move even one small speck of dust
Deaf to my words and deaf to all my strength
Nothing but silt that clogs my body's engine.
What's left? Hand, you're my shovel; hand, my bucket.
And Heracles is Heracles my bull.
(*Manual labor.*)
I'd rather move the world than its manure!
(*Building a dike.*)
Look: your mountain's walking with my legs.
Look: your river's rising at your mountainside.
(*Thunder.*)
Did I forget to ask you? Permit me to change your world, Papa.
Augias, drive your cattle from your stable
I'm coming, Heracles, two rivers strong
Lord of the waters and your stableboy
The river is my hand and is my strength
He who was conquered by my hand
He who was conquered by my weakness.

AUGIAS: My stable! My cattle!

SHOUTS FROM THEBES: Our beef to the fish!

HERACLES: (*Opens the dam.*)
Out of my way, you cattlebaron. Here
I come and wash your stable, Heracles
The river, steered by Heracles, the pilot
Of the rivers.
(*Thunder.*)
                     I know that you can thunder.
And I can steer your rivers, look, unbridled,
     wherever I like to.
(*Winter. The river stops in its tracks, frozen.*)
Hey, what is that supposed to mean?

AUGIAS: Heracles, the pilot of rivers.

HERACLES: (*To the above.*)
You've started it.

(*Rips the sun from the sky, holds it in his hand until the ice melts. Hand and stable are burning.*)

Where's your winter, Zeus?

AUGIAS: My stable's burning.

HERACLES: (*Looks at his hand, it is black.*)

Is it?

Not for long. Make way, Augias.

(*The river washes the stable.*)

AUGIAS: Seven oxen!

(*Rejoicing from Thebes.*)

VOICES: Long live Heracles! Bravo. Da Capo.

HERACLES: (*Whistles mountain and rivers back to their places.*) The job is done. And now: Where's my reward?

(*Thunder and lightning.*)

AUGIAS: Why don't you ask my cows for your reward.

See you again in your muck of tomorrow.

HERACLES: Did I hear you say: My cows?

AUGIAS: And your muck.

HERACLES: My river will take care of your muck gratis.

Your stable and your cattle, they are mine.

Now, play your final scene.

(*He rips* AUGIAS *in two and throws the halves into the river, pulls down the sky, reaches for* HEBE. *Before the wedding, the two* THEBANS *enter.*)

THEBANS: He who strangled the Nemean Lion and beheaded the Hydra

He who captured the hind and the boar, destroyer of harvests

He who cleaned the stable of Augias, stinking fleshpot

Heracles, son of Alcmene, sired in Amphitryon's bed.

(*They grin.*)

Not by Amphitryon—

(*They dodge. Silence.*)

Not by Amphitryon—

(*They shout.*)

Not by Amphitryon!

Doer of five great deeds. Lend us your arm for the sixth one.

(HERACLES *rolls up the sky and puts it in his pocket.*)

Tales of Homer

1

Often talked, and in abundance, with Homer his pupils,
Elucidating his work, and demanding correct explication.
Because the old man loved to discover himself anew
And, when extolled, he wasn't stingy with wine and a roast.
During such feasts, with meats and the wine, the talk often turned to
Thersites, the much despised one, the gossip who rose in assembly.
Cleverly using the war lords' quarrel about their spoils
Said he: Look at the peoples' shepherd who's shearing and killing
His sheep like all shepherds do with their flock, and showed the bloody
Empty hands of the soldiers to the soldiers as empty and bloody.
There then the pupils asked: What is that about this Thersites
Master? You give him the right words but then with your own words
You prove him wrong. This seems to us difficult to understand.
Why did you do that? Said to them Homer: To please the princes.
Asked the pupils: Why's that? The old man: From hunger. For laurel?
Too. But he liked it as much in his fleshpot as on his temple.

2

Amongst his pupils, they say, was one exceptionally bright
A great one for questions. Each answer he questioned to find
The one and only definitive answer. He asked the old man
Sitting with him at the river again the often asked question.
Quizzically looked the old man at the youngster and said serenely:
The truth is an arrow that's poisoned for all hasty archers! Even
Bending the bow is much. The arrow will still be an arrow
If someone hides it in reeds. Truth dressed as a lie is still truth
And the bow won't die with the archer. Said it and rose.

Oedipus Commentary

Laius was king in Thebes. The god told him from the mouth of the
Priests his son would walk over him. Laius, unwilling
To pay the price of a birth that would cost his life, tore from
The breasts of the mother the new born and pierced its toes
Careful that it wouldn't walk over him, and sewed them up threefold
Gave it so that he would serve it to the birds on the table of mountains

To an old servant, *this my own flesh won't overgrow me*
And so he spread the foot which would trample him by his own caution:
To the winged hunger the servant refused to offer the child
Gave it to other hands that they might save it in other countries
There the highborn grew up on his misshapen feet
Nobody walks like me, his blemish his name, on his feet
And on others' fate took its course, resistible every
Step but the next one, irresistibly one step took the other.
See the poem of Oedipus, Laius's son from Jocasta
Unbeknownst to himself, in Thebes a tyrant through merit:
He solved, since his crippled foot forbade him to flee, the riddle
Posed by the three times born Sphinx, a curse on the city of Thebes
To the stone he offered to eat the three-headed man-eating monster
And Man was the solution. For years in a happy city
He plowed the bed he was conceived in, a lucky bringer of luck.
Longer than good luck is time, and longer than bad luck: The tenth
Year out of the unknown the plague came and struck the city
Many years happy. Bodies it broke and the order of things.
Ringed by those he ruled, the new riddle crushing his shoulders
Stood on too big a foot, around him the screams of the dying,
The solver of riddles and threw into darkness his questions like nets:
Is the messenger lying, his ear he sent to the priests, mouth of the gods?
The blind man who points his ten fingers at him, does he speak the truth?
Out of the darkness the nets bounce back, and there in their mesh
On his own tracks overtaken by his own steps: He.
And at the bottom he is at his peak: he overtook time
Caught in the circle, *I and no end,* he caught himself.
In his eyesockets he buries the world. Stood here a tree?
Is there still flesh aside of his own? None, there are no trees
With voices his ear is talking to him, the ground is his thought
Mud or stone, whatever his foot thinks, and from his hands
Sometimes a wall grows, *the world is a wart,* or his finger creates
Him once again in intercourse with the air, until he
Wipes out the image himself with his hand. And so
He lives, his own grave, and is chewing his dead.   ·
See his example, he who jumps from a bloodied start
In the freedom of Man, caught in the teeth of Man
On feet far too few, with not enough hands, he grasps at space.

Mauser

A Performance Text

Mauser, written in 1970, was first performed in an English version December 1975, at the University of Texas, Austin, while Heiner Müller was Poet-in-Residence with the university's Department of German. This version, by Helen Fehervary and Marc Silberman, was published with the German text in *New German Critique, #8,* 1976.

Mauser is Müller's response to Bertolt Brecht's *Die Massnahme* (*The Measures Taken,* in Eric Bentley's translation). *Lehrstücke* both, the plays examine the failure of loyal revolutionaries and the consequent acceptance of a death deemed necessary by their party. Brecht's protagonist failed due to spontaneous empathy and compassion with the oppressed. One of Müller's characters fails due to a similar weakness. Yet, his protagonist, who in an early draft was named Mauser, embraces executions as a rewarding part of his revolutionary mission and begins to kill for killing's sake. Only his own execution can stop his excesses, an execution he learns to accept as his last service to the revolution.

Brecht's text reflected, in 1930, on the struggle of the German Left against the rise of Hitler, distancing his fable by way of an East Asian setting. Forty years later, Müller's play represented a post-Stalinist view of violence in service to the revolution. Employing as well as criticizing the model of *The Measures Taken* and quoting also from other Brecht texts, such as *The Mother,* the play reflects its author's experience of Stalinism. Already in the early fifties it had engaged his imagination, as a brief text in ABC reveals. *Mauser* could be neither published nor performed in the GDR; it was the only play of Müller for which a written instruction was issued: "Publication and dissemination of this text in the territory of the GDR is forbidden."

The title refers to a famous pistol, designed by the German weapons manufacturers Mauser Brothers, which became the handgun of choice with the Red Army during the Russian Civil War, 1918–20. The poet Mayakovsky praised it in his *Left March* of 1918: "Silence, you orators / You / Have the floor / Comrade Mauser." The German word *Mauser* also denotes the molting undergone by birds in spring and autumn, while the verb *mausen* signifies the catching of mice by a cat, as well as petty larceny.

C.W.

CHORUS: You have fought at the front of the civil war
    The enemy hasn't found any weakness in you
    We haven't found any weakness in you.
    Now you yourself are a weakness
    The enemy must not find in us.
    You dispensed death in the city of Witebsk
    To the enemies of the Revolution by our order
    Knowing, the daily bread of the Revolution
    In the city of Witebsk as in other cities
    Is the death of its enemies, knowing, even the grass
    We must tear up so it will stay green
    We have killed them, using your hand.
    But one morning in the city of Witebsk
    You yourself have killed with your hand
    Not our enemies, not by our appointment
    And you must be killed, an enemy yourself.
    Do your work now at the last place
    The Revolution appointed you to
    The place you won't leave on your feet
    At the wall which will be your last one
    As you have done your other work
    Knowing, the daily bread of the Revolution
    In the city of Witebsk as in other cities
    Is the death of its enemies, knowing, even the grass
    We must tear it up so it will stay green.
A: I have done my work.
CHORUS: Do your last one.
A: I have killed for the Revolution.
CHORUS: Die for her.
A: I have committed a mistake.
CHORUS: You are the mistake.
A: I am a human being.
CHORUS: What is that.
A: I don't want to die.
CHORUS: We don't ask you if you want to die.
    The wall at your back is the last wall
    At your back. The Revolution doesn't need you anymore.
    It needs your death. But until you say Yes
    To the No that has been pronounced on you

You haven't finished your work.
Facing the gun barrels of the Revolution which needs your death
Learn your last lesson. Your last lesson is:
You, who stand at the wall, are your own enemy and ours.

A: In prisons from Omsk to Odessa
On my skin the text was written
Once read under school benches and on the john
PROLETARIANS OF ALL COUNTRIES, UNITE
Written with fist and rifle butt, with boot heel and shoe cap
On the son of a middle-class father who owned his own samovar
Prepared on floorboards which were hollowed from kneeling
Before the icon for a cleric's career.
But soon I left the starting post.
At meetings, demonstrations, strikes
Ridden down by orthodox Cossacks
By sluggish officials listlessly tortured
I learned nothing of life after death.
Killing I learned in the everlasting combat
Against the mortal clinch, at the time of Die or Kill.
We said: He who won't kill won't eat.
To ram the bayonet into an enemy
Cadet, officer, or a peasant who hadn't understood anything
We said: It's work like any other work
To smash a skull or shoot.

A (CHORUS): But one morning in the city of Witebsk
The noise of battle not far off, the Revolution gave me
With the Party's voice the mandate
To take charge of the Revolutionary Tribunal
In the city of Witebsk, that dispenses death
To the enemies of the Revolution in the city of Witebsk.

CHORUS: You have fought at the front of civil war
The enemy hasn't found any weakness in you
We haven't found any weakness in you.
Leave the front and take the place
The Revolution needs you at right now
Until it needs you at another place.
Conduct our struggle in our back, dispense
Death to the enemies of the Revolution.

A (CHORUS): And I agreed with the mandate.

Knowing, the daily bread of the Revolution
Is the death of its enemies, knowing, even the grass
We must tear up so it will stay green
I agreed with the mandate
The Revolution had given me
With the party's voice in the noise of battle.
And this killing was another kind of killing
And it was work unlike any other work.

CHORUS: Your work begins today. He who did it before you
Must be killed before tomorrow, he himself an enemy.

A (CHORUS): Why he.

B: Before my revolver three farmers
Enemies of the Revolution out of ignorance.
On their backs the hands, tied by rope
Are ruined by work, tied to the revolver
By the Revolution's mandate is my hand
My revolver aimed at their neck.
Their enemies are my enemies, I know it
But those standing before me, facing the quarry
Don't know it, and I who know it
Have no other lesson for their ignorance
But the bullet. I have dispensed death
The revolver my third hand
To the enemies of the Revolution in the city of Witebsk
Knowing, the daily bread of the Revolution
Is the death of its enemies, knowing, even the grass
We must tear up so it will stay green
Knowing, the Revolution kills with my hand.
I don't know it anymore, I cannot kill anymore.
I retract my hand from the mandate
The Revolution gave me
One morning in the city of Witebsk
With the Party's voice, in the noise of battle.
I cut the rope off the hands
Of our enemies that are marked
With their work's trace as my own kind.
I say: Your enemies are our enemies.
I say: Go back to your work.

CHORUS (THE PERFORMERS OF THE THREE FARMERS):

And they went back to their work
Three enemies of the Revolution, uninstructed.
When he retracted his hand from the mandate
The Revolution had given him
One morning in the city of Witebsk
With the Party's voice, in the noise of battle
It was one hand more at our throat.
Namely, your hand isn't your hand
Just as my hand isn't my hand
Until the Revolution has finally triumphed
In the city of Witebsk as in other cities.
Namely, ignorance can kill
As steel can kill or fever
Since knowledge isn't enough, but ignorance
Must end once and for all, and it isn't enough to kill
But killing is a science
And must be learned, so it will end
Since what is natural isn't natural
But we must tear up the grass
And we must spit out the bread
Until the Revolution has finally triumphed
In the city of Witebsk as in other cities
So the grass will stay green and hunger will end.
He who insists on himself as his own property
Is an enemy of the Revolution like other enemies
Because our kind isn't our kind
And so aren't we, the Revolution itself
Isn't one with itself, but the enemy with
Tooth and nail, bayonet and machine gun
Writes into its living image his hideous features
And his wounds will be scars on our face.

B: Why the killing and why the dying
If the price of the Revolution is the Revolution
Those to be freed the price of freedom.

A: These or other words he shouted against the noise of battle
That had increased and still was increasing.
A thousand hands at our throat, there was
Against doubt in the Revolution no
Other remedy but the death of the doubter.

And I had no eyes for his hands
As he stood before my revolver, facing the quarry
If they were ruined by work or were not ruined
But they were tied firmly with rope
And we killed him with my hand
Knowing, the daily bread of the Revolution
Is the death of its enemies, knowing, even the grass
We must tear up, so it will stay green.
I knew it, killing others on another morning
And at a third morning others again
And they had no hands and no faces
But the eye with which I looked at them
And the mouth with which I talked to them
Was the revolver and my words the bullets
And I didn't forget it when they screamed
As my revolver hurled them into the quarry
Enemies of the Revolution to other enemies
And it was work like any other work.
I knew, if you shoot into a human being
Blood will flow from him as from all animals
Little differentiates the dead and
The little not for long. But man is no animal:
The seventh morning, I saw their faces
The hands on their back, tied with rope
Marked by the trace of their various work
While, facing the quarry, they waited
For death from my revolver, and doubt
Lodged itself between finger and trigger, burdening
With those killed during seven mornings
My neck which carries the yoke of the Revolution
So that all yokes will be broken
And my hand which is tied to the revolver
By mandate of the Revolution, given
One morning in the city of Witebsk
With the voice of the Party, in the noise of battle
To dispense death to its enemies
So the killing will end, and I spoke the command
This morning just as the first morning
DEATH TO THE ENEMIES OF THE REVOLUTION

And dispensed death, yet my voice
Spoke the command like it wasn't my voice and my hand
Dispensed death like it wasn't my hand
And the killing was a killing of another kind
And it was work like no other work
And at night I saw my face
That looked at me with eyes not my own
Out of the mirror, many times cracked
From the shelling of the city many times taken
And during the night I was not a man, burdened
With those killed during seven mornings
My sex the revolver that dispenses death
To the enemies of the Revolution, facing the quarry.

A (CHORUS): Why I. Relieve me of the mandate
I am too weak for it.

CHORUS: Why you.

A: I have fought at the front of civil war
The enemy hasn't found any weakness in me
You haven't found any weakness in me
Now I myself am a weakness
The enemy must not find in us.
I have dispensed death in the city of Witebsk
To the enemies of the Revolution in the city of Witebsk
Knowing, the daily bread of the Revolution
Is the death of its enemies, knowing, even the grass
We must tear up, so it will stay green.
I did not forget it on the third morning
And not on the seventh. But on the tenth morning
I don't know it anymore. To kill and to kill
And each third one, maybe, is not guilty who
Stands before my revolver, facing the quarry.

CHORUS: In this struggle that won't end
In the city of Witebsk as in other cities
But with our triumph or fall
With two weak hands each one of us does
The work of two thousand hands, broken hands
Hands tied with chains and rope, hands
Hacked off, hands at our throat.
A thousand hands at our throat, we don't

Have the breath left to ask for guilt or innocence
Of each hand at our throat, or their extraction
If they are ruined by work or are not ruined
If misery twined them around our throat and
Ignorance about their misery's root
Or fear of the Revolution which will tear it up
By its root. Who are you, different from us
Or special, who insists on his weakness
He who says: I with your mouth, is not you.
Not until the Revolution has finally triumphed
In the city of Witebsk as in other cities
You are your own property. With your hand
The Revolution kills. With all the hands
With which the Revolution kills, you kill too.
Your weakness is our weakness
Your conscience is the breach in your consciousness
Which is a breach in our front. Who are you.
A: A soldier of the Revolution
CHORUS: So you want
The Revolution to relieve you of the mandate
You are too weak for, yet which needs to be achieved
By some man or other.
A (CHORUS): No./And the killing continued, facing the quarry.
Next morning before my revolver a farmer
As before him his kind at other mornings
As before me my kind before other revolvers
Cold sweat at his neck: four fighters of the Revolution
Were betrayed by him to our enemy and his
Cold sweat at their neck, they stand before other revolvers.
His kind has been killed
And my kind, for two thousand years
By wheel gallows rope garrote knout katorga
By my enemy's kind who is his enemy
And my revolver aimed at his neck now
I wheel gallows rope garrote knout katorga
I before my revolver, facing the quarry
I my revolver aimed at my neck.
Knowing, with my hand the Revolution kills
Abolishing wheel gallows rope garrote knout katorga

And not knowing it, before my revolver a man
I between hand and revolver, finger and trigger
I breach in my consciousness, in our front.
CHORUS: Your mandate is not to kill men but
Enemies. Namely, Man is unknown.
We know that killing is work
But Man is more than his work.
Not until the Revolution has finally triumphed
In the city of Witebsk as in other cities
Will we know what that is, Man.
Namely, he is our work, the unknown one
Behind the masks, the one buried in the dung
Of his history, the real one beneath the leprosy
The living one in those petrifications
Because the Revolution will tear off his masks, efface
His leprosy, wash from the petrified dung
Of his history his image, Man, with
Teeth and nail, bayonet and machine gun
Rising from the chain of generations
Rending his bloody umbilical cord
In the lightning of the real beginning, recognizing himself
The one the other, according to their difference
By the root, digs up Man from man.
What counts is the example, death means nothing.
A: But in the noise of battle that had increased
And still was increasing, I stood with bloody hands
Soldier and bayonet of the Revolution
And asked with my own voice for assurance.
A (CHORUS): Will the killing end when the Revolution has triumphed.
Will the Revolution triumph. How much longer.
CHORUS: You know what we know, we know what you know
The Revolution will triumph or Man will not be
But disappear in the increasing mass of mankind.
A: And I heard my voice say
This morning as at other mornings
DEATH TO THE ENEMIES OF THE REVOLUTION and I saw
Him who was I killing a thing of flesh blood
And other matter, not asking for guilt or innocence
Not for its name and if it was an enemy

Or no enemy, and it stopped moving
But he who was I didn't stop killing it.
He said:
CHORUS: I have thrown off my burden
On my neck the dead don't trouble me any longer
A man is something you shoot into
Until Man will rise from the ruins of man./
And after he had shot again and again
Through the bursting skin into the bloody
Flesh, at cracking bones, he voted
With this feet against the corpse.
A (CHORUS): I take under my boot what I have killed
I dance on my dead with stomping steps
For me it isn't enough to kill what must die
So the Revolution will triumph and the killing end
But it shouldn't be here anymore and be nothing forever
And disappear from the face of the earth
A clean slate for those who will come.
CHORUS: We heard his roaring and saw what he had done
Not by our mandate, and he didn't stop screaming
With the voice of Man who is devouring Man.
Then we knew that his work had used him up
And his time had passed and we led him away
An enemy of the Revolution like other enemies
And not like others since also his own enemy
Knowing, the daily bread of the Revolution
Is the death of its enemies, knowing, even the grass
We must tear up so it will stay green.
But he had thrown off his burden
That had to be borne until the Revolution had triumphed
On his neck the dead didn't trouble him any longer
They who will trouble us until the Revolution has triumphed
Since his burden had become his spoils
Hence the Revolution had no place for him any longer
And he had no place any longer for himself
Other than before the gun barrels of the Revolution.
A: Not until they took me away from my work
And took the revolver away from my hand
And my fingers were still crooked as around the weapon

Separate from me, did I see what I had done
And not until they led me away did I hear
Again my voice and the noise of battle
Which had increased and still was increasing.

A (CHORUS): But I am led to the wall now by my own kind
And I who understand it, do not understand it.
Why.

CHORUS: You know what we know, we know what you know.
Your work was bloody and like no other work
But it must be done like any other work
By some man or other.

A: I have done my work. Look at my hand.

CHORUS: We see that your hand is bloody.

A: How not so.
And louder than the battle noise the silence was
In the city of Witebsk for one moment
And longer than my life was this moment.
I am a man. Man is no machine.
Kill and kill, be the same after each death
I couldn't do it. Give me the sleep of machines.

CHORUS: Not until the Revolution has triumphed
In the city of Witebsk as in other cities
Will we know what that is: Man.

A: I want to know it here and now: I ask
This morning in the city of Witebsk
With bloody boots on my last walk
He who is led to dying, who hasn't time left
With my last breath here and now
I ask the Revolution about Man.

CHORUS: You are asking too early. We cannot help you.
And your question doesn't help the Revolution.
Listen to the noise of battle.

A: I only have one time to live.
On the other side of the battle noise like black snow
Is waiting for me: silence.

CHORUS: You only die one death
But the Revolution is dying many deaths.
The Revolution has many times, not one
Too many. Man is more than his work

Or he won't exist. You don't exist any more
Since your work has used you up
You must disappear from the face of the earth.
The blood you have stained your hand with
When it was a hand of the Revolution
Must be washed off by your own blood
From the name of the Revolution which needs each hand
But not your hand any longer.
A: I have killed
By your mandate.
CHORUS: And not by our mandate.
Between finger and trigger, the moment
Was your time and ours. Between hand and revolver, the span
Was your place at the front of the Revolution
But when your hand became one with the revolver
And you became one with your work
And had lost any consciousness of it
That it had to be done here and now
So that it won't have to be done anymore and by no one
Your place at our front became a gap
And no place for you at our front any longer.
Terrible is what is custom, lethal what's easy
With many roots the past is dwelling in us
That is to be torn up with all its roots
In our weakness the dead are arising
Those to be buried, again and again
We have to give up ourselves, each one of us
But we shouldn't give up one another.
You are the one and you are the other
Whom you have mangled under your boot
Who has mangled you under your boot
You gave yourself up, the one the other
The Revolution won't give you up. Learn to die.
What you learn will increase our experience.
Die learning. Don't give up the Revolution.
A: I refuse. I won't accept my death.
My life belongs to me.
CHORUS: Nothingness is your property.
A (CHORUS): I don't want to die. I throw myself on the ground.

I hold on to the earth with all my hands.
I bite with my teeth into the earth to hold on
To what I don't want to leave. I scream.
CHORUS (A): We know that dying is work.
Your fear belongs to you.
A (CHORUS): What will come after death.
CHORUS (A): He still asked but got up from the ground
Not screaming anymore, and we answered him:
You know what we know, we know what you know
And your question won't help the Revolution.
When life will be an answer
It might be permitted. But the Revolution needs
Your Yes to your death. And he didn't ask anymore
But went to the wall and spoke the command
Knowing, the daily bread of the Revolution
Is the death of its enemies, knowing, even the grass
We must tear up so it will stay green.
A (CHORUS):
DEATH TO THE ENEMIES OF THE REVOLUTION.

NOTE

Mauser, written in 1970 as the third piece of an experimental sequence, of which the first was *Philoctetes,* the second *The Horatian,* presupposes/criticizes Brecht's theory and practice of the Learning Play. *Mauser,* a variant of a theme from Sholokhov's novel *Quiet Flows the Don,* is not a play for the repertoire; the extreme case is not the topic, but the example with which the continuum of a normality that has to be exploded is demonstrated; death—in the theater of individuals tragedy was based on its glorification, comedy on its inhibition—is shown as a function of life that is regarded as production, one kind of work among others, organized by the collective and organizing the collective. SO THAT SOMETHING CAN ARRIVE SOMETHING HAS TO GO THE FIRST SHAPE OF HOPE IS FEAR THE FIRST APPEARANCE OF THE NEW IS TERROR. Performance for an audience is possible if the audience is invited to control the performance by its text, and the text by its performance, through reading the Chorus part, or the part of the First Player (A), or if the Chorus part is read by one group of spectators and the part of the First Player by another group of spectators—the text not read by each group should be blotted out in the script—or through other devices; and if the audience's reaction can be controlled through the nonsynchronism of text and performance, the nonidentity of speaker and performer. The proposed distribution of text is variable, the mode and degree of variants a political choice that has to be made in each individual case. Examples of possible variants: the Chorus provides to the First Performer for certain speeches a performer of the First Performer (A 1); all Chorus performers at once or one after another, perform the part of the First Performer; the First Performer speaks certain segments of the Chorus's speeches while A 1 performs his role. No performer can assume another's role all the time. Experiences are only transmitted by and in a collective; the training of the (individual) capacity to make experiences is a function of the performance. The Second Performer (B) is played by a member of the Chorus who, after his killing, will again assume his place in the Chorus. All tools of the theater should be totally visible when employed: props, costume pieces, masks, makeup utensils, etc., are on stage. The city of Witebsk is representative of all places where a revolution was is will be forced to kill its enemies.

H. M., 1970

The Wound Woyzeck

A Public Address

Die Wunde Woyzeck is a speech Heiner Müller made at Darmstadt, 18 October 1985, when accepting the Georg Büchner Prize of the German Academy of Language and Poetry, Germany's most coveted literary honor. The text was originally published in *Theater Heute, #11,* Berlin, 1988. Müller prefaced his address with a comment on the execution of the black poet Benjamin Moloise at Central Prison of Pretoria the same morning. He stated that it had been a shock to see his text immediately corroborated by this murder, a sordid demonstration of apartheid, which was still the law in South Africa at the time.

The speech embarks upon a stream of associations that explore the connections between Büchner's antihero and a number of vastly dissimilar writers that includes J. M. R. Lenz, von Kleist, Heine, Kafka, Georg Heym, Samuel Beckett, Konrad Bayer, and Rolf Dieter Brinkmann. Müller also refers to a prominent figure in German politics of the 1970s, the former terrorist Ulrike Meinhof, who had died in a West German penitentiary—according to the police a suicide, though many remain convinced she was murdered in her cell. The author compares her to the fictional character of the Young Comrade in Brecht's *Lehrstück The Measures Taken.* In his autobiography, *War without Battle* (*Krieg ohne Schlacht*), Müller commented on the shocked silence with which the West German audience hearing his acceptance speech at Darmstadt (it included the then President of the Federal Republic, von Weizsaecker) responded to his mentioning of Meinhof.

Dismissing the fashionable theory of a so-called Post-Histoire, Müller quotes in his final paragraph a German proverbial saying, "*Da liegt der Hund begraben*" (That is where the dog's been buried). The meaning is, roughly, "That is where you'd find the root of it all." In conclusion Müller articulates his frequently stated belief that humankind's future will be determined by the "South," just as the recorded history of the past two millennia has been dictated by the peoples of the northern hemisphere.

C.W.

1   Woyzeck still is shaving his Captain, eating the prescribed peas, tor-
turing Marie with the torpor of his love, the play's population has become
a state, surrounded by ghosts: The Fusilier Runge is his bloody brother,
proletarian tool of Rosa Luxemburg's murderers; his prison is called Stalingrad, where the murdered woman faces him in the mask of Kriemhild;
her monument is erected on Mamaia Hill, her German monument the
Wall in Berlin, the armored train of the Revolution curdled to politics. HIS
MOUTH PRESSED AGAINST THE SHOULDER OF THE POLICEMAN WHO NIMBLY LEADS
HIM AWAY, that is how Kafka has seen him disappear from the stage, after
the fratricide WITH DIFFICULTY STIFLING THE LAST NAUSEA. Or as the patient, in
whose bed the doctor is placed, with his wound open like a mine pit from
which the maggots swarm. Goya's giant was his first appearance, he who
sitting on the mountains counts the hours of the rulers, father of the
guerilla. On a mural in a cloister cell in Parma I have seen his broken off
feet, gigantic in an Arcadian landscape. Somewhere, his body perhaps
swings itself forward on his hands, shaking with laughter perhaps, toward
an unknown future that perhaps will be his crossbreeding with a machine,
propelled against the force of gravity in the frenzy of rockets. In Africa he
is still on his Way of the Cross into history; time doesn't work for him anymore, perhaps even his hunger isn't an ingredient of Revolution any longer
since it can be quenched with bombs, while the Drum Majors of the world
devastate our planet, a battlefield of Tourism, runway for the final emergency; they don't see the Fire that the Rifleman Franz Johann Christoph
Woyzeck saw race around the sky near Darmstadt as he was cutting
switches for the gauntlet. Ulrike Meinhof, a daughter of Prussia and the
late-born bride of another erratic block of German letters who buried himself at the shore of Lake Wannsee, female protagonist in the last drama of
a bourgeois world, the armed RESURRECTION OF THE YOUNG COMRADE FROM
THE LIME PIT, she is his sister with Marie's bloody necklace.

2   A text many times raped by the theater, a text that happened to a
twenty-three-year-old whose eyelids were cut off at his birth by the Weird
Sisters, a text blasted by fever to orthographic splinters, a structure as it
might be created when lead is smelted at New Year's Eve since the hand
is trembling with anticipation of the future; a sleepless angel, it blocks the
entrance to Paradise where the innocence of playwriting was at home.
How harmless the Pill's equivalent in recent drama, Beckett's *Waiting for
Godot,* faced with this fast thunderstorm that moves with the speed of another age, in its baggage Lenz, the extinguished lightning from Livonia,

the time of Georg Heym bereft of utopia in his space under the Havel River's ice, of Konrad Bayer in Vitus Bering's eviscerated skull, of Rolf Dieter Brinkmann in the right-hand traffic in front of Shakespeare's Pub. How shameless is the lie of Post-Histoire in the face of the barbaric reality of our own prehistory.

3   THE WOUND HEINE begins to scar over, crooked. WOYZECK is the open wound. Woyzeck lives where the dog is buried; the dog's name: Woyzeck. We are waiting for his resurrection with fear and/or hope that the dog will return as a wolf. The wolf will come from the South. When the Sun is in its zenith, he will be one with our shadow and in the hour of white heat History will begin. Not until History has happened will our shared de-struction in the frost of entropy or, abridged by politics, in the nuclear lightning, be worthwhile; the destruction that will be the end of all utopias and the beginning of a reality beyond mankind.

Dove and Samurai;
A Letter to Robert Wilson
Two Prose Texts

Dove and Samurai (*Taube und Samurai*) and *A Letter to Robert Wilson* (*Brief an Robert Wilson*) were written in the 1980s. Heiner Müller first observed Wilson's work when the latter rehearsed his *Death, Destruction & Detroit* at the Schaubühne in what was then West Berlin in 1978. The same year, Müller wrote a text, *Terror Is the First Appearance of the New*, in which he stated, "The theater of Robert Wilson, as naïve as it is elitist, infantile toe dance and mathematical child's play, doesn't make any difference between amateur and professional actors. Prospect of an Epic Theater as Brecht conceived it yet never realized it, with a minimum of dramaturgic labor and beyond the perversity that makes out of luxury an occupation."

Müller and Wilson then met briefly in Cologne, in 1981, and became friends in 1983 when the latter was directing the German segment of his project *CIVIL warS,* to be shown at the 1984 Olympic Arts Festival in Los Angeles. It was planned to consist of several parts that were to be staged in Germany, Holland, Italy, Japan, and other places. Due to financial reasons, the project was eventually canceled. When Wilson desired a text for the German segment, Müller was recommended to him as a feasible author. They discovered they had much in common in spite of their vastly different backgrounds. Müller: "The beginning of our relation was his remark, `We are so different.' " Wilson used in his production texts by Müller about Frederick II and Prussian-German history and also other authors' texts which Müller had selected. The production was presented in Cologne, in 1984, and at the ART in Cambridge, Massachusetts, in an American version, in 1985. It was the beginning of their intensive collaboration and close friendship. Wilson went on to employ Müller's text *Explosion of a Memory* in his staging of *Alcestis,* at Cambridge (1986) and Stuttgart (1987). He then directed Müller's *Hamletmachine* in New York and Hamburg (1986), as well as *Quartet* in Stuttgart (1987) and Cambridge (1988). In 1987, when Wilson staged *Death, Destruction, & Detroit 2* at the Schaubühne, he wanted a text from Müller, who instead wrote his *Letter to Robert Wilson*; and in 1988 Müller contributed texts to Wilson's version of the Gilgamesh epic, *The Forest,* produced at the Freie Volksbühne Theater in West Berlin. Their last collaboration was the first European high-definition video-film, *The Death of Molière,* which Wilson produced for the French Institut de L'Audovisuel in 1994. At his friend's funeral, 16 January 1996, Wilson gave a eulogy, and he recently included Müller's *Landscape with Argonauts* in his staging of Brecht's *The Ocean Flight* at the Berliner Ensemble, 1998.

Dove and Samurai was first published in *ERSTE, Magazin für das Deutsche Schauspielhaus Hamburg, May–June 1986.* (The German title, *Taube und Samurai,* is difficult to translate since it conveys more than one meaning: *Taube* translates as *dove* but also as *deaf woman* and *deaf persons,* the plural. *Dove* appeared to be the most appropriate English title in view of the text's topic.) A slightly different version was originally sent by Müller as a telegram to Wilson, in 1984, after the planned production of *CIVIL warS* at Los Angeles had been canceled.

Letter to Robert Wilson appeared first in the program brochure for *Death, Destruction & Detroit 2,* at the Berlin Schaubühne, 1987. Wilson had asked Müller to contribute text to the production, based on writings by Kafka, and later, the mentioned text by Tshingis Aitmatov. The result of his efforts, as Müller explains it, was the *Letter.* Wilson used it eventually in the production, along with other texts.

Müller once pointed out, "The essential aspect of Wilson's theater is the separation of the elements, a dream of Brecht."

C.W.

Dove and Samurai

Robert Wilson comes from a space Ambrose Bierce disappeared into after he had seen the horrors of civil war. The one who returns carries the horror under the skin, his theater is the resurrection. The dead are liberated in slow motion. On this stage Kleist's marionette theater has a playroom, Brecht's epic dramaturgy a dance floor. An art without exertion, the step is planting its path. The dancing god is the marionette. His/her dance designs humans of a different flesh that is born from the wedding of fire and water of which Rimbaud was dreaming. Just as the apple from the tree of knowledge has to be eaten once again so that humans may return to the state of innocence, the tower of Babel has to be built anew so that the confusion of languages will come to an end. With the fairy tales' wisdom that the history of humans cannot be separated from the history of animals (plants, stones, machines) but for the price of extinction, Robert Wilson articulates the theme of our age: war of classes and races, species and genders, civil war in every sense of the term. When the eagles come gliding down and tear the banners of separation asunder and panthers walk about between the counters of the World Bank, the theater of resurrection will have found its stage.

Its reality is the union of humans and machines, the next step of evolution.

A Letter to Robert Wilson

For one week I have been trying to produce a text which could serve as a gravitational center to your production of *DD&D II*, a creation that more than any of your earlier works consists of its own explosion. My efforts have failed. Maybe, the explosion already had progressed too far, the degree of its acceleration (I'm not talking of Greenwich time) was already too high, that a text which willy-nilly means something could still inscribe itself in the vortex of the detonation. To speak of progress in context with an explosion seems paradoxical, but maybe for a long while now the liberation of the dead hasn't been happening in slow motion anymore but in quick motion. What remains to be done is the effort of describing my failure so that it will at least become an experience. The starting point was a text by Tshingis Aitmatov that describes a Mongolian torture which served to turn captives into slaves, tools without a memory. The technology was simple: the captive, who had been sentenced to survival and not designated for the slave trade but for domestic use by the conquerors, had his head shaved and covered with a helmet made form the skin of a freshly slaughtered camel's neck. Arms and legs shackled, his neck in the stocks so that he couldn't move his head, exposed on the steppe to the sun which dried the helmet and contracted it around his skull so that the regrowing hair was forced to grow backward into the scalp, the tortured prisoner lost his memory within five days—if he survived them—and was, after this operation, a laborer who didn't cause trouble, a Mankurt. There is no revolution without a memory. An early design of total utilization of labor, until its transformation into raw material in the concentration camps. I couldn't represent this event—the disintegration of thinking, the extinction of memory—only describe it, and any description is silenced, as our experiment with Kafka texts already was, when confronted with the centrifugal force of your images: Literature is experience congealed. The dead are writing with us on the paper of the Future at which flames are licking already from all sides. (Technology merely trains reflexes, it prevents experience. Our camel's skin, the computer, it is nothing but the present.) Yesterday I dreamed the end of libraries: next to workmens' barracks and engine rooms where geometrical modules were manufactured—I couldn't figure out their function or intended use—stacks, heaps of books, books in the grass, books in the mud, in the excavated building sites, putrid paper, decomposed letters. On his way to the toilet a worker with an empty face. Another dream of the same night: we were eating, tightly packed at narrow tables, in the spacious inner court of a castle in Switzerland, beneath helicopter flights. Sirens interrupted the meal: air raid warning. A waiter or the castellan in his armor informed us what had triggered it. Seventeen coaches of the Federal Soccer League had run over two children while driving in France. When I tried to translate the news for you, hoping for your coyote-like laughter, I discovered you weren't sitting at the table anymore but standing on the castle's ramparts, harnessed in a spacious steel construction, nearly grown together with it, because of your headphones not reachable by my voice, unreachable also for the sirens of the Swiss air raid warning. Next to my typewriter on the desk, which is full of burn marks and hasn't been cleaned up in years, there lies a reproduction, a picture postcard, of Tintoretto's *Miracle of Marcus*. Perhaps you have seen the painting in Milan, at the Pinacoteca Brera. I haven't seen it there, maybe it was just being restored, or I cannot remember it and have to be content with the postcard. That offers the advantage of the imprecise view, like at times a bad seat during a performance of yours. (The ideal audience of *DD&D II* would be one single spectator, enormously stretched between the four playgrounds of the dead in the vault of the stage space, crucified by geometry as in Leonardo's drawing after Vitruvius's text about *homo circularis* and *homo quadratus*: "If a man lies on his back, his arms and legs stretched out, and you place your drawing compass's needle at the point of his navel and draw a circle, such a circle will touch the fingertips of both hands and the tips of the toes. As there is a circle to be found at the body, there also will be the figure of the square. Namely, if you take measure from the soles of the feet to the crown of the head and then apply such measure to the stretched out hands, it will result in equal width and height as with surfaces that are laid out in a square by means of a T-square." This One-Person-Audience should have one eye that is attached to a pillar rising from the navel, circular and catholic, or turning with great speed as the eye of a certain reptile whose name I have forgotten. (Maybe, it only exists in my dreams.) Back to the Tintoretto: What I'm seeing is a church nave, vaulted by Roman arches, diagonally tapered toward the back, the right wall with its moldings and balconies is fully visible. Two men standing on ladders, the one with his right, the other one with his left hand holding on to the parapet, lower from the foremost balcony a naked old man, maybe a corpse, head first towards the ground. A white cloth with which he probably was clothed serves as a rope; his sex isn't important anymore. A third helper reaches from below for his right arm that is hanging down. He is the only one in the room who is wearing a turban. Behind him a man with arms spread out, expectation or salutation, how does one salute a dead man whose resurrection still is in the future. The left foreground is dominated by the Saint himself. With stretched out left arm he directs—like a foreman the crane—the labor at the balcony that is a deposition from the cross. The right hand holds the tablet or the book with Future's diagram. Before the Saint's feet a gray-white corpse. The skin color of the muscular body is meant to indicate that the soul has already left it: it belongs to art and putrefaction. On the right behind the corpse, a mourning father figure. The dead's head is twisted, as if to avoid the father's blessing hand. And so forth the personnel of the legend. The picture's secret is the trap door in the background, held open by two men. From the depths light emanates: the heavens are below. Hit by the light from the depths, the group of figures in the right foreground reels: Two men on their knees, the upper trunks thrown backwards, the faces turned away from each other. The stronger one of the two, head and breast in a different light which emanates from the Saint and the dead man, tries with both his arms to prevent the fall of the second man who, falling, clutches the knees of a woman. The woman is the counterpart of the Saint, one hand in front of her eyes, protection against the imperious gesture of Future's architect or against the light from the underground. The light is a hurricane. Written as the crow flies between the two German capitals Berlin, separated by the chasm of their shared and not shared history, piled up by the latest earthquake as a borderline between two continents. Accept this letter as an expression of my desire to be present in your work.

Heiner Müller
23 February, 1987

Shakespeare a Difference
Text of an Address

Shakespeare eine Differenz is the revised version of an address Heiner Müller gave at a conference of Shakespeare scholars, Shakespeare Tage, in Weimar, April 1988. The text was first published in *Explosion of a Memory, Heiner Müller DDR, Ein Arbeitsbuch*, Berlin, 1988.

When reading the speech, one should keep in mind that less than two years later the East German Democratic Republic collapsed. The ruling party, SED, used to refer to the country's socioeconomic system as "Real Existing Socialism." Müller cites in his speech numerous writers, artists, and politicians, from the (West) German pop singer Udo Lindenberg to the genocidal Khmer Rouge leader Pol Pot, the German early-nineteenth-century poet Friedrich Hölderlin to the English twentieth-century poet W. H. Auden, from the nineteenth-century philosopher Friedrich Nietzsche to the conservative twentieth-century professor of constitutional law Carl Schmitt and a contemporary Russian writer, Vassily Grossman. As in other writings, Müller often quotes the original English; passages where he does so are indicated by asterisks.

From the age of thirteen, when he first struggled through the English text of *Hamlet*, Müller immersed himself in a discourse with Shakespeare's work. He translated plays such as *Hamlet* and *As You Like It*, adapted *Macbeth*, and eventually went on to deconstruct and revise two of the Elizabethan's texts in *Hamletmachine* and *Anatomy Titus Fall of Rome: A Shakespeare Commentary* (based on *Titus Andronicus*). He has staged his *Macbeth* version, and also *Hamlet* coupled with *Hamletmachine*, his interpretation of "Hamlet as Our Contemporary" (to paraphrase the title of the Polish critic Jan Kott's book, *Shakespeare Our Contemporary*). Müller's premature death has deprived us of other reinterpretations of Shakespeare's work, to our great loss.

C.W.

The attempt to write about Shakespeare, between Berlin, Frankfurt, Milan, Genoa. With the growing pile of notes the horror of its wording grows. Closest to Shakespeare in Genoa, at night in the medieval inner city and near the harbor. Narrow alleys—during the Middle Ages they were barricaded with iron chains against the people—between the palaces of the city-state's aristocracy, the Dorias, for instance, who have been made popular by Udo Lindenberg. On a wall the sprayed graffiti WELCOME TO HELL NO PITY HERE.* All this is like the way to the Globe* as Giordano Bruno described it, past taverns, brothels, and dens of cutthroats. Memories of the first reading: *Hamlet* from the school library, defying the teacher's warning to the thirteen-year-old about the original's difficulty. A black leatherbound volume, on the title page the stamp of the former grand-ducal grammar school. I imagined more than I understood, but the leap creates the experience, not the step.

The play itself is an attempt to describe an experience that has no reality in the time of its description. An end game at the dawn of an unknown day. BUT LOOK THE MORN IN RUSSET MANTLE CLAD / WALKS O'ER THE DEW OF YON HIGH EASTERN HILL. Nearly four hundred years later another version: IN RUSSET MANTLE CLAD THE MORN WALKS O'ER / THE DEW THAT GLISTENS FROM ITS STEPS LIKE BLOOD.

In between, there is for my generation the long march through the hells of Enlightenment, through the bloody swamp of the ideologies. Hitler's geographical lapsus: genocide in Europe instead—as usual and today's practice as it was yesterday's—in Africa Asia America. The St. Vitus's dance of dialectics during the Moscow trials. The lidless view at the reality of the labor and extermination camps. The village-against-city-utopia of the Hegel-reader and Verlaine-lover Pol Pot. The belated Jewish vengeance upon the wrong object, a classical case of belated allegiance. The lockjaw of a party, once beaten into the victor's role, when it is exercising its bestowed or force-fed power in the shortage-ridden economy of a Real Socialism. THE SCARS CRY OUT FOR WOUNDS AND THE POWER / HAS COME UPON THEM LIKE A HEAVY BLOW. The clinch of the Revolution and Counterrevolution as the basic pattern of the century's mammoth catastrophes.

Shakespeare is a mirror through the ages, our hope a world he doesn't reflect anymore. We haven't arrived at ourselves as long as Shakespeare is writing our plays. The opening line of *Miranda's Song** from Auden's commentary on *The Tempest: My Dear One is Mine as Mirrors are Lonely** is a Shakespeare metaphor that is reaching beyond Shakespeare. NO MORE HEROES! NO MORE SHAKESPEAROS* goes the refrain of a

Punk song. A fragment by Hölderlin describes the unredeemed Shakespeare: FIERCELY ENDURING! IN THE FEARFUL ARMOR! MILLENNIUMS. Shakespeare's wilderness. What is he waiting for, why in armor, and how much longer.

Shakespeare is a mystery, why should I be the one who betrays it, assuming I would know it, and why in a Weimar so distant from Shakespeare. I accepted the invitation and stand now before you, sand in my hands that's trickling through my fingers. Hamlet is an object of desire for critics. For Eliot the Mona Lisa of literature, a botched play: the remnants of the revenge tragedy—a marketable genre of the age as today the horror film—are butting awkwardly into the new construct and impede Shakespeare's material in its unfolding. A discourse that is broken by silence. The dominance of the soliloquies is no accident; Hamlet has no partner. For Carl Schmitt a text that is consciously confused and obscured for political reasons, begun during the rule of Elizabeth, concluded after the first Stuart assumed power, son of a mother who had married the murderer of her husband and died under the axe, a Hamlet figure.

The invasion of the times into the play constitutes myth. Myth is an aggregate, a machine to which always new and different machines can be connected. It transports the energy until the growing velocity will explode the cultural field. The first hurdle during my reading was Horatio's surprising speech, surprising from the mouth of a Wittenberg student, after the dead man's entrance at the coast of Elsinore. IN THE MOST HIGH AND PALMY STATE OF ROME / A LITTLE ERE THE MIGHTIEST JULIUS FELL / THE GRAVES STOOD TENANTLESS AND THE SHEETED DEAD / DID SQUEAK AND GIBBER IN THE ROMAN STREETS / AS STARS WITH TRAINS OF FIRE AND DEWS OF BLOOD / DISASTERS IN THE SUN AND THE MOIST STAR / UPON WHOSE INFLUENCE NEPTUNE'S EMPIRE STANDS / WAS SICK ALMOST TO DOOMSDAY WITH ECLIPSE . . . History in the context of nature. Shakespeare's view is the view of the epoch. Never before did interests appear so naked, without the drapery, the costume of ideas. MEN HAVE DIED FROM TIME TO TIME AND WORMS HAVE EATEN THEM BUT NOT FOR LOVE. The dead have their place on his stage, nature has the right to vote. That spelled in the idiom of the nineteenth century, which still is the idiom of conferences between the rivers Oder and Elbe, Shakespeare had no philosophy, no understanding of history: his Romans are of London.

Meantime the war of the landscapes, which are working toward the disappearance of Man who has devastated them, isn't a mere metaphor anymore. Dark times, when a discourse about trees was nearly a crime. The times have become brighter, the shadows fade out, it's a crime to be silent about trees. The horror that emanates from Shakespeare's mirror images is the recurrence of the same. A horror that drove Nietzsche, the God-forsaken reverend's son, from the misery of the philosophies into his dance of knives with the ghosts from the future, from the silence of the academies onto the white-hot high wire of history, stretched BY AN IDIOT FULL OF SOUND AND FURY* between TOMORROW AND TOMORROW AND TOMORROW.*

The accent is on the *And,* the truth is a steerage passenger, the abyss is the hope. Vassily Grossman has Stalin—the Meritorious Murderer of the People, as Brecht once called him—see in the German tank turrets moving towards Moscow a thousand times the murdered Trotsky, Creator of the Red Army and Executioner of Kronstadt. A Shakespeare variant: Macbeth sees Banquo's ghost, and a difference. Our task—or the rest will be statistics and a matter of computers—is the work at this difference. Hamlet, the failure, didn't accomplish it, this is his crime. Prospero is the undead Hamlet: after all, he smashes his staff, a reply to Caliban's, the new Shakespeare reader's topical rebuke to all hitherto existing culture:

YOU TAUGHT ME LANGUAGE AND MY PROFIT ON'T
IS I KNOW HOW TO CURSE.

Mommsen's Block
A Poem / Performance Text

Mommsen's Block was written in the early nineties and published in *Drucksache 1,* Berlin, 1993, a publication of the Berliner Ensemble. It was first staged in an English translation at the Nitery Theater of Stanford University's Drama Department in November 1994.

Theodor Mommsen (1817–1903) was one of the eminent historians of the nineteenth century. Appointed a professor at Berlin University in 1858, he won the 1902 Nobel Prize in literature for his *History of Rome.* This work was "an unmatched recreation of Roman society and culture," according to the *Concise Columbia Encyclopedia.* It was the fruit of exhaustive studies of ancient coins, inscriptions, literary texts, and other concrete relics of Roman culture and history. Mommsen was also a liberal politician passionately opposed to Bismarck, the conservative Prussian prime minister whose politics triggered the Franco-Prussian war of 1870–71. Bismarck created the Imperial German Reich, which united the previously sovereign German states; he also planted the seeds of World War I through his insistence on annexing Alsace-Lorraine from France. In spite of his liberal positions, Mommsen was not free of the widespread anti-Semitism of his time.

In its references Müller's text alludes to European history and to many of its protagonists, from Caesar, the emperors Augustus and Nero, to Bismarck and Mussolini, and on to Eisenhower, Shukov, and a former head of state and party in the GDR, Ulbricht. He also invokes the voices of other writers, from St. John and St. Paul to Humboldt, Marx, Nietzsche, Dilthey, and Toynbee; from Virgil and Tacitus to Dante, to Kafka and Pound. There were two events which seem to have inspired the text: the first publication of Mommsen's fragmentary notes for his lectures on the later Roman empire, and the replacement of a statue of Karl Marx with one of Mommsen at the entrance to Berlin's Humboldt University, which was Mommsen's academic home when it was Friedrich-Wilhelm University, named after the Prussian king who founded it, in 1809, following the advice of his secretary of education, Wilhelm von Humboldt. The government of the former East German Republic had changed the university's name and replaced Mommsen's statue with one of Marx.

The text not only represents a reflection on European history but also explores the perplexing difficulty in trying to capture history in the pages of a book—or on the stage. It also might be read as the author's reckoning with a creative crisis of his own. He had always cited the Berlin Wall as the concrete manifestation of our age, that is, the Cold War, and of the fratricidal divisions of German history. When the wall disappeared, with it went a paradigm that had informed much of Müller's work.

Whichever way it is interpreted, the text raises a multitude of questions while refusing to offer any answer. In its form it continues a line of experimentation Müller began with some sections of *Gundling's Life Frederick of Prussia Lessing's Sleep Dream Scream* and pursued further with *Hamletmachine* and *Explosion of a Memory*. In these texts Müller probed the limits of a theater in which the visual image is of equal significance as the spoken language. His re-visioning of performance and its vocabulary might well be compared to the experiments of such contemporary theater artists as Robert Wilson, Pina Bausch, Bill Forsythe, and the Wooster Group.

The text asks a lot of the reader and even more of a spectator. The barrage of references, paraphrased quotes, names mentioned, and incidents alluded to invites many pages of explanation and annotation. Here is not the place for it, alas. The reader is advised to have a good encyclopedia at hand. Yet, this problem was of little concern to Müller, who believed in the acumen of the unconscious which is at work in the spectator's mind while watching a performance.

C.W.

> What authorities are there beyond Court tittle-tattle.*
>> —*Mommsen to James Bryce, 1898*

The question why the great historian
Didn't write the fourth volume of his *Roman History*
The long-awaited work on the age of emperors
Kept occupied the minds
Of the historians who came after him
Good reasons are offered wholesale
Handed down in letters rumors conjectures
The lack of inscriptions He who writes with a chisel
Has no signature The stones don't lie
No trust in literature CONSPIRACIES AND
COURT GOSSIP Even the silvery fragments
Of the laconic Tacitus simply a reading matter for poets
To whom history is a burden
Insufferable without the dance of vowels
On top of graves against the gravity of the dead
And their dread of the eternal return
He didn't like them those Caesars of the later empire
Not their languor not their vices
He'd had enough of the peerless Julius
Whom he liked as much as his own tombstone
Even TO WRITE ABOUT CAESAR'S DEATH he had
When he was asked about the still missing
Fourth volume NOT ENOUGH PASSION LEFT
And THE PUTRESCENT CENTURIES after him
GRAY IN GRAY BLACK UPON BLACK   For whom
The epitaph   That the midwife Bismarck
Was as well the gravedigger of the empire
That afterbirth of a counterfeit dispatch
Could be concluded from the third volume
Jaded had become in Charlottenburg—
Twice daily the trip with the horse-drawn trolley
In the dust of books and manuscripts forty
Thousand in the Mommsen house Number Eight Mach Street
Twelve children in the basement—THE COURAGE TO ERR

---

* Asterisks indicate text that appeared in English in the original.

Which MAKES THE HISTORIAN   NOW I KNOW
ALAS WHAT I DIDN'T KNOW For instance Why
Does an empire collapse The ruins don't answer
The silence of the statues gilds the decline
THE INSTITUTIONS ARE ALL WE UNDERSTAND
BUT HE IS TIRED AND QUITE DUSTY
The pious Dilthey wrote to Count York
FROM TREADING THE BACKROADS OF PHILOLOGY
INSCRIPTIONS AND PARTY POLITICS
HIS MIND ISN'T HOMESICK FOR THE IN-
VISIBLE EMPIRE His empire was what is manifest
In a letter to one of his daughters Mrs. Wilamowitz
He dreams of a villa near Naples
Not so he'd learn how to die Comes time comes death
And no grace to be granted A BLIND FAITH
FOR COUNTS AND BARONS Christianity
A tree disease that starts at the root
A cancer infiltrated by intelligence services
The twelve apostles twelve secret agents
The traitor provides the proof of divinity
And the trademark Saul a colonized
Bloodhound plays the part of the Social Democrat
Turned into Paul by a fall from his horse
Bellwether of the Unknown God
For Him he lures the sheep into the fold
For the Selection Salvation or Damnation
Only for the maggots the dead are alike
A police informer the first pope
Only John in Patmos amid the fumes of drugs
The heretic The guide of the dead The terrorist
Has seen the New Beast that is rising
The dream of Italy is a dream of writing
The stimulant of moonlight on ruins
With the divine arrogance of MY YOUNG YEARS
THE YOUNGER ONES AT LEAST YOUNG I NEVER WAS
What remains is the DIVINE BLUNTNESS—A POOR
SUBSTITUTE* In the swamp the eagles Why
Write it down just because the mob wants to read it
That there is more life in swamps than

In high altitudes is known to biology
How should you make people understand
And for what reason that the first decade of Nero's reign—
The frustrated artist the bloody one
Music is highly prized during the decline
When all has been said the voices sound sweet—
Was a happy time for the people of Rome
The happiest perhaps in their long history
They had their bread their games The massacres
Took place in the dress circle
And they achieved high ratings
A fire in the Mommsen house caused
Not by Christian zeal against libraries
As two thousand years earlier in Alexandria
But by a gas explosion at Number Eight Mach Street
Gave rise to the horrible hope
The great scholar might have written after all
The fourth volume the long-awaited one
About the age of the emperors
And the text had been burnt
With the rest of the library for instance
Forty thousand volumes plus manuscripts
Rescued was the *Academy Fragment*
Seven pages of a draft framed by the fire
IN POINTED BRACKETS THE SCORCHED WORDS
OF MOMMSEN as the editors write
One hundred and twelve years after the fire
The fire is reported in the papers
The newspaper reader Nietzsche writes to Peter Gast:
"Have you read of the fire at Mommsen's
house? And that all his excerpts are destroyed, the
weightiest preliminary studies perhaps made by any living
scholar? It is said he repeatedly
plunged back into the flames, so that finally
force had to be used to restrain him who was covered
with burns. Undertakings such as Mommsen's
must be very rare, since a colossal memory
and a corresponding sagacity in the evaluation and
classification of such sources rarely go together

but rather tend to work against each other.—When
I heard the story it truly wrung my heart
and even now I am in physical distress when I
think of it. Is this compassion? But what is
Mommsen to me? I am not at all fond of him."
A document from the century of letter writers
The fear of solitude is hidden in the question mark
He who writes into the void has no use for punctuation
Permit me to speak of myself Mommsen Professor
Greatest historian after Gibbon according to Toynbee
(Or did he say beside him That ever gnawing fear
Of the praised that the yardstick is lying)
In life resident at Number Eight Mach Street Charlottenburg
Two three pages long For whom else do we write
But for the dead omniscient in their dust A thought
That perhaps doesn't please you teacher of the young
To forget is a privilege of the dead
After all you yourself forbade
The publication of your lectures in your will
Since recklessness at the lectern commits treason
Against the toils at the desk Even the *Aeneid*
You wanted to see it burnt in accord with the will
Of the failure Virgil Immortality
Was forced on him by Augustus
Masterbuilder of Rome himself deferring completion
Because it conceals the abyss
The *Divine Comedy* would not
Have been written or would be less enduring
Had he not ruled against the fire
And I'd wish you could read Kafka Professor
On your pedestal in your marble vault
The bombs of World War II You know they
Did not spare Mach Street Nor
Was spared your Academy of Sciences
From the fall of the Asiatic despotism Product
Of an erroneous reading and falsely called
Socialism after the great historian
Of capital Whom you didn't notice
A worker in a different quarry

Until his monument stood on your pedestal
For the duration of one state The pedestal is yours again
Before the university that was named after Humboldt
By the rulers of an illusion
(They never had read your Roman history
Nor Marx who kept mum about reading it
Had he lived longer one could have claimed
He envied perhaps the money of your Nobel Prize the Jew)
Ensnared in the knitting pattern of the red Caesars
Who scanned HIS text with combat boots
How do you clear a minefield asked Eisenhower
Victor of World War II another
Victor With the boots
Of a marching battalion replied Shukhov
THE GREAT OCTOBER OF THE WORKING CLASS—extolled
Voluntarily with hope or in a twofold stranglehold
By too many and even after their throats had been cut—
Was a summer storm in the World Bank's shadow
A dance of gnats above the graves of Tartars
WHERE THE DEAD ONES WAIT*
FOR THE EARTHQUAKES TO COME*
As Ezra Pound perhaps would say the other Virgil
Who bet on the false Caesar he too a failure
Because the ghosts do not sleep
Their favorite food is our dreams
Pardon Professor the bitter tone
The university named after Humboldt
Before which you stand upon your pedestal again
Long after your death it is shoveled out
Right now from the suspected rubbish of the new
Blind faith that's not for counts and barons
Yesterday while eating in a four-star restaurant
In the once more resurrected capital Berlin
I leafed through the notes of your lectures
On the Roman age of Caesars fresh from the book market
Two heroes of the new times dined at the next table
Zombies of capital brokers and traders
And as I listened to their dialogue greedy
To feed my disgust with the Here and Now:

"This four million / Must come our way at once // But that won't work //
   But that won't be conspicuous at all // If you haven't mastered the rules
   of this game / You're lost You've seen that in the X case / He didn't master them // You've got to drum them / Into his brain or he's going belly
   up Too bad // Well I'm afraid / They're going to smash him against the
   wall Like a jellyfish // He'll hang there Just squirming and squirming //
   I figure he's good as a buyer During the preliminaries / But when you
   cut right to the bone . . . // Then he's got to hand it over // But then
   you've got to ask Are our hands strong enough / To turn the table //
   You've got to bring him into line // We have to bag him for Deutsche
   Bank // We'll haul him in for ourselves / As soon as I put the screws on /
   I'll teach him a lesson Then he'll make / Serious money."
Five streets away as the police sirens indicate
The poor are clobbering the poorest
And when the gentlemen turned to private matters Cigars and Cognac
Strictly according to the textbook of Political Economics
Of capitalism: "They wanted to send me / To a remedial school // My
   mother was hard as nails / Against all of them You'll get your final
   diploma / The faculty was always split / There were teachers who
   thought I was stupid."
Animal sounds Who would write that down
With passion Hate is a waste Contempt an empty exercise
For the first time I understood your writer's block
Comrade Professor facing the Roman age of Caesars
The as we know happy times of Nero's reign
Knowing the unwritten text is a wound
Oozing blood that no posthumous fame will staunch
And the yawning gap in your Roman history
Was a pain in my—how long still?—breathing body
And I thought of the dust in your marble vault
And of the cold coffee at six in the morning
In Charlottenburg at the Mommsen house Number Eight Mach Street
At your workplace fenced in with books

The Future Is Evil

A Discussion

Translated by Matthew Griffin

The Future Is Evil (*Das Böse ist die Zukunft*), Frank M. Raddatz's interview with Heiner Müller, first appeared in the Hamburg journal *Trans-Atlantik* 3 (1991). Raddatz has published two volumes of his interviews with Müller and a study on the philosophy of history in Müller's plays, *Dämonen unterm Roten Stern*, Stuttgart, 1991.

Müller turned increasingly in the 1980s to the interview as a form of literary production that allowed him a freedom to formulate ideas without the pressures of writing. When asked in 1985 whether he would consider the interview to be a literary genre, Müller responded that the spread of the technological media, which make it possible to record an author's conversations, had given literature a new autonomy, freeing it from its former obligations to represent reality in much the same way that photography had freed painting around the turn of the century (*Gesammelte Irrtümer*, Frankfurt am Main, 1985). Müller's remarks illuminate the relation between his theater texts and the large body of interviews and conversations that seem to have become his preferred mode of expression during the 1980s and early 1990s. His writing for the theater, with its dense language and flood of verbal imagery, resists the facile production of meaning and reduction of the text to an ideological core. Müller's interviews, on the other hand, tend to expose the author's ideological investments in the various topics they engage. For this reason he intends these interviews, which he has also labeled "performances," to be considered as a literary production separate from his writing for the theater. The interviews, however, are perhaps most provocative when the lines between theater and literature become blurred and the discussion reveals contradictions in Müller's thought that offer new perspectives from which to read his theater texts. (For a comprehensive bibliography of Müller's interviews and conversation protocols see Ingo Schmidt and Florian Vaßen, *Bibliographie Heiner Müller,* 2 vols., Bielefeld, 1993 and 1996.)

At the time of Raddatz's interview, Müller was involved in directing his own plays at the Deutsches Theater in Berlin. *The Scab* premiered in January 1988 and *Hamlet/Maschine* in March 1990; his production of *Mauser* was first performed in September 1991. Müller's work in the theater is not, however, the subject of *The Future Is Evil.* The interview is much more an effort by Müller to address societal ills at a specific historical moment, while drawing on important concepts and themes from his work.

The occasion for the interview was the Gulf War (January–February 1991) between the United States and Iraq over Kuwait, but the topics discussed in the interview have more to do with questions arising out of German reunification. The conflict between the former East and West German people provides the framework for a discussion of such issues as the struggle between capitalism and communism, the loss of utopia with the collapse of the GDR, and the status of Marxist theory after Gorbachev's reforms in the Soviet Union and the dismantling of the Eastern Bloc. Müller's conceptual vocabulary in his discussion of the changes taking place in German society after reunification includes terms such as *functionalization, differentiation,* and *individualization*; and these terms address the effects of capitalism and technology, for example, the "destruction of the subject" and the "extinction of memory."

Müller's reflections on the political situation after November 1989 are mixed with references to literature and film in what comprises a discourse on the relation of art to politics. Among the references Müller uses to illustrate his ideas are: *Bladerunner,* directed by Ridley Scott, a film in which androids revolt against their human makers because they want to live longer, that is, live a human life span; Jean Paul (the pseudonym of Johann Paul Friedrich Richter [1763–1825], a German novelist whose works, immensely popular in the first twenty years of the nineteenth century, bridge the gap between Weimar classicism and early romanticism;

Gayev's dialogue with a bookcase in Anton Chekhov's *The Cherry Orchard* (1904), Act I, in which Gayev addresses his family bookshelf, praising it for what he calls its ability to uphold "confidence and faith in a better future . . . fostering in us the ideals of virtue and social consciousness."

Müller's reference to the British-born poet and critic W. H. Auden (1907–73) is perhaps the most significant in assaying the breadth of intellectual influences on the ideas that Müller expresses in the interview. In his posthumously published book of aphorisms from 1939, *The Prolific and the Devourer,* Auden takes up William Blake's distinction in *The Marriage of Heaven and Hell* between "two classes of men," "the devourer" and "the prolific," who, according to Blake, can only be reconciled at the price of the destruction of existence. In Auden's interpretation, the prolific are producers, for instance, artists, scientists, and skilled laborers, while the devourers are politicians, judges, and critics. Müller confuses Auden's definitions, equating the politician and scientist with the "doer" and the artist with the "maker," but the resulting dichotomy between art and politics is fundamentally Auden's. The appeal of Auden to Müller is that of a poet trying to reconcile his artistic production with his communism. Auden was a champion of communism in the 1930s before his turn toward Christianity in the early 1940s, and many of the ideas on communism and art in this interview have parallels in Auden's writings from the 1930s. Raddatz quotes Vladimir Mayakovsky (1893–1930), a leading poet of the Russian Revolution in 1917 and the early Soviet period; see Müller's 1983 adaptation, written with Ginka Tscholakova, *Wladimir Majakowski Tragödie* (in *Kopien 2,* Berlin, 1989), as well as his poem *Mayakovsky* in this volume.

Another significant influence on Müller's thought was contemporary French philosophy, in particular the works of Jean Baudrillard. Müller's comments on the abstraction of the senses in the Gulf War, as well as Raddatz's introductory remark on the end of utopia, can be understood as references to Baudrillard's essays that appeared at the time of the war and were published in the U.S. as *The Gulf War Did Not Take Place.* Müller's comments on speed, mobility, and the Mongols furthermore bear the marks of the chapter entitled "Nomadology: The War Machine" in Gilles Deleuze and Félix Guattari's *A Thousand Plateaus.* Acknowledging his debt to the thinkers of modernity but also the distance between his thought and the nihilistic theories of a collapse of utopia, Müller cites the French poet Arthur Rimbaud's (1854–1891) well-known phrase, "I is someone else."

The Future Is Evil reads as a response to the victory of capitalism over communism that ended the Cold War. Müller's effort to rescue what remains for the future is an example of the unorthodox thought of an artist who constantly strove in his work to explore alternatives to the existing cultural and historical paradigms.

M.G.

FMR: Heiner Müller, one could perhaps say, to put it rather simplistically, that the Gulf War is a war between the forces of American speed and Arabian slowness, in which, apart from the tyranny of Saddam Hussein, the technology of the future is meeting with past arts of war. Our topic, however, is not the Gulf War but this epochal conflict. So far, the future has always been occupied by utopia. Does the failure of socialism mean this is over?

HM: The loss of the escape hatch utopia isn't only negative, because utopia demands sacrifice and renunciation from the individual. It lowers the value of the present in favor of a fiction of the future. Utopia always exists at the expense of real life. The important question is whether the future can still be thought of as a quality. In the still unsettled structures that have at present arisen, the individual is not meant to exist, only to function. This paves the way for the computer to take over power.

In this constellation, mortality, memory, history—everything that makes a subject a subject and disrupts functionalization—suddenly becomes charged with utopia. In the science fiction film *Bladerunner* the computers go on strike because they want to be mortal. That's because whoever cannot die also cannot live. In the face of the total functionalization of the subject through technology, Jean Paul's beautifully naïve sentence first makes sense: "Memory is the one paradise from which no one can be driven."

FMR: Memory as the last bastion of the subject?

HM: That's the precondition. The point is no longer the destruction of some class or other, or a lifestyle, rather the destruction of the subject itself. The trend is such that people no longer talk, like Gayev in Chekhov's *The Cherry Orchard,* with their bookcases, that is, with old bits of memory, but rather with the television, which has an answer for and can remember everything. That's deadly because, first, it slowly hollows out the subject, then it engulfs it. Only art can counteract this. Making art means nothing other than talking with yourself. If you can't talk with yourself, you can't accomplish anything. But when you do something, then there is no more reason to be preoccupied with the old. A text can first be finished when you are already generating the next in your mind. One child brings forth the other. It's a genetic code. The materials are relatively random. But the rhythm of writing, painting, music, or whatever, is a very subjective, physical matter, a form of communication with one's own individual code. It's objective chance as to what will finally group itself around these molecules.

FMR : Memory is also central to psychoanalysis, which attempts to bring the repressed and the forgotten to light in order to stabilize identity.

HM: Forgetting is counterrevolutionary, because all technology is geared towards the extinction of memory. Psychoanalysis is, however, the opposite of art. Art can be described as a flight from self-analysis. If I know who I am, I have no more reason to exist, to go on, to write, or to do something else. Psychoanalysis does not communicate with the code. Rather it rapes it, bending it back until the subject functions again efficiently in society; it stimulates the process of dying in the living.

It's normal for a person's entire biography to appear in the final seconds of life, like a film. This is when you know who you are. It's the first clear view we get of our genetic code, and it's also a form of paying one's dues to pass away. Art is the attempt to slow down time to this point, to bring it to a halt. The drive for knowledge is a death drive, and art is the attempt to anesthetize and to build up defenses against the drive for knowledge.

FMR: The inscription in the Temple of Delphi read: "Know Yourself." This was, so to speak, an exhortation to deal with the oracle rationally. Perhaps, too, a verdict against art . . .

HM: W. H. Auden differentiates between the "maker" and the "doer of things," that is, between makers and doers. Artists belong to the makers, and politicians, scientists, managers to the doers. These two groups share a mutual contempt, and their attitudes are irreconcilable. Whoever does things has to know how things are actually created, how they function in reality, in order to master them. The maker is not concerned with this. The connections between the individual structural elements become more and more complex, and are charged with an energy that can't be controlled. The artist plays with the structural elements, reconfiguring the particles of reality and partially nullifying reality. This can be controlled less and less by society, which is why civilization always becomes more hostile towards art. Art is a threat to any existing order.

It's subversive to play with reality, because it undermines reality. The art market counters this by turning artworks into cultural commodities. It attempts to sterilize them and make them safe by bringing them into the circulation of the market. Works of art need to be left alone if their destructive force is to be tapped. The same thing happens in theater or on the festival circuit. The function of the festival is to strip a production of what might be called its aura, its effect. As long as a work of art—be it a play, a picture, a book—circulates, it can't puncture reality or our conception of reality. The doers secretly know that reality is only a fiction, and they have a mortal fear that the illusory conceptions of reality will spring leaks. Any and all means are used to defend the ground of facts upon which one has to live or upon which one believes one has to live. Artworks don't have a function, they have an effect, in the sense that they cancel out the gravity of the old. What we experience as reality is always the product of tradition. Art, on the other hand, exists basically in the sphere of the nontraditional.

FMR: But we understand art in principle as a moment of history.

HM: The point is to separate literature from the libraries, artworks from the museums, to separate reading from writing. Who would dispute, for example, that a text by Shakespeare isn't at the moment more timely than one from this century. The tendency towards the museolization of art stems from the fact that we all live in museums. This most basic human experience serves as the standard for our conception of reality. As a child one plays with objects, pieces of furniture, for instance, that are older than oneself. What we live from and where we live are always older than we ourselves are. Fashion just scratches the surface, but it never affects anything at its core where the gravity of the old prevails. You have to be clear in your mind about this most basic experience in order to shake it off. History, too, or at least our conception of history, is nothing complete, rather it has to be constantly held in flux.

There is a theory that Lenin was a dadaist and the October Revolution was a dadaist performance. Even though that's sheer nonsense, it's correct in principle. It's an attempt to force history out of the museum. Once it's outside the museum, it can speak and the dead can speak with us. Expelling art and history from the museum means tearing them away from death and establishing the discourse of the living. Only the production of ever newer perspectives on the old makes it at all possible to live. Everything else turns one into a zombie.

FMR: What was unattractive about the GDR was the dust always in the air. It had an antiquated atmosphere. New fashions, new types of music, new technological gadgets from the photocopier to the Walkman were perceived to be provocations that had to be repressed.

HM: The GDR's one legitimization came from antifascism, from the dead, the victims. For a time this was laudable, but at a certain point it began to be a burden to the living. It became a dictatorship of the dead over the living—with all the economic consequences. The dead don't need jeans, kiwis, or Walkmans. The products of the GDR were, at best, gifts for the dead. That was the devilish thing about this structure, its Christian legacy—the waiting for the Messiah who comes from the realm of the dead. But the Messiah always arrives too late. You have to put up with this, even though it's intolerable. There are two types of civilization: one is oriented towards the dead, the other towards the living. Socialism feels indebted to the dead, the victims. It was a refuge of slowness because the dead have an endless amount of time. The economic disaster is a product of what is perhaps the more lofty, noble type of civilization, while the other, which is based on the living, is cheaper but works.

FMR: It's amazing that a form of society based on historical materialism would tend towards metaphysics. In the GDR they said, "The teachings of Karl Marx are omnipotent, because they are true." And Mayakovsky said, "Lenin is more alive than any living person."

HM: Only when he's outside the mausoleum. Then the virus is set free once more. It really doesn't matter what philosophical model a society bases itself upon. As long as it takes the utopia seriously, it is bound to mobilize religious energies. Without the Messiah there would be no utopia, no salvation, because we still don't know of another utopia than that of the Jewish. Even after thousands of variations it's still the same utopia, the archetype. The National Socialist as well as the communist utopias are two variations of Jewish philosophy. The major problem of this century was the collision of two theocracies, the one wanted to save only Germans, the other the entire world, which is, of course, more humane. This is the basic pattern for the century. It's also the original reason for anti-Semitism—the father must be killed. The oedipal structure is a purely European problem, because, for an African, it's not a spiritual-moral dilemma to kill the father or to sleep with the mother. An African does not organize his life around this structure.

FMR: But the idea to construct a society based on the criteria of equal rights and social justice is not at all theocratic or pathological but seems quite reasonable . . .

HM: Only as an idea. Every society that has a goal and pursues utopia consciously makes history, moving in another time, the messianic. The Federal Republic moves within empirical time. No political party would make the claim "If we gain power, we will have a paradise on earth in thirty years." Everyone knows that society thrives as long as there is growth, otherwise you have a recession, which may or may not matter to those who have enough. The Federal Republic has cashed in on the promises of National Socialism. Every German can race his Volkswagen across the autobahn, foreigners without any rights sweep up the garbage, and the bordellos are full of women from Africa and Asia.

There start to be problems when a society becomes mobile. The Jews had no place of their own, which is why they invented a home-land, and that was the utopia, the "no-place." They shifted the home-land from space into time. The nomad moves in cycles from place to place and retains a mythical conception of the world. But the Jews had no place, and so they had no present. Whoever has no place also has no time. This calls for a different time, namely, messianic time. The Jews didn't have a place for their dead. So they couldn't converse with their ancestors—the idea of resurrection is the result. This is the beginning of an uncanny sort of abstraction that explains the congruence of anti-Semitism and anti-intellectualism. All intellectuals are actually Jews. The affinity between Jews and money is also tied to mobility. Money and capital are something that have no place. The Jews could only survive by linking their placeless structure, their civilization's movement and upheaval, with a monetary structure that was just as mobile and flexible.

The Jews are a disturbance to time. This disturbance has an unset-tling effect on states, fortifications, settlements; it undermines, in the final analysis, the structure of the state. The only people today who still uphold this mobile, stateless structure are the Gypsies. Their sheer pres-ence is a provocation. As exponents of the mobile structure, they place in question everything upon which the state is based. The real tragedy is the creation of the state of Israel. It's a trap, a reaction to anti-Semitism and the pogroms. Israel has made the Jews a state-building people and led them to give up their actual structure, which is anti-state. In the end, it was Hitler who turned the Jews into Romans. Rome is the nucleus of the state and its imperial structures.

FMR: In biblical tradition Cain stands at the beginning of this development—the fratricide was also the founder of the first city.

HM: The relation between mobile and sedentary societies is rife with conflicts. If the Jews are the head of the structure of mobility, then the Mongols were the arm. From a purely military standpoint, their superiority rested upon their invention of the saddle, which allowed them to deploy their weapons more effectively. The Mongols never wanted to found an empire; they only wanted to destroy empires. Under Ghengis Khan in Russia, the first thing the Mongols did after having captured a city was to slaughter its craftsmen. Craftsmen are vectors of stability. They build houses, fortify, repair, in short, stabilize. The Mongols, who conquered half of Europe, Turkey, and a large part of the Orient, never founded a city. They buried their dead so that they couldn't be discovered, trampling the ground with their horses until the grave could no longer be seen. Even today, no one knows where Ghengis Khan lies buried. Without the dead, however, a state cannot be founded. Mobility is a form of life. Stability is an ideal, a program. The best day in school is the field trip, which isn't a lesson, but a surprise. Everything that can be lived out by means of mobility has to be locked away in a climate of stability, and that poisons life. Explosions result.

FMR: The fundamental problem for the next century will be the mass migration of peoples from the Third World to the First.

HM: As long as there was a Second World, there was still hope for the Third World. This isn't so anymore. Hitler's stroke of genius was to see that Europe could only survive—be held—by means of mobility. Europe was always a center out of which movement originated, but it had itself never been moved. The actual function of the October Revolution was to set the world in motion against Europe. The price was the freezing up of the idea of communism. Hitler realized that only mobility, the conversion of Europe into a liquid state, could oppose a world set in motion against Europe by the October Revolution. His real problem was that he had too little fuel for his program, for the strategy of mobility. This is going to be the problem of the future as well. The Americans can do headstands—there just isn't enough energy.

While we were all thinking in phases and sticking to tradition, Gorbachev was the first to think the lessons of this century through to their conclusion. He deconstructed the Eastern Bloc and put into practice Lenin's thesis on the reduction of the state through socialism in a way that was quite different from what Lenin had in mind. He needed the bolt of speed in order to disturb the static of the October Revolution. He revived the strategy of mobility in the era of the atomic bomb, that is, made it possible. Mobility was the privilege of the West, at least within a specific economic framework. Gorbachev destroyed this framework, taking a phrase from Baudrillard, "We have left the silent film era of the political." Gorbachev brought an end to the Cold War by dissolving the East-West conflict, the battle of ideologies, in the North-South conflict. The point now is not ideas, but rather realities. He reduced the conflict between capitalism and socialism to its material core, the opposition between rich and poor. This conflict now is acquiring its world-historical significance and force.

In contrast, the idea of making Europe into a stronghold is totally stupid. Nothing will come of it. The tide of the October Revolution can no longer be stemmed. Tens of millions of poor and oppressed are standing outside the gates and want in. The belief that Europe can still be held, if defended, is an illusion. The victory of capitalism is the beginning of its end, because you can't conquer something that has already thrown itself at your feet. It can only trip you up. Capitalism, traditionally the aggressor, is now surrounded by Asia and Africa and stands with its back against the hole in the ozone layer.

By putting Lenin's thesis on the abolishment of the state under socialism into practice, Gorbachev liberated socialism from the dictatorship of the dead and discharged the Christian legacy. Now all that is bad for bourgeois society is free to develop its many variations; it is impossible to conceive of this in traditional categories. According to certain heretic traditions, the Messiah comes out of the tradition of evil: at the final judgment someone stands up and says, "J'appelle" (I appeal). And the one who objects is Jesus.

Bourgeois society is based on differentiation, but when it is no longer able to identify evil it ceases to be able to define its own limits and determine itself. It needs the other for this, the empire of evil. This empire is currently dissolved. The downfall of bourgeois society is this—the future is evil. What remains of bourgeois society is Rimbaud's phrase "I is someone else." The dream of the avant garde is now ac-

quiring the quality of a nightmare. Bourgeois consciousness, which is
no longer able to define itself, is dissolving as a historic subject.

FMR: Can this—the "new world order"—also be understood as an aspect
of emancipation?

HM: Only negatively, because you can only emancipate yourself as an individual. A conglomerate of the individual and the other cannot be
emancipated. Groups cannot be emancipated either. As an individual
you can still have a consciousness, but in a group or as the other you
can only have a false consciousness. Each individual who lives in a
group construction has to renounce a part of him or herself. Everything
that is valid for two people is wrong. The only thing right is what is true
for the individual. This begins with the relationship between a man and
a woman. The very idea that there could be a union between a man
and a woman is mistaken, because in the first place the preconditions
are far too different. Only a false consciousness can make you oblivi-
ous to this difference, and love is a metaphor for false consciousness.
The true content of communism is individualization, and this includes
the abolishment of love. Communism is total individualization and the
recognition of that individualization. "Community" is always a phrase
used to legitimize the invasion of the individual. You have to learn—
and this is the essence of emancipation—to bear being alone.

Auschwitz ad Infinitum

A Discussion

Translated by Matthew Griffin

Auschwitz ad Infinitum (*Auschwitz und kein Ende*), a discussion with young French directors, edited by Holgar Teschke, first appeared in *Drucksache* 16 (1995), the program brochure for the Berliner Ensemble's 1995 production of Bertolt Brecht's *The Resistible Rise of Arturo Ui*, directed by Heiner Müller.

The title of Müller's interview, which refers to Goethe's Shakespeare study *Shakespeare ad Infinitum* (*Shakespeare und kein Ende*, 1813–16), is an indirect reference to Müller's proposal as the artistic director of the Berliner Ensemble to make his own plays and those of Brecht and Shakespeare the focal point of the theater's work. His choice to include the interview in the *Arturo Ui* program alongside scene 4 of *Germania 3* points to his desire to address questions of German fascism with his Brecht production in the year marking the fiftieth anniversary of the end of World War II.

The Holocaust does not figure prominently as a subject in Müller's work. His plays do not directly deal with the genocide of European Jewry or the roots of German anti-Semitism. Müller approaches the period of German fascism from the perspective of antifascism in plays such as *The Battle* (1951, 1974), *Germania Death in Berlin* (1956, 1971), and *Volokolamsk Highway* (1984, 1987). Plays such as *Philoctetes* (1958, 1964) and

Mauser (1970), in which Müller discusses historical violence in the context of Stalinism and communist revolution, likewise, elide the question of the relation of German fascism to anti-Semitism. These plays adhere to the claim of the GDR to be a state founded on antifascism. One has to turn to the fragmentary scenes from one of Müller's earliest attempts at writing drama, his unfinished 1952 play about Werner Seelenbinder, to find the author directly addressing the subject of anti-Semitism in Nazi Germany; four scenes have been published in *Explosion of a Memory: Heiner Müller DDR, Ein Arbeitsbuch* (Berlin, 1988), and the scene "The Larder" (*Der Gemüsekeller*) appears in English as "Boots Have a Memory" in *Germania* (New York, 1990).

The interview *Auschwitz ad Infinitum*, perhaps Müller's most straightforward commentary on the Holocaust, provides an important supplement to the critique of German fascism in his plays. The interview is also an investigation into the aspects of modernity that produced the technological disaster to which we have given the name Auschwitz. By suggesting that Auschwitz, literally, has "no end," Müller deprives the Holocaust of its singularity as a historical event in order to discuss the ways in which Auschwitz represents a trauma that remains with modern society.

Müller draws in the interview upon his own texts as well as those of other authors. The reference to speed with respect to the Nazi Blitzkrieg has parallels in Paul Virilio's *Speed and Politics*. Müller also refers to a touring production of his play *The Battle* that had its premiere in 1975 in Budapest.

The reference to Heinrich von Kleist draws upon remarks in Müller's 1990 acceptance speech for the Kleist Prize, "Germany without a Place," published in *Jenseits der Nation* (Berlin, 1991). Karl Korsch (1886–1961) is a Marxist philosopher whose major work is the 1923 *Marxism and Philosophy*. Korsch's unorthodox Marxism exercised a major influence on Bertolt Brecht, and his letter to Brecht on the Blitzkrieg as "bundled-up energy from the left" is likely to have been familiar to Müller, who cites Korsch's letter in his introduction to a German translation of Italian novelist Curzio Malaparte's (1898–1957) war reportage on the Russian front in 1941 for *Corriere della Sera* (*Die Wolga entspringt in Europa*, Cologne, 1989.) Müller was fascinated by Korsch's definition of the Nazis' appropriation of the anticapitalist energies of the working class. He writes: "Malaparte describes the war in Russia, that is, its initial phase of an apparently unstoppable German advance, as a war between two armies of workers, defined by the relation of the worker to the machine, which also

143

determines the ethic of the war: it has the precision of work, the war is a production."

Müller injects his discourse with references to a number of artists, artworks, and public figures. These include the Russian master of the short story Nicolay Leskov (1831–95). His story *The Iron Will* begins with a statement by one of the characters that "the Germans are endowed with an iron will, which Russians lack." The character adds, "Maybe they are iron, while we are just plain, soft, raw dough—but you would do well to remember that dough, if there's enough of it, can't be chopped through even with an axe: what's more, an axe can get buried and lost." Wernher von Braun, the leading rocket scientist under the Nazis, became the head of the U.S. rocket program after the war. The Stephen King story to which Müller refers is *Survivor Type,* published in *Different Seasons* in 1982 and made into the movie *Apt Pupil* in 1998 by Brian Singer. Rostock and Hoyerswerda are the two East German cities that became synonymous in the early 1990s with violence against foreigners, due to racist attacks and demonstrations by former East Germans. Eberswalde is a suburb of East Berlin known for its dreary, modernist housing projects. Dostoyevsky's 1866 novel *Crime and Punishment* tells the story of Raskolnikov, a student who is racked by guilt after putting to the test his theory that humanitarian ends justify evil means, by murdering a pawnbroker.

Walter Benjamin (1892–1940) is the German Jewish philosopher and critic whose writings have been an important source for Müller's philosophy of history. Müller contributed the anecdote about the cat and the cricket to a festschrift for Ernst Jünger, *Thrakischer Sommer* in *Magie der Heiterkeit: Ernst Jünger zum Hundertsten,* Stuttgart, 1995.

The Roßbach brigade was one of the paramilitary organizations known as Freikorps that sprang from the demilitarized army after World War I and performed acts of right-wing terrorism. Gerhard Roßbach published a memoir, *Mein Weg durch die Zeit: Erinnerungen und Bekenntnisse,* and Rudolf Höß's autobiographical sketches were published posthumously as *Kommandant in Auschwitz.* Konrad Wolf (1925–82), a leading East German film director, created a montage of personal memories from the end of World War II in his 1967 film *Ich war neunzehn* (*I Was Nineteen*).

In *Auschwitz ad Infinitum* Müller discusses issues from twentieth-century history that reappear in his final play *Germania 3,* whose subject is World War II in Russia and its effects in East Germany. Müller often spoke in this context about his desire to become a repository for German memory, because, as he declared on occasion, "I stand in the void of the communist utopia" (*Germania*, New York, 1990). If it can be said of Müller's plays that they are an attempt to fill this void by putting it on stage, then the interview *Auschwitz ad Infinitum* must be read as a measure of the author's commitment to preserving the experience of the twentieth century.

M.G.

Q: Heiner Müller, you have written a lot about German history, especially about National Socialism in Germany. Is there something specifically German about this theater material?

HM: Mao Tse-tung once said that as long as National Socialism was on the attack it was unbeatable. It was an attack in a void, in empty space, a pure movement, without reserves. The moment the attack ground to a halt outside Moscow, it was over. The first stop was already the last. The battle for Stalingrad is Attila the Hun's coffin. The only national material is the saga of the Nibelungs.

Q: Isn't Auschwitz also a national material? Is it at all possible to deal with this material in the theater?

HM: It's difficult. I once risked my life in Yugoslavia during a tour of a Volksbühne production of *The Battle*. After the performance a discussion took place, and I remarked—somewhat off the cuff—that Hitler had been bad at geography. He did in the middle of Europe what an upstanding European would only do in Africa, Asia, or Latin America. Genocide was normal in the colonies, but in Europe it was an aberration. That's where Hitler deviated from the norm. The other point is that German anti-Semitism was probably so virulent because it is based on an ancient trauma. From our standpoint today it seems strange that the terminology used by the Nazis was often Jewish, for example, the "thousand-year empire." Until 1933 anti-Semitism was more evident in Poland, Russia, and Eastern Europe. In Germany, in contrast to France or the USA, it was less prevalent. There is a theory for this that I find quite interesting. After the fall of Rome, the first Christian missionaries came to the Franks, who were the main Germanic tribe in France and Germany and the missionaries told the Franks, "You are the chosen people, therefore, having been chosen, you must take up the cross." And they took up the cross. A hundred years later the Jews, another chosen people, arrived in Europe. There cannot be two chosen peoples, one has to go. It's totally irrational, but that's what the Nazis dredged up out of the national subconscious.

This also has to do with Hitler himself. There is a legend that after the annexation of Austria Hitler's first secret order was to evacuate and destroy a small village in upper Austria. It was to be turned into a training ground for troops. This was supposedly the village in which one of Hitler's grandmothers lay buried, and the rumor had circulated that this grandmother had had a liaison with a Jew. So Hitler's energy was also a result of his fear of and hatred for the Jewish blood he believed he had in his own veins. Perhaps another aspect of this energy is that National Socialism could only be conceived of as a permanent movement. Hitler never spoke of "the Party," rather it was always "the Movement." There is a parallel in Kleist: the Germans are always trying to get away from themselves, but this movement has its limits.

The Jews were the main problem in this context, because they couldn't be assimilated. They embodied a resistance. The Jews served as an alibi as well, since to a large portion of the population, they were the capitalists, an ersatz for all the anticapitalist energies from the Left and the Right. Capitalism came to Poland and Russia by way of a monetary economy. In the Middle Ages only the Jews were permitted to collect interest, since the Bible considered it un-Christian. So they founded banks and lending houses and became the ideal ersatz enemy. This also explains why the original energies of National Socialism were anticapitalist. There is evidence that in 1933 the SA [*Sturmabteilung*] consisted, to a large part, of former communists. The Nazis thus were able to appropriate a great deal of energy from the Left. When the Wehrmacht occupied Crete, Karl Korsch wrote in a letter to Bertolt Brecht, "The Blitzkrieg is bundled-up energy from the Left." National Socialism was, in fact, the greatest historical achievement of the German working class.

Q: Are you serious?

HM: It can also be reformulated: the Blitzkrieg, or the war of speed, was— after the failed revolution in 1848—the transformation of the German working class from the status of the exploited to that of the hunter. By going to war, they became hunters. One hears this over and over in every neighborhood bar. The memory of war is the greatest experience of freedom. War was an ersatz for revolution, just as the present-day violence against foreigners is once again an ersatz for a revolution that wasn't carried out fully. The Jews became ersatz enemies because the real capitalists were needed, in effect, to finance the war. They stood behind Hitler, which is also why no one could get at them.

Q: But Jewish capitalists were also disenfranchised and killed in the camps.

HM: Yes, but the industries important to the war, essentially the heavy industries, were in German hands—Flick, Krupp, Thyssen. German industry has always dreamed about what is now happening in the East. They tried it first with Hitler, but it didn't work. Now they've got what they've always wanted. Eastern Europe is spread out at their feet, both as a marketplace and as a labor pool. As early as 1943 secret conferences took place in Madrid and London between German, British, and American industrialists who were worried about the division of the market in the East after the war, since they already knew that it wasn't going to work out with Hitler. They miscalculated then and are bound to miscalculate again. They have never understood Russia. There is a nice story by Leskov about Russia at the time of Napoleon. Leskov writes that Russia is like a dough ball, one can pound it with a fist, kick it with a boot, hack at it with an axe, but when one removes the boot or the axe, the dough expands, rises and is just the same as ever.

Q: How do you explain the aggressiveness of the Germans?

HM: There is perhaps a historical-economic explanation for this: the Germans always came too late, especially when it came to dividing the world. While Frederick the Great was waging his regional wars, the French and the English were divvying up the world, which is why the Germans didn't get any colonies. It also made German capitalism, which was possessed by a spirit of invention and an incredible capacity for production, the most dynamic in Europe. This is a historical-economic explanation for the later invention of technologized mass murder. Colonies make it easier for a nation to disperse its aggressive energies around the globe. In Germany these forces remained concentrated.

There are a few other events in German history that have also formed the national character. Germany is in the center of Europe, so all wars inevitably took place in Germany. The Germans have never been able to imagine a war that isn't also a war with two fronts. The English or the French could send their criminals to Australia or Algeria where they could carry out their massacres, but in Germany the criminals stayed home and so did the criminal energy—this naturally includes the criminal energy of capital. There was, however, a discrepancy between the ideology of the Nazis and the interests of German industry. German industry saw the war as a war for the forces of labor. The Nazis, as a result of Hitler's racial theories, understood the war to be about the annihilation of labor. The West German economic miracle is a result of Auschwitz. All the major German corporations used workers in Auschwitz and other camps in alliance with American and British industry.

Q: Is there actual proof of this?

HM: There are documents in Washington which show that the Americans knew about the camps early on from aerial surveillance photos. Churchill knew about their existence as early as 1941. This knowledge was kept secret, because IG Farben, Krupp, and Thyssen had close ties to American firms. Actually, the only real interest for the Americans was the destruction of the Soviet Union.

Q: Why do you think the Left still has trouble dealing with the Jewish question?

HM: In 1962 I wrote a text for a documentary film about the concentration camp Buchenwald. We had material showing that Wernher von Braun had been a frequent visitor to the outlying camp Dora, where parts for the V-1 and V-2 rockets were being assembled. Naturally, we wanted to use this footage in our film, but we were forbidden with the argument that in the concentration camp Oranienburg, where the V-2 had also been built, Manfred von Ardenne, our head physicist, had also had work done, research that would later form the basis for space travel and space medicine. Ardenne later went to work for the Russians. You also can't forget the massive Nazi propoganda machine, which succeeded in suggesting to the general population that the Jews were vermin. The majority of people didn't know exactly what was going on in the camps, because the Western powers withheld their information in the hope that Hitler would crush the Soviet Union. Hitler was the German shepherd who had been given a long leash so that he could snap at the communists, but when he went wild he had to be put down.

Q: But isn't it dangerous to reduce National Socialism to the phenomenon of Hitler?

HM: A distinction must be made here. The gas for the gas chambers was not manufactured by the same people who later used it. German industry supplied it. The industrialists knew how it would be used. These people are either retired today or still hold high-ranking positions in German industry. People talk mostly about the animals in SS uniforms but forget the animals seated on the board of directors. I'm not arguing that the SS or the army is innocent, but one has to understand the connections. The concentration camps were big business for German industry. Technology was developed and tested in the camps. The technologies for killing were always state of the art, and torture is one of the oldest services in the history of mankind. The British strapped Indians to the barrels of their canons—they hadn't come up with anything better. Churchill was in Egypt when the machine gun was first tested. The English used their new military technology on the Africans. New technologies have always been tested and implemented against minorities, that is, against the threat of their becoming majorities. All modern technologies for killing will one day be implemented. The dropping of the atomic bomb on Japan was totally pointless and unnecessary from a military perspective, but it was a signal directed towards the Soviet Union. The problem is that Auschwitz has lowered our inhibitions.

Q: This brings us back to one of our first questions: Is Auschwitz a material for the theater?

HM: I once read a good story by Stephen King about a thirteen-year-old boy in California. The boy has a hobby: he collects documents, photos, whatever he can get his hands on about concentration camps. His interest is that "they just did those things." They did what one always dreams about. One day, while waiting for his school bus, he sees an old man who looks familiar. He searches through his collection, and then he finds the man in SS uniform in one picture. The next day at the bus stop he follows the man home to a small house on the edge of the city. The boy rings the doorbell and shows the man the picture. The old man trembles, he can't lie, it's him. He thinks the boy wants to report him, but the boy says, "No, I want you to tell me how you did those things. How did you shove the Jews in the ovens? How did you torture them?" The old man doesn't want to tell, but the boy threatens to go to the authorities. So the old man is forced to divulge every detail. After a while the boy says, "Now I want to see it done." The old man has an oven and one day the boy brings a dog. The boy says, "Take the dog and shove it in the oven. Show me how someone can do that." They set up a "Murder Inc.," a murder corporation. First, they take dogs, then later indigents, and they shove them into the oven one after the other.

That's the youth growing up today. The most horrifying thing about the violence in Rostock and Hoyerswerda is that it is a part of this society—it isn't just some barbarous excrescence—and by the same token fascism is a product of a market economy. In the U.S. this form of violence is by now customary, but here it's something new. There is, for example, a term used among German youth bands called *Bordsteinclashing* (street-curb bashing). After they've beaten the foreigner and he's lying on the ground, they take his head and lay it on the street curb, then they jump on it with their Springer boots. The skinheads did that to an African in Eberswalde. They talk about it as if it were totally natural, "His head was lying there on the ground, and I think to myself, why not jump on it?" The young man who said that on television is nineteen, a locksmith, he has a job, and speaks about it matter-of-factly, without a trace of emotion.

Q: I'd like to return one more time to the subject of Auschwitz. For me the concept of "la grace," is an essential element in my life. When I hear you trying to explain Auschwitz, I have to ask myself how one can still call upon Grace and retain a transcendental hope in a world in which such a thing is possible?

HM: That's a good question. Auschwitz is the model for this century and for its principle of selection. Not everyone can survive. So selection takes place. Whenever I try to understand what heroism means, I think of a little story. On one of the last ships out of Germany there was a heavy-set Jewish sportswriter from Berlin. The ship was torpedoed and began to sink. Naturally, there wasn't enough room in the lifeboats for everyone, but the portly Jewish sportswriter had found a spot. Suddenly a mother with her child appeared at the railing, but the lifeboats were all full. The fat little Jew let himself fall overboard into the Atlantic, and then there was room for the woman. That is the only answer.

Q: I'm not sure I understand.

HM: It's not meant to be understood. It's Dostoyevsky's problem, the Raskolnikov question. Dostoyevsky, too, can only find one answer in the end and that is Grace. Assuming that Auschwitz is the model for selection, then there is no political answer. There is probably only a religious answer. The problem with this civilization is that it does not have an alternative to Auschwitz.

Q: Now I understand.

HM: The same topic comes up again and again in Walter Benjamin. Socialism, communism, or whatever other utopia stands no chance, if it doesn't also offer a theological dimension. This is also a fundamental problem today. I have another story that relates to this. Once I took LSD in Bulgaria. In the house where we were staying there was a sort of cellar, a washroom, and there was a large cricket on the door. The radio was playing Turkish or Arabic music, desert music with a very strange undercurrent, a flat sort of music. There was also a cat that lived in the house, and this cat suddenly came in through the door. I showed the cat the cricket and I knew what would happen next. After five or ten minutes the cat had somehow managed to get the cricket down and had begun to chase it up the steps, biting, then letting go, then biting again. The cricket began to limp. Meanwhile the Arabic music was playing. I observed it all very intently, the drug warping my perception of time. I enjoyed it, but at the same time I was repulsed—because I was enjoying it. I will never forget the self-repulsion I felt at my pleasure in watching in slow motion. What distinguishes the cat from the SS soldier is that the cat needs such food now and again to keep the stomach juices in order. It's a biological necessity. Man doesn't need it by necessity, that's what distinguishes him from the cat. Every time killing is made more abstract, inhibitions drop. I can't imagine stabbing another human being. But I can imagine shooting one, and that's the way it works. It only takes the push of a button and the people who have just been killed also disappear. The news coverage of the Gulf War was the height of abstraction, an entirely abstract war.

Q: Is this a phenomenon which first became apparent in Germany after World War II?

HM: No. I read something interesting in the memoires of Roßbach, a well-known leader of the Freikorps after World War I. One episode relates how a member of the Roßbach brigade has, on assignment from the Freikorps, killed someone—it's a contract killing. After the man has finished the job, he meets with Roßbach and tells him, "I feel terrible. I don't know how I can go on living. How could I kill another man the way I did, not in war, man against man, but from behind and for hire? I will never kill another man again, and I will never again pick up another weapon." The man who said this to Roßbach was Rudolf Höß, later the commander of Buchenwald and Auschwitz. And I have another story. At the concentration camp Oranienburg there was an extremely brutal SS soldier. After the war the Russians went to his wife and told her about the things her husband had done in the camp. The wife didn't understand. He had only done his job, and he had always been a good father to his children, always very loving. The Russians persisted, asking whether nothing at all had seemed odd to her? She considered, then said, "Now and then he would come home with bloody boots." When she asked him where the blood came from, he would say, "We killed a pig today." All those years, the woman never knew. She killed her children, set fire to the house, went mad, and ran screaming across the moor. In the concentration camps the low-ranking members of the SS were often farmers' sons, so they were accustomed to killing animals. All that had to be done was to supply them with the ideology that the prisoners were not humans but animals.

Q: But didn't these low-ranking SS soldiers have the choice to refuse to follow orders, say, for example, when women and children were selected for the gas chamber?

HM: Of course, they had a choice. There is an answer to your question in a film by Konrad Wolf. One scene shows a former prisoner of a concentration camp who survived because he had the job of shoving the corpses in the ovens. This job was always done by prisoners in the camps. Each day these prisoners were faced with the decision: "Either do it or die." What do you do in such a situation? That's the real question, even today. The only answer to this question is that each of us is alone with ourselves and our decision.

Ajax for Instance
A Poem / Performance Text

Ajax for Instance (*Ajax zum Beispiel*) was written in 1994–95 and first published in Germany's leading national newspaper, *Frankfurter Allgemeine Zeitung,* 29 October 1995. The poem presents a stream of associations that have been triggered by the view of the Mercedes logo on top of Europa Center, a high-rise office building in the heart of what used to be West Berlin. The author, conducting a dialogue with himself, contemplates the difficulties he encountered in writing a tragedy based on Sophocles' *Ajax* and what might be causing them. The text, however, concerns itself not so much with a reinterpretation of the classic Greek play as with the last play Müller completed a draft of, namely *Germania 3.* Many incidents inscribed in the poem are reappearing in the play, in a more or less paraphrased fashion.

A major theme of the text is the writer's disgust with the results of German unification: the triumph of an unbridled market economy and its consequences for Germany's social and cultural life; the ugly stirrings of a new German nationalism; and the concurrent efforts to erase anything that might remind of German socialism and its history. *Bild,* the most popular West German tabloid, stands here for all the media that continue to beat the dead horse of the former East German Republic and its socialist agenda.

The text refers to numerous historical events and personalities. The gold from the Jews who had been killed in Auschwitz; writings concerning German history by Brecht and other authors; the present day altercations about the future of the Berliner Ensemble and other Berlin theaters (as, for instance, with the quote about Peter Zadek, the prominent stage director who vied with Müller for the leadership of Brecht's former company, or the reference to Einar Schleef, whose stagings at the Berliner Ensemble provoked Zadek's protest)—these and other references are woven into the stream of consciousness the author embarks upon.

The text ends with the conclusion that the act of writing itself may have become useless. There are hints that Müller might identify with Ajax, at least to a degree. Didn't he himself once suffer from his work's rejection by the group he wanted to be accepted by, namely the establishment and the ruling party of the GDR? Hadn't he often attacked what might in retrospect be regarded as mere surrogates of an enemy? Didn't a socioeconomic system he despised triumph while Ajax/Müller became an object of derision for many in the cultural establishment of postunification Germany? Not to mention that Müller was aware that his own death was closing in when he wrote this text. Yet, the last line might be read as a stubborn effort to continue writing. To paraphrase Beckett: He can't go on—but he goes on.

C.W.

The pill's a rotten hoax and mean
Ajax keeps your oven clean

Popular German saying

In the bookstores piling up
Bestsellers a literature for idiots
Who aren't satisfied with their TV
Or the more slowly stupefying cinema
I dinosaur but not one of Spielberg's sit
Pondering the possibility
Of writing a tragedy   Holy simplicity
In a hotel in Berlin the unreal capital
My gaze through the window is caught
By the Mercedes star
Rotating in the night sky dolefully—
Above the gold fillings from Auschwitz and other branches
of Deutsche Bank—on top of the Europa Center
Europa   The bull has been butchered the beef
Is rotting on the tongue Progress doesn't spare a single cow
Gods won't visit you anymore
What you are left with is the Ah! of Alcmene
And the stench of burning flesh carried daily
By the landless wind from your frontiers to you
And sometimes from the basements of your affluence
Whisper the ashes sings the bone meal
A letter board at Kurfürstendamm announces to the world
PETER ZADEK SHOWS BERLIN HIS TEETH
BEWARE OF DENTISTS* you would like to tell him
In the Peasant Wars the greatest calamity
Of German history—I shook my head in disbelief when I read this
In a state of innocence nineteenfortyeight
How can a revolution be a calamity?
In Brecht's notes on *Mother Courage*—
The Reformation had its fangs extracted
Today I can write the sequel   The
French Revolution in the Napoleonic Wars
The prematurely delivered Socialism in the Cold War

---

*Passage in English in original.

History is dancing the tango again ever since
A digression about revolution and dental surgery
Written in the century of dentists—
Two dental protheses one Büchner Prize—
That is coming to its end   The next one
Will belong to the lawyers   The times
Are for sale as real estate
In the high-rise under the Mercedes star
On the floors of the city's Administration of Culture—
What a term   Who administered Phidias
A carpet dealer from Smyrna according to POLYDORUS
Even the arts don't live by dust alone—
The lights are still on   The heads are smoking forced to economize
Those who were amputated rehearse the upright walk
With borrowed crutches made of fiber glass
Supervised by the Senator of Finance
TO MONEY THRONG AT MONEY CLING ALL THINGS
Groans Faust in Goethe's sarcophagus in Weimar
With the broken voice of Einar Schleef
Who is rehearsing his choruses in Schiller's skull
I dinosaur in the air conditioner's drone
Myself being choked by the stranglehold of taxes
The state's power depends on money Money
Must acquire Work makes unfree Home is
Where the bills arrive says my wife—
I read Sophocles AJAX for instance Description
Of an animal test Faded tragedy
Of a man with whom a whimsical goddess
Plays blindman's buff before Troy in the ages' abyss
Arnold Schwarzenegger in DESERT STORM—
To make myself clear to contemporary readers—
I AJAX VICTIM OF TWOFOLD DECEPTION
A man in Stalinstadt in Frankfurt Oder district
When he received news of the climate change in Moscow
Took from the wall in silence the portrait of the beloved
Leader of the Working Class of World Communism
Trampled with his feet the image of the dead dictator
And hanged himself from the now available hook
His death wasn't newsworthy A life

For the shredder ALL OR NONE
Was the wrong program   There isn't enough for all
The final war's objective will be the air we breathe
Or KAULICH liberated by the Red Army
From Hitler's Gulag hears after four days of walking
His wife scream behind a shattered window
Sees a soldier of the glorious Red Army
Who throws her on the bed forgets the ABC
Of Communism smashes the Comrade Liberators'
Skull conducts a self-critique in conversation with the corpse
Has got no ear for the still screaming woman
Is seen for the last time on a transport
To Stalin's Gulag his second epiphany
Sings in the cattle car the International
And if he died is still singing today
With the dead Communists beneath the ice
The bliss of writing in the fifties
When your safe harbor was the blank verse
Amidst the planks of the capsizing ship of ghosts
Sheltered by doggerel's ironic pathos
Only the stresses count
Against the rock slide of the monuments
In the infinity of the moment
In the wretchedness of information BILD FIGHTS FOR YOU
Narration turns into prostitution BILD FIGHTS
Tragedy gives up the ghost Stalin for instance
Since his totems are for sale
Blood curdled into medals' tinsel
At Brandenburg Gate for Hitler's grandsons
What kind of text should I put in his mouth
Or stuff it down his throat depending on the point of view
Into the corral of his yellow teeth
Fangs of a wolf from Caucasus
In his night at the Kremlin while waiting for Hitler
When speechless Lenin appears in his vodka
Babbling and howling after the second stroke
Mover of the world whose tongue
Will obey no more LENINDADA
His world a square by Malevich

The Tartar to whom the law of the steppe
Is no longer familiar having become a Roman at the wrong time
His executor has it in his blood the Caucasian
Or Trotsky the axe of Macbeth still in his skull
The fist raised in the Bolshevik salute
In a German tank's turret Hamlet the Jew
Or Bukharin singing in the basement
The Party's darling child of AURORA
Perhaps with Hitler he can talk from man to man
Or beast to beast depending on the point of view
He who buries the dead with the leader of the dead
After ten years of war Troy was fit for the museum
An object of archeology
A bitch alone still wails for the city
On the avengers' bones Rome was founded
The price a burning woman in Carthage
Mother of Hannibal's elephants
Rome nursed by the she-wolf the victors' legacy
Greece a province to draw culture from
3000 years after the bloody
Birth of democracy with bath   net   ax
O NIGHT BLACK MOTHER in the house of Atreus
The forceps guided by Athena born from the head
The third Rome pregnant with calamity
Plods toward Bethlehem to its next incarnation
The rapture of the old images   The fatigue
In your back the never-ending muttering
Of the TV   WITH US YOU SIT
IN THE FRONT ROW The difficulty
Of sustaining the verse against the staccato
Of commercials inviting the voyeurs to dinner
GIVE US OUR DAILY MURDER TODAY
In my memory a book title surfaces
THE FRONT ROW a report on deaths in Germany
Communists fallen in the war against Hitler
As young as today's arsonists are   knowing
Little perhaps as the arsonists of today
Knowing other things and not knowing other things
Devoted to a dream that makes you lonely

Within the traffic circle of commodities
Their names forgotten and effaced
In the Nation's name from the memory of
The Nation whatever that may be or might become
In the current fusion of violence and amnesia
In the dreamless chill of the universe
I AJAX WHO POURS OUT HIS BLOOD
BENT ON HIS SWORD AT THE BEACH OF TROY
In the white noise
Return the Gods after the TV programs sign off
Is burnt the longing for the pure rhyme that
Turns world into desert   day into dreamy haze
Rhymes are mere jokes in Einstein's curved space
Light waves will never spin foam into lace
Brecht's monument a barren plum tree's face
And so on whatever the language tolerates
Or the dictionary of German rhymes
The final program is the invention of silence
I AJAX WHO . . . HIS BLOOD

The Death of Seneca
A Dialogue

The Death of Seneca (Der Tod des Seneca) is the edited transcript of a discussion with Alexander Kluge, broadcast on television in April 1993. It was published in Ich schulde der Welt einen Toten, Gespräche, Hamburg, 1995. The text is one of several conversations Heiner Müller conducted on television with Kluge (1932–), a noted author, filmmaker, and academic who had been an influential intellectual in the former West German Republic, as Müller was in the East German counterpart. Between 1983 and 1994, they discussed a great variety of topics, among them the myth of the House of Atreus, the West German elections of 1990, tank warfare and the character of the warrior, the "castration" of artists and intellectuals when they are in service of political power, etc. Müller opens their conversation with the quote from a Nietzsche letter that also appears in Mommsen's Block; later on he mentions a remark of Mommsen about the reign of Nero, likewise to be found in the poem.

The discussion first centers on the function of "greed" in the arts, that is to say, the virtue of being insatiable in pursuit of all things that might feed the artist's imagination and production. Eventually the focus shifts to Seneca's role as an intellectual in the service of power who persuaded himself of being able to influence his emperor and pupil, Nero, quite like the philosopher Martin Heidegger (1889–1976), for instance, who believed he might provide guidance to Hitler. It is a topic Müller often explored, as, for instance, in *Gundling's Life Frederic of Prussia Lessing's Sleep Dream Scream*. He believed this illusion to be an especially German fallacy. In the final section the conversation turns to Seneca's suicide, a suicide as a theatrical performance before an audience. While dying, the actor kept record of his physical and mental experience so it might be read by future generations and procure a kind of afterlife for him. In other words, Seneca treated his own suicide as material that feeds the "greed" of the dying writer-philosopher. The source of the concluding poem is Tacitus's description of Seneca's death.

The text spells out Müller's own thoughts on death and dying. He obviously identified with the Roman stoic's acceptance of a death he couldn't escape.

C.W.

HM: There is a letter by Nietzsche, addressed to Peter Gast, I believe. He writes there that he received news about the fire in Theodor Mommsen's house. He writes quite emphatically that actually he could stand neither Mommsen nor what and how he writes. The letter relates how Mommsen keeps running into his burning house and coming back again, to rescue manuscripts and books. His hair is smoldering and he is covered with burns. Nietzsche says that he nearly cried when imagining it. And then follows the extraordinary question, or rather a sentence that is questioning: Is this compassion? This fear of compassion. That was quite extraordinary.

AK: It isn't compassion, but greed; he would have liked to have the fourth volume of [Mommsen's] Roman history. He thinks as a philologist.

HM: Yes, of course. But this fearful question, "Is this compassion?" is also something else: "I cannot afford this. I am not allowed to feel compassion."

AK: Nietzsche characterized himself as a philologist. How would you interpret such a sentence in 1992–93? What is a philologist? You are one, aren't you?

HM: Yes, I think so. The impulse to do philology is actually greed. There isn't only *Neugier* [German for *curiosity,* literally: greed for the new], there is also *Altgier* [greed for the old]. It is nearly the same. Simply wanting to have everything, to grab, to know everything. And I believe, without it nothing at all is going to work.

AK: It has been said that Montaigne was so greedy when he was eating that he kept biting his finger and hurting his tongue, out of sheer appetite.

HM: I don't think appetite is the correct term. There is a difference. Let's take another example. I was just in Paris, I don't know how many times I have been there, because I wanted to show to Brigitte the modern art in the permanent exhibition at the Centre Georges Pompidou. It was awful for me to see that for the third time. All this modernism is so boring, so dead . . . Matisse . . . patterns for wallpaper, absolutely boring. Then you suddenly enter a room. It's the room of Giacometti. And immediately you are in a temple. I don't mean this in the sense of being "holy," but suddenly you're in the presence of art. Everything else you can throw away. There you clearly feel the actual cut. Picasso was the last universal artist, or the last Renaissance artist if you like. And he was still hungry. After him, everybody merely had his own special appetite. If you look at it this way, the difference between hunger and appetite is very important. And the harder it becomes to feed the populace of the globe, the more obviously the hunger in the arts is declining. Art without hunger isn't going to work at all. That is, art without the assumption of a desire to devour and possess everything isn't going to work.

AK: And how would you define greed? What is greed?

HM: Greed is something quite positive in the arts, it is actually a precondition for the arts.

AK: Let's go back to our theme: Seneca is a high-ranking Roman aristocrat of some wealth and sufficiently educated to be appointed the teacher of Prince Nero. He is mentor to a young dictator, a young emperor.

HM: I believe this was from the beginning a mediated kind of power, not an unmediated one.

AK: That is to say, Seneca merely creates the appearance of power? In the hope of attracting clients?

HM: He also has, of course, the illusion that he has power.

AK: People are paying him money for that.

HM: Yes, of course. He also enriched himself. I believe Seneca had a cynical relation to power. There is a bust of Seneca that is of interest in the context. Actually, I wanted to bring it along today . . .

AK: How does he look. A bald head?

HM: In a way, yes.

AK: A narrow face?

HM: No, not narrow, but . . .

AK: His character . . . chiseled features?

HM: No, not at all chiseled. Rather like someone you would characterize as decadent and morbid, more the type of a bonvivant who likes to indulge himself. I believe that always goes together.

AK: Really? A decadent man, a split persona. There is very much that is merely appearance and relatively little that is substance?

HM: In any case a desire to indulge himself. That is evident in this bust.

AK: But a self-indulgence of a very elevated kind of greed. I'd rather die than give up my self-indulgence?

HM: He even tried to make his suicide enjoyable and turn it into a performance.

AK: And it has succeeded for nearly two thousand years.

HM: As for another aspect, I became interested in the right of dispensing with your own life, a right that was obviously quite clear to the Romans. It was natural to dispose of your own life. There were scores of suicides of this kind, surely not as theatrical as Seneca's, not so well staged, but . . .

AK: There is, by the way, a Japanese attitude that expresses, "I am not the emperor's subject in the final analysis, as long as I still am the master of my life and my death."

HM: Yes, there were evidently no scruples at all attached to it, and also not that much fear.

AK: Armed with the rationale that I will keep my property when I kill myself. When being killed by the emperor or his henchmen I will lose my property, and so will my descendants.

HM: Yes, but it also has to do with the fact that there was no belief in a beyond at the time. You knew: with your death life will have ended, there is nothing else.

AK: But I achieve an eternal life . . . as a rumor; namely that of Seneca's death.

HM: Yes, okay. But not the idea or the illusion that there is something else.

AK: No, no, but Heiner Müller later will make a poem about me. Do you actually believe Nero was a villain? It has been, after all, only successors, only usurpers, who have reported on his life.

HM: I have forgotten to mention: There is a strange remark by Mommsen concerning why, apart from other reasons, he never wrote the fourth volume. He says, "How can you explain to students that the rule of Nero probably was the happiest time the Roman people ever experienced?"

AK: The usurpation of an empire by an artist was indeed a completely new phenomenon. That is to say, the Roman state as a performance is incomprehensible to anyone who is a legionary or militarist. It is a most elevated form of luxury, to use your words.

HM: Yes, and also because Nero didn't have the slightest interest in military actions, he was too much of a coward.

AK: Could you retell for me the historical events of Seneca's death? How did it happen?

HM: The information we have is from Tacitus. I have read Tacitus since a very early age; it is a perpetual reading matter for me; I keep reading Tacitus again and again.

AK: A crystalline narrative structure.

HM: And also the laconism and even the mannerism of Tacitus. There is this peculiar division of Latinity into a golden and a silver period. And Tacitus belongs to the silver period, that is in the view of classical philologists a lower genre.

AK: The garrulity of Cicero was considered golden, in his time grammar was still respected? It doesn't play a role with Tacitus. Substance displaced grammar.

HM: That's what is interesting in Tacitus. There is a very precise description of Seneca's suicide. He was the teacher of Nero and an author of stage plays in one person. There also existed an elder or younger one, I believe, but it is certain that the teacher of Nero was also the author of the plays. It was, however, very much later that I became familiar with the plays.

AK: Those are highly dramatic works, works of pathos?

HM: Yes, it is interesting that Seneca was the favorite author of the Elizabethans, of Shakespeare and his contemporaries. They didn't know the classic Greek plays. That was important for the origin of their kind of drama.

AK: So, the Elizabethans' reception of Greek drama was by way of Seneca's adaptations?

HM: Yes, and with Seneca the atrocities, the murders, etc., happen on stage, in contrast to Greek plays. His plays were never performed, they were dramas to be read. That's why all the atrocities and murders were taking place on stage, in writing only. But exactly that was the important impulse for Elizabethan drama. And then there is also a history of the subject matter, of course, especially a German history of subject matter, concerning the theme of Seneca's suicide. There was Lessing who had thoughts about a play, there is a play by Ewald von Kleist, *Seneca's Death*. It was always a topic of German literature in the eighteenth century, at a time when the illusion of an education of princes still existed but already was losing its hold: the effort of intellectuals to meddle with politics and exert an influence and, at the same time, their disillusionment. Seneca offered the topic and the central character for it.

AK: So here is one of the few examples that an intellectual exerted an important influence for many decades.

HM: But at the same time, of course, a failed one.

AK: Yes, he had to die for the sake of it.

HM: And he didn't achieve anything. But he tried.

AK: Heidegger had the idea that he eventually might have a role as the educator of "prince" Hitler.

HM: Yes, this is very much a German illusion, I believe. And it is obviously also a GDR illusion.

AK: How did the actual death take place? There are reports from Nero's court that a proscription, a ban is considered?

HM: There was suspicion of a conspiracy, that was the conspiracy of Piso, and Seneca—a case like Jünger's if you like—was suspected of being a participant in this conspiracy.

AK: Even without this suspicion, he had too large a fortune. The emperor would have had an eye on it.

HM: Yes, though Seneca's wife survived. Nero spared her. There was a last inhibition in regard of Seneca. Normally the emperor would have exterminated all members of the family.

AK: Exterminate? Or expropriate?

HM: No, expropriate the fortune and exterminate the people, so as to expropriate the fortune. But Seneca's wife was left alone.

AK: He is in danger, and he anticipates it and kills himself.

HM: No, it was not an anticipatory action, it was quite simple. It was really the way it was with Stalin. It was clear that when the centurion arrives, who is the captain of the Praetorian guard, and brings the order that you should kill yourself, then you must do it, otherwise you will be killed.

AK: Like Rommel. Rommel was visited by two officers from the general staff and they handed him some poison.

HM: The only possibility of administering your own death was to kill yourself before you were killed.

AK: And now he has some difficulty because he is an old and self-indulgent man, since his blood doesn't flow as quickly any more.

HM: That is described by Tacitus. He must, you may say, warm his blood to make it flow. At the end in a steam bath and even that isn't sufficient.

AK: If you think of your own death—we are all going to die, after all—what kind of death do you wish for yourself?

HM: I believe I wouldn't think of it that way, I wouldn't formulate that kind of a wish.

AK: Are you saying it's none of my business?

HM: No, it's none of my business. I would rather assume there are alternatives: either it is a quite sudden death or a quite protracted one. [*Heiner Müller picks up his manuscript and reads:*]

Seneca's death / What was Seneca thinking / and didn't say / when the captain of Nero's bodyguard silently drew the death sentence from his breast plate / sealed by the pupil for his teacher: / Writing and sealing he had learned and the contempt of all deaths but his

own. / Golden rules of all statesmanship. / What was Seneca thinking and didn't say it / when he forbade their crying to his guests and
slaves / who had shared his last meal. / The slaves at the low end
of the table. / Tears aren't philosophical. / What has been decreed
has to be accepted / and as far as this Nero is concerned / who has
killed his mother and his siblings. / Why should he make an ex-
ception with his teacher? / Why forsake the philosopher's blood /
who didn't teach him the shedding of blood? / And when he let his
veins be opened / first at the arms / and his wife's / who didn't want
to survive his death / with a cut probably done by a slave / even the
sword Brutus impaled himself on / at the end of his republican hope /
had to be held by a slave. / What was Seneca thinking and didn't
say / while the blood was leaving too slowly his too old body and
the slave obediently cut also open the veins of the legs and the
crooks of the knees of his master? / A whisper from dried up vocal
chords / My pain is my property. / The wife to the other room! /
Scribe come hither! / The hand couldn't hold the stencil anymore /
but the brain was still working / the machine produced words and
sentences / took notes of the pain. / What was Seneca thinking and
didn't say / between the letters of his final dictation / stretched out
on the philosopher's couch / and / when he drained the cup / the
poison from Athens / since his death still kept him waiting / and the
poison / that had helped many a man before him / could only write
a footnote / into his by-now nearly bloodless body / no clear statement. / What was Seneca thinking speechless at last / when he
walked toward death in the steam bath / while the air was dancing
before his eyes / the terrace darkened by the whirring beating of
wings / most likely not those of angels. / Death, too, is no angel. / In
the glimmer of columns when meeting again the first blade of grass /
that he had seen on a meadow near Cordoba, as high as no tree
would be.

AK: What makes you think of Cordoba now?

HM: Because he was born there. Seneca was a Spaniard.

Dreamtexts
Two Prose Texts

Dreamtexts (*Traumtexte*), published in the 1990s, continue what had become an increasingly important project for Müller, namely the recording
of dreams in as faithful a manner as possible. He claimed that a good text
contains knowledge the author was not aware of during the act of writing and that dreams know more than their dreamer. Müller began during
the seventies to insert dream texts into his plays, such as *Heracles 2 or the
Hydra* and *Prometheus* in *Zement,* the von Kleist and Lessing sequences
in *Gundling's Life Frederick of Prussia Lessing's Sleep Dream Scream,* several parts of *Hamletmachine,* the text *The Man in the Elevator* in *The Task,*
and not to forget the dream in his *Letter to Robert Wilson.*

The Night of the Directors was published in the magazine *Theater der
Zeit,* Berlin, March–April 1995. Müller had the dream in April of 1994.
The intimate intersection of the author's private and professional life is one
intriguing aspect of the text. The dream recognizes no border between
these domains. Whenever a separation becomes perceivable, the dream's
narrative quickly fuses again both sides of the writer's conscious and unconscious memory into one traumatic tangle of events. Many of the narrative's characters refer to persons who played a major or minor role in
Müller's life during the early nineties. "L.B." suggests Luc Bondy, the
French-German director who works in Paris, at the famed Berlin

Schaubühne, the Salzburg, and other festivals, and who was treated for cancer at the time. "Z." Stands for Peter Zadek, who, like Müller himself, had been a member of the Berliner Ensemble's directorate since 1993. Zadek had complained to the weekly *Der Spiegel* about "fascistoid tendencies" he claimed to have recognized in the work of several German stage directors, mentioning Heiner Müller among others. When asked about Zadek's interview, Müller laconically remarked: "Zadek is a stage director. As a journalist he is of no interest to me." Their controversies eventually resulted in Zadek's resignation from the Ensemble's directorate, in the spring of 1995, and the subsequent appointment of Müller as the "speaker" of the directorate, that is, the person responsible for the artistic leadership of the Berliner Ensemble. "M." refers to the director Fritz Marquardt, also a member of the directorate, who staged in the 1970s and '80s at the East Berlin Volksbühne several of Müller's plays which previously had been banned by the East German authorities. The "Composer" may stand for the East Berlin poet Dieter Schulze, whom Müller once supported when he applied for a stipend from the GDR Cultural Ministry in the early 1980s. Schulze, who had achieved little success as a writer, in January 1993 accused Müller of having been an I.M., an "unofficial collaborator" of the Stasi, East Germany's secret police. The intended scandal quickly fizzled, since no evidence of Müller's activities as an informer was found in the archives of the so-called "Gauck bureau," the body appointed to screen the files of the GDR security service and named after its director, the Reverend Mr. Gauck. Lastly, the hoodlum who attacks the dreamer in a junk yard elicits memories of the assaults on foreigners and the elderly by right-wing skinheads, which had become a daily item in the German press at the time of Müller's dream. *Dreamtext October 1995* (*Traumtext Oktober 1995*) was written in October 1995 and published in *Drucksache 17*, Berlin, 1995, a publication of the Berliner Ensemble. The narrative's imagery articulates the dreamer's awareness that his death has become inescapable and that soon he can't protect his young child anymore. This may well be the last literary text Müller completed. It is also a most personal one. History and the world it dominates have receded behind the walls and the fog which enclose the author/father and his child. The only view beyond that is briefly allowed reveals a teeming world where, however, a man is dying in utter solitude. The isolation and finality evoked in the text bring to mind the late writings of Samuel Beckett.

C.W.

The Night of the Directors

The dream begins in a café with two entrances that look like arches or vaulted church doors and are facing each other. The space occupies all of the ground floor of an old house. The house is close to the theater where I occasionally work. I sit with the director L.B. at one of the round tables. B. is cheerful, as always when in company, a master of his illness, it quickens his life instead of his death: he is playing with it. He orders a drink that is unfamiliar to me, dark brown and heavy. Three young men with empty faces sit down at our table without a word and stare at us. Their eyes have the shrouded gaze that the natives of the dictatorship share. After exchanging glances with the others, one of them addresses me. He pretends to know me. He is from a quarter where for a long time I used to live. I can't remember having seen him or having heard of him. He claims to be a composer. In any case, he is adept at talking about music. It is impossible to determine if he is interested in the topic. His face comes alive when he is talking. I am annoyed by his confidential demeanor. It hides a menace. His gaze, when he is opening the curtain behind his eyes, is the touch of a snake. I know this reptilian gaze from conversations with functionaries of the state and the secret police. The composer's companions belong rather to the species of zombies signified in popular parlance as snitches, an allusion to their snitchlike squint. At the entrance facing me, Z. has entered, another director who is more famous for his scandals than B., at my table, for his successes. He is staging his entrance with a long gaze all over the space, in the stance of the strategist taking measure of the battlefield where he wants to be victorious. I call out to him, an occasion to break off the conversation with the composer, which has been tedious for quite a while now. Z. ignores my calling, our relation is not friendly at the present, or he could not hear me with the din in the joint; and, passing our table without a glance, he leaves through the entrance behind me in the direction of the theater. With a look at his exit B. says, "He is on his way to rehearsal." Then another reality catches up with me. On a narrow muddy path between heaps of trash and rubble I am standing face to face with one of the young men from the café. I remember now that at the table he offered me a cheap cigar, which I didn't smoke. When I ask him how we got from the café into this waste land, his face contorts itself into the familiar features of a scornful grimace. He picks a broken-off board from the ground and swings it high above his head. At the same time he performs a wild dance in the splashing mud. Then he freezes for seconds (To me they feel like hours. Why don't I run), takes a wide swipe, and suddenly strikes. I can parry the blow, but a nail that sticks out of the board rips my palm. He laughs as he sees my blood, the first sound from him. At the second blow I succeed in yanking the board from his hands. I don't forget to turn it around and pound the nail into his head. Screaming he tugs the board from the wound, falls face forward into the mud that slowly stifles his voice. The path is a dead end, a wall of trash is blocking it. I take the way back in the direction we, the dead one and I, must have come from at a time that has been erased from my memory. The mud is sucking at my shoes. Frightened by a sound in my back, a hissing or a whisper, I turn around and see my dead one crawling after me on hands and knees, his face a mask of blood and mud. His lips are moving and trying to articulate a word. My fear overcomes my curiosity and I walk on. I shall never know what he wanted to tell me: a plea or a curse. A confused thought takes hold of my brain and moves as a sharp pain through my veins: his hate was the hate of a son which behooves the fathers in this world; the sons are crucified. The path narrows, a wind is starting, whirling dust, paper, and tin cans from the trash heap; as it increases, the dust is obscuring the sight. The path ends in a part of town I know only from the newspapers. No wind, no sound. The quarter is one of the hunting grounds of the poorer populace, the undead of prosperity. You don't enter it without compelling reason, but I have no choice. Anyway, I must once before have passed this road with the old tank tracks that now is void of human beings, its run down tenements with the stink of clogged toilets and overflowing trash bins, of sweat and urine, accompanied by the dead man now behind me on the mud path between the trash heaps, who perhaps had been my protection, since he dwelled in one of those caverns where now perhaps a woman is waiting for him. I regret I didn't take along the board that served me so well, a weapon. I control my desire to walk faster or look behind me. From the corner of my eyes I notice shadows that soundlessly stalk my course. I am sweating. After minutes of a fear that escalates into a panic I am assailed by the discovery that the heat doesn't come from inside my body but looms oppressively in the air. Something like an abrupt change of climate has occurred. From the pale dusk a rusty red sky is rising. The street vanishes into a brown steppe with hard, knee-high grass. In a great distance a band of molten lead is gleaming. Behind it a forest is swimming in the mist. The trees are gigantic mushrooms. At second glance the forest is a city, stepped pyramids that stand on their heads, slantingly leaning against each other, the tiers displaced as if from earthquakes, an assault of geometry. For a moment I have misgivings if I shouldn't walk back into the bleak quarter that now seems like home to me, to the shadows who are of my own kind and may be waiting for me with knives. After hours which the dream shrinks to the blink of an eye—time is a cut through space—I stand at the bank of a wide, quietly flowing river that is teeming with people. Women crawl out of the water, men on their backs. The women are laughing and talk to each other, the men appear to be no burden to them. It occurs to me that the men don't share in the laughter: they converse in another language. Nobody takes notice of me or even seems to see me. Until a woman stands before me—naked like the others, water dripping in pearls from her breasts, glistening on the hair of her crotch—and speaks to me with the voice of all the women I have loved, in a language whose sounds are alien to me, not to mention the words. Here the thread is torn, the tangle of the dream dissolves into fragments that flash like lightning through my memory and submerge in oblivion. I still recall that I stand with the woman who now is clothed, her dress a gray blot, in a space the size of a gymnasium; in front of me, in the center of the space, M. leans against a pillar, enveloped in a cocoon of a plasticlike, dimly transparent substance, his face shows no expression through the dimness. M. is the third director to populate my dream. It is the night of the directors. I tear the cocoon open, the material is tough and my fingers are bleeding. The woman has some design on him, maybe on us. I follow her instructions. The text tries to describe the dream. The description can only be an extemporization, a falsification. The obsession of presenting the torrent of images as a sequence, like dead moths in a show case, results in the essential lie of coherence, the illusion of meaning. The dream works with other material than what is available to the writing mind. The colors the text assigns to the images are already an interpretation, protection against the suction exercised by the other reality of the dream, the radiant force of its images, the destructive potential of the dark side where perhaps its curative powers rest. The commentary, too, merely a rationalization, fear for the imagined supremacy of the author that the dream puts in doubt every night. The dead man from the salt mine disintegrates in the sun. The last image is a funeral chamber that is illuminated by a dusty light from above, along the walls shelves with drawers in which men are stacked, naked. Women in gray walk from one to the other and masturbate them, the way cows are milked. Before I am next in line, the dream stops and without any transition the next one begins. I sit naked in an armchair in my apartment in Berlin. In comes, without a word of greeting, not impeded by the locked door, an unknown woman. She is naked under a wide overcoat. She masturbates me in silence with a firm hand, drinks my semen and leaves without a parting word, just as she came without a greeting. (At the awakening the terrible certitude: this will not happen).

7 APRIL 1994

Dreamtext October 1995

I walk, my daughter—she is two years old—on my back in a basket woven of bamboo, along a narrow strip of concrete with no railing on the bank of a huge water basin; right or left of me, depending on the direction of my circular walk (the only choice I have), an unsurmountably high wall that is also made of concrete. The wall has no opening, no exit from this kettle, a mystery how I entered it, the child on my back and the path so narrow that my right or left shoulder grazes the concrete when my step, afraid of the water that reveals no visible bottom, becomes insecure. At every change of direction—I don't know how many aimless rounds back and forth I already have walked—when I dig my fingernails into the concrete to keep my balance against the swaying of the bamboo basket on my back wherein the child is moving, my eye is caught by a fog bank that encloses our basin and hides the outer world from my sight. Why don't I stop instead of tiring my legs. Why don't I sit down to rest, the basket in my lap and my arms. Why don't I lie down to sleep a little, the basket on my chest. My breathing, quieter when I'm asleep, would move the rib cage up and down and could rock the child into sleep. I am not allowed to stop or sit down to rest, tired as I am. I am not allowed to sleep. I could wake up in the water, rescueless, no steps are leading from the water, too, and then, next to me the basket with the perhaps already drowned child. At the next change of direction, one heartbeat long, the demented hope: if I for a long enough time and at the same spot would dig with my fingers—my nails will grow back the concrete won't grow anymore—into the concrete, with the passing years steps would appear, fit for climbing even if dangerously, but what is death compared to the danger. On doomsday perhaps, which is known to be the shortest day since the longest night will precede it, derisively my reason replies, there is no escape. The fog bank suddenly is torn before my eyes and opens the view on a high-rise that stands alone in the flat landscape. Twenty floors where people are teeming behind windows without curtains, on balconies and verandas, on the flat roof. The foreboding, or is it already a certainty, that I shall not partake of this life anymore, or rather the tearing pain with which my body, which craves for sleep, is perceiving this certainty, propels me into the next senseless walk around the black water that doesn't betray any bottom. Looking back over my shoulder while I'm walking, I see—on the twelfth or thirteenth floor of the lonely highrise, on a veranda beneath an umbrella in a deck chair—a man die. The man is fat, the dying begins with his ripping open his shirt. Probably the buttons are popping. I can't see it from the distance. I observe his convulsive movements which, starting from his chest, quickly seize the whole body. I never have seen a man die, my curiosity is unquenchable, the fatigue that descends on him like a large bird and slows down his movements, his body only a wave on the surface of the ground now, stirred by a mild earthquake, until he comes to rest in harmony with the laws of gravity that we are accustomed to call death.

My too-long gaze at the dying man in the deck chair must have confused my step, as if through the cut in a film have I fallen into the bottomless water. When surfacing again I see with relief that the bamboo basket with my daughter is standing askew above me on the concrete strip and with horror that she is trying to crawl from the basket, her eyes fixed on me who can't get out of the water, the concrete bank is too high. STAY AWAY FROM ME WHO CANNOT HELP YOU my only thought, while her demanding and trusting look tears my, the helpless swimmer's, heart asunder.

Germania 3 Ghosts at Dead Man

A Play

*Germania 3   Ghosts at Dead Man (Germania 3   Gespenster am Toten
Mann)* is the last play Heiner Müller worked on. The text was published
as a book, Cologne, February 1996. Müller intended to start rehearsal of
it at the Berliner Ensemble on 15 January 1996. His death two weeks before that date halted the project. The play received its premiere at the
Bochum Theater, 24 May 1996; it was performed at the Berliner Ensemble on 19 June 1996, in a staging by Martin Wuttke, who had been appointed artistic director as the successor Müller himself had proposed.
Müller might have revised or even drastically altered the text while exploring it with actors in rehearsal. In previous stagings of his plays, such
as *The Scab, Hamlet/Machine* and *Mauser,* he inserted text from various
other sources into the performed piece. *Germania 3 Ghosts at Dead Man*
is already rich in shorter or longer citations from German classics, fairy
tales, folk songs, songs of the working-class movement, and other sources;
a list of texts from which major inserts were culled is to be found at the
end of the play; within the play, the quotations are set in italic type. An
audience would hardly be able to recognize the sources, nor would the
reader who is not intimately familiar with German history, literature, and
folklore. The *Ghosts at Dead Man* of the title refer to a hill in northeast-
ern France, called Dead Man, which was a notorious site of trench fight-

ing during the World War I battle for Verdun. Shell-shocked soldiers claimed to have sighted the ghosts of the dead continuing to fight in the skies. (The title is borrowed from a novel about World War I trench warfare, *Gespenster am Toten Mann*, by P. C. Ettighoffer, published in 1931.)

Müller had been thinking about a play on World War II, Hitler, and Stalin, since the mid-eighties. Traces of its germination can be found in writings such as *Ajax for Instance*. The text's nonlinear narrative spans German and Eastern European history from 1941, when Hitler's armies were poised to attack Moscow, to 1991, when the two postwar German states had been united again. In between, it touches on the Battle of Stalingrad, which broke the spine of German military strength in 1943; on the final days of World War II in 1945 when Germany was overrun by the armies of the Allies; 1956, the year Stalin's crimes were denounced by Khrushchev during the Twentieth Congress of the Soviet Party, the year Bertolt Brecht died and a group of East German intellectuals was arrested in the aftermath of the failed revolution in Hungary; and the period of 1961–89, when the Berlin Wall stood as a monument of the divided Germany, of a world split by the Cold War, and of a socialism that had been utterly discredited by the so-called "Real Existing Socialism" in Eastern Europe.

Twenty-five years earlier Müller had written a comparable dramatic treatment of German history, *Germania Death in Berlin*, a play which pulled together events from the year 10 A.D., eighteenth-century Prussia, the aborted German revolution of 1918, Hitler's taking power in 1933 and his final days in the bunker in 1945, the founding of the GDR in 1949, and the quickly suppressed East German uprising in June of 1953. The play's ambiguous ending revealed Müller's doubts about the future of a German socialism, even as he still was committed to it. (One might ask: Was there once a project called *Germania 2*?)

Germania 3 opens with Ernst Thälmann and Walter Ulbricht guarding the Berlin Wall. Thälmann was the head of the German Communist Party (KPD) in 1933 when Hitler became chancellor; he was arrested by the Nazis and spent time in prisons and concentration camps until early 1945, when he was murdered in Buchenwald Camp. Ulbricht was head of party and state of the former GDR when he ordered the sealing of the GDR borders and construction of the Wall in 1961. Müller places Thälmann's ghost with Ulbricht on guard duty at the Wall, debating the failure of German socialism. They observe the arrest of a defector who is followed by Rosa Luxemburg, one of the founders of the Spartakusbund, which later became the German Communist Party. She is taken away not by the East German People's Police but by the members of the Imperial Guards regiment who had assassinated her in January of 1919. Luxemburg embodied for many a concept of socialism that had been betrayed and perverted in the GDR. Thus is, in the scene's concluding image, the theme of the play established.

The next image is of a paranoid Stalin in the Kremlin, taking stock of his murderous rule. While awaiting the German onslaught in the fall of 1941, he is haunted by ghosts: his predecessor, Lenin, his erstwhile "brother" Hitler, and his victims Trotsky and Bucharin. Both scenes explore reasons and the specific motivations for the way the communist project went awry and eventually became doomed.

The Stalingrad scenes' title, *Siegfried A Jewess from Poland,* is a reference to the Nibelung Saga as well as to Rosa Luxemburg, who was Jewish and born in what used to be Russian Poland, in 1871, where she later cofounded a socialist party before she became a leading figure in the German Social-Democratic Party. (Müller discusses the connection in *A Conversation in Brecht's Tower.*) The scenes depict both sides of the front. Soviet soldiers, one of them a former inmate of Stalin's forced labor camps, find a killed German, a lover of the poet Friedrich Hölderlin's play *The Death of Empedocles* (1799) who also appears to enjoy the hanging of Russian partisans. Then the German side: Officers cannot maintain their sense of duty and dignity anymore and consequently kill themselves. (A scene from Heinrich von Kleist's play *The Prince of Homburg* [1811] shows how that sense of duty once had been cruelly instilled in the Prussian officer corps.) Infantrymen debate German politics during the Weimar Republic and devour what might well be a dead comrade. A scene from Friedrich Hebbel's tragedy *The Nibelungs* (1862) reminds us how that medieval saga anticipated in an uncanny way the fate of all those who tried to conquer the vast expanse of the East and its people. In Hitler's bunker, the end of the German dictator plays out like an opera that turns into operetta, observed by Stalin as the King of Rats. Hitler's minister of propaganda, Göbbels, appears after having poisoned his children, as the real Göbbels did before he committed suicide with his wife Magda, in April 1945.

The end of World War II, when Germany had been invaded by armies from east and west, is shown from two aspects. In the manor house of an estate near Parchim, three widows of German aristocrats and officers would rather die than be victimized by the approaching Red Army soldiers. They enlist the help of a Croatian SS man; Croatia was at the time a German satellite state that supplied many volunteers to the SS divisions. (The incident is based on an event that happened in the province of Mecklenburg in spring of 1945.) While the women are being killed, their dead husbands' ghosts debate the loss of the war and its reasons. The oldest, a general, had taken part in the conspiracy to kill Hitler that didn't succeed, on 20 July 1944. His son and grandson accuse him of treason. The Croatian, having done his job, goes home and later becomes a "guest worker" in West Germany, as many of his Yugoslavian compatriots did during the sixties and seventies. He eventually applies his skills with the axe to his own family, to get rid of what might impede his integration into prosperous West German society. In 1991, a distant heir of the former owners of the estate has reclaimed the land and buildings expropriated after World War II by the East German land reform of 1945. The story of the widows' suicide has stimulated the young man's imagination and he recalls a play, *The Foremother,* by the Austrian nineteenth-century playwright Franz Grillparzer.

In the following set of scenes, a liberated concentration camp inmate surprises and kills the Red Army soldier who has raped his wife. When taken to Stalin's gulag, the inmates are jeering at his loyalty to communism.

The 1956 segments consist of a multilayered scene, supposedly after Brecht's death at the Berliner Ensemble's office, and the farcical depiction of a party at the house of a local official in provincial Saxony. Both scenes conflate historical events that didn't occur at the same time. Brecht died on 14 August 1956; the Hungarian uprising did not happen until October, the arrest of Wolfgang Harich, a professor of philosophy at East Berlin's Humboldt University, not until November of the same year. There was no rehearsal of Brecht's adaptation of Shakespeare's *Coriolanus* during those months. The play was eventually staged at the Ensemble in 1964. The taking of measurements for Brecht's coffin is a rumor never reliably confirmed. However, Fritz Cremer was a highly esteemed sculptor who later created the Brecht monument in front of the Berliner Ensemble's Schiffbauerdamm theater. The three widows are fictional characters based on Isot Kilian, wife of Harich and Brecht's last lover (Woman 1); Helene Weigel, Brecht's wife from 1929 and leading actress and managing director of the Berliner Ensemble (Woman 2); and Elisabeth Hauptmann, a former lover and an important collaborator of Brecht before and after his exile from Germany (Woman 3). The Burning Woman refers to Ruth

Berlau, a Danish actress and writer and longtime lover of Brecht, who died in 1974, in a fire started by her cigarette when she fell asleep in bed at the East Berlin Charité Hospital. Peter Palitzsch and Manfred Wekwerth were collaborators of Brecht who became the leading stage directors of the Ensemble after his death; Palitzsch left for the West in 1961 and had a very successful career as a director and the manager of companies in Stuttgart and Frankfurt; Wekwerth eventually became artistic director of Brecht's former theater, 1977–91. Ekkehard Schall is the actor who played Coriolanus in the Ensemble's 1964 production; he also is Brecht's son-in-law. The scene's title refers, of course, to Brecht's Lehrstück, *Die Massnahme;* the term *Massnahme* connotes the steps taken to a specific end but it also can mean the taking of measurements, as by a tailor.

In the original German version, published in 1995, extensive excerpts from Brecht's plays *Galileo* and *Coriolanus* are recited by some of the characters. These Brecht quotes were subsequently excluded from any publication of Müller's play, by legal action brought by the Brecht estate. In our version, the original position and act and scene numbers of those quotes have been indicated. (After this volume had been typeset, Germany's Supreme Court reversed the lower court's decision, so the quotations can be included in future publications of this work.)

The party scene at the house of Frankenberg's town architect reflects Heiner Müller's experience during the time his father was mayor of the town in the late forties. His parents defected to the West in 1951. The events supposedly take place in 1956, the year Stalin's crimes were for the first time acknowledged by the Soviet Party; they are fictional to a degree. Several details can be found in other writings of Müller. Aside of the mayor and the architect there are three functionaries who embody three generations of Socialist Unity Party (Sozialistische Einheits Partei, or SED) office holders in the former GDR: a veteran of the old Communist Party from its founding days in 1919, a somewhat younger man, probably of the former Social-Democratic Party during the Weimar years before Hitler's Reich, and a recent but quickly rising member who was a Nazi until 1945. The mayor's son, a fictional portrait of the author himself, his father, and the architect comment with acerbic wit on the results and the sudden reversal of Stalinism. The senior functionary's suicide is based on a factual incident, as is the story of the former concentration camp inmate in *The Second Epiphany;* both events are related as well in the poem *Ajax for Instance.* The mayor's son recites a section from Müller's play *Philoctetes,* which describes Ajax's suicide; he also quotes Kafka and an early-twentieth-century German playwright and poet, Klabund. Songs of the communist movement are quoted or referred to by several of the characters.

The concluding scene is based on the case of a serial killer who was shocking Germany during the period of reunification: five women and a baby were found murdered between October 1989 and April 1991, at a time the Red Army units on East German territory were waiting to be moved back to Russia. The tabloid press baptized the killer "The Pink Giant," due to descriptions of his appearance. The killer's monologue contains numerous quotes from German fairy tales, such as *Rumpelstiltskin*.

The very last line of the play, "Dark, Comrades, is outer space. Very dark," was the message sent back to earth by the Soviet cosmonaut Yuri Gagarin, the first person to travel in space. It may be interpreted as Müller's comment about the future an ever-expanding technology will have in store for us.

C.W.

Military Parade at Night

Night. The Berlin Wall. THÄLMANN *and* ULBRICHT *keep sentry.*

THÄLMANN: The mausoleum of German Socialism. Here is where it's been buried. The wreaths made of barbed wire, the salute fired at the bereaved. With dogs against our own populace. This is the red hunt. This is the way we imagined it in Buchenwald and Spain.

ULBRICHT: You know something better.

THÄLMANN: No.

ULBRICHT: If you put your ear to the ground, you can hear them snoring, our people, fuck cells with district heating from Rostock to Johanngeorgenstadt, their skulls hugging the TV screen, the compact car outside the door. (*Shots. Tracer shells.*) Another one. I hope it isn't my sector.

(*Enter soldiers with a young fugitive.*)

ULBRICHT: What do you want from the capitalists. What else should we stuff down your gullets.

FUGITIVE: Next time I'll do better.

ULBRICHT: In three years, maybe. Take him away.

THÄLMANN: A comrade in Buchenwald told me about Spain. How his stomach turned after the battle of Teruel when he saw the dead Moroccans lying around, torn to shreds by our grenades, a victory. How should they know who their enemies are.

ULBRICHT: He isn't dead. He can still learn.

THÄLMANN: In prison. What did we do wrong.

(*Lieutenant* VOGEL *and gendarme* RUNGE *pass by with* ROSA LUXEMBURG.)

Song: A HUNTER BLEW INTO HIS HORN AND ALL THAT HE BLEW WAS MOST FORLORN.

Tank Battle

Kremlin. STALIN *is drinking.*

STALIN: Comrade, why are you drinking when it's night.
What do you fear, your power is the law.

I know of everyone something that kills him.
Behind my back no enemy is alive,
Is he. The dead are sleeping lightly.
They are conspiring in our foundations
And their dreams are the force that's choking us.
Trotsky, the Jew, playing the role of Banquo
The axe stuck in his skull. It is a chair,
And nothing else. Why fear an empty chair.
Koba, why did you need my death.
That was Bucharin, darling of the Party
I needed him as enemy, he was
The best. He learned it well, his lesson, the
Darling of the Party, if under torture.
Two tears for the best enemy. One-sixth
Of our globe is twitching in my fist. And
Will shatter no god knows into which pieces
When death will break my fist at the wrong time.
My arm is short, right. And my arm is longer
Than any arm has ever grown in Russia
And Russia's the dominion of long arms.
It is mere child's play: Paper beats the stone.
No man is heavier than his file, and ink
Drinks blood. The Remington replaced the Mauser
And each file is the Holy Book.
Who'll count the corpses when the graves are empty.
Not until mankind rises from their knees
Out of the blood that we have spilled at the
Last Party Congress, will the monuments bleed.
And what if our seed won't sprout, Lenin.
With blood I've fertilized this country
And forged new industries with human bodies
Ground into bonemeal in my grinders, I
The great Stalin, leader of nations.
I'm the bloodhound. My private property
Two pairs of boots. It's always only one
Who dies, you answered if someone asked you
About your corpses. Did you ever count them.
I am your death, can't count them anymore.
Because they are the ground we're walking on

On our way into your shining future.
Mankind is just a poor material
Ants under your boot. How shall I while Russia's
Sluggish bulk is squatting on my nape
Create the new man if the old one isn't
Liquidated. Yesterday for your tomorrow.
The mass grave is now pregnant with the future
The age is needing men of a new flesh
I'm baking them from their own blood
And no Prometheus will ever cross me
There is still room at the Caucasus rock.
Who am I. Dead is Dead. I am my prison
Where I'm locked up until the day I die.
And who could kill Stalin aside from Stalin.
They hate me and are waiting for my death
And no one risks a word, they all are cowards.
And if I'd sign my own death warrant
Stalin is a traitor kill Stalin
Stalin has ordered it, they will obey
Since no one dares to contradict me.
Or they won't, afraid it is a trap.
What's whispering in the hallways now. Guard.
Treason is human. Am I still a human.
Who besides Stalin could betray Stalin.
In every human there's a Hitler hiding, a
Capitalist, kulak, and saboteur.
I can't wait till he slips out of his skin.
If you'll choke him maybe he'll see reason
Or whipped with hunger, or with fear
Of Asia or rebellion from the sewers.
I know the dreams that waft about, Churchill,
In your brain that has been steeped in whisky:
You exorcise the devil with the devil
One of them has to break the other's neck
Brown against red Red against brown makes white
The corpses carpet of three continents
Upon which you are dancing your last tango.
Whoever doesn't want to love me got to fear me
We're each one dancing on his own dance floor.

My trump's called Hitler, there are no rules to heed
In times of need.
OFFICER: The Germans are attacking, Comrade Stalin.
STALIN: Guards. Tear his tongue out. He is lying.
I should have known it, I before anyone.
A joke, the eagle who trusted the vulture.
And I stand naked facing his divisions
My army has no head. I wished I hadn't
Have them shot, all my best generals.
I had to have them shot, or didn't I.
Suspicion equals guilt, traitors everywhere
Better one death too many than a dagger
In your back. What noise there at my borders.
The Germans are attacking. Who are the Germans
A flock of small fry at Asia's western margin.
Why do I feel cold sweat upon my brow.
Forgotten who I am. The Great Stalin.
I am afraid of my own shadow.

(One after the other, three apparitions enter: LENIN, babbling and screaming after his second apoplexy; TROTSKY, with Macbeth's axe still in his skull,
in the turret of a German tank; HITLER, who is barking one of his speeches.)

STALIN: (To Lenin.) There it is, your German revolution you were dreaming
of in October. They will drag your corpse from the mausoleum and
feed it to their dogs. Fodder for Hitler's German shepherd, that's what
you are now, Lenin, for your beloved German working class.
(To Trotsky.) Trotsky, the executioner of Kronstadt. Now you know
where's your place, Bronstein, with your perpetual revolution, your de-
formed fetus from a Viennese coffee house: in a German turret, in a
Nazi tank.
(To Hitler.) Hitler, my friend of yesterday. Brother Hitler.
You're burning down my villages, That's good.
Because they're hating you, they'll learn to love me.
Your trail of blood will wash my name snow white.
You've got your time but not more time than I have.
Go on and conquer. Drive your tanks into the snow
That buries them when its time has come.
My back's called Asia, my wolves are waiting

They've learned it well while they were in my gulag.
Your war is now their hope that they will march
To Germany along the tracks your tanks made.
The sluices you have opened, now the flood comes.
And you shall be the first who will be drowned.
The final conqueror is always death.
In a rat's cage you'll see Moscow at last
Before your dead and mine will rise again.

(*Enter* THE DEAD.)

Siegfried   A Jewess from Poland

1

Stalingrad. Two Russian soldiers.

1: Comrade, you are new at our front.
   Where did you come from.
2:                              From the gulag.
1: Are you a murderer or a thief.
2:                              A traitor.
1: And whom did you betray.
2:                              Not Russia.
1: Who'd you like better, Hitler or Stalin.
2: They both have blood on their hands, it is ours.
1: The fathers beat you harder than the stranger.
2: And harsher tastes the blood.
                              Watch out. A German. (*Shoots.*)
1: Where did you learn this. Not in the gulag.
2: In the army. It was my life. I was
   An officer.
1: (*Points at the German.*)
             He's very young, a kid still.
   I can't look at his eyes. You bury him.
   Snow we have plenty now.
2:                              There is a book
   Inside his boot. Friedrich Hölderlin.
   Empedokeles

Since ever-more violent
Like water the wave of wild mankind crashed
Against my breast, and from the uproar sounded
The poor people's voice into my ear.
And when, while I was silent in the great hall,
At midnight the riot began to lament
And raced across the fields and, tired of living,
Broke with its own hand its own house,
When brothers fled each other, and the lovers
Blindly passed each other, and the father didn't
Recognize his son, and human speech was not
Intelligible anymore, and human laws
Dissolved   in flames,
Then the meaning grasped my trembling mind,
It was my people's God who took his leave!
It was him I heard

1: A photo. Seven partisans
   Strung up. And he in front of them and laughing.
   The wolves shall eat his eyes out of their sockets.
   (*He spits on the corpse.*)
2: Maybe he did believe their lies.
   The German's human, we are the animals
   (*Tears up the photo.*)
   There are no pictures of the gulag. No
   Mirror in the gulag shows your face
   Only the eyes that gaze at you, ice cold
   And strange as if they never had seen you
   And no one else, they are sometimes a mirror
   For your face that's not your face anymore
   Forgotten who you are what was what will be
   Only your hundred grams of bread and soup
   Tomorrow if you're lucky you'll wake up
   With bones the frost forgot to bite
   That was the gulag The Germans are my godsend
   Since Russia is more than the gulag and
   Stalin is breaking Hitler's neck with our
   Bones that were three times broken by him.
1:   Amen

2

Two German officers discover a parachute drop with provisions.

1: The Führer won't let us perish.

2:                             Heil Hitler

   (*Tries to eat.*)

1: These are provisions for a company
   I shoot you if you are going to eat.

2: And why are your hands trembling, Captain

1: You couldn't feed a company with it.

2: Have you counted them. The company
   Is seven men now. We are two of them.

2: The hunger turns us into animals.
   (*He eats.*)

2: (*Eats, too.*) Why was it we marched into Russia.

1: I didn't hear you ask that question, Lieutenant.

2: Because it's our duty to save Europe
   From Bolshevism. That's what I have learned.

1: Europe. What do I care for Europe.
   It is for Germany. Schiller and Goethe.

2: Oil and wheat.

1:                 Thinking of such a base kind
   Is alien to me, Lieutenant.

2:                    Napkin, Captain.

1: I do admit, not everything that shines
   Is gold. The thing about the Jews perhaps
   Was a mistake. I for instance knew one
   In World War I. He was an officer.

2: Everybody knows a Jew. I'm full.

1: Our soldiers are starving.

2:                 We're pigs.

(*Each one goes into his bunker, shaves or is getting a shave, shoots himself.*)

HOMBURG: *Now, immortality, you are all mine!*
   You're radiating even through my blindfold,
   With the splendor of a thousand suns!
   Wings are growing forth from both my shoulders,

Through silent realms of ether soars my mind,
And as a ship, abducted by the wind's breath,
Watches the noisy port sink in the sea,
All of life is fading from my sight:
Now I still recognize colors and forms,
And now a fog is everything below me
ELECTOR: *Let roaring cannon bring him back to life!*
HOMBURG: *No, say! Is this a dream?*
KOTTWITZ: *A dream, what else?*

3
Three German soldiers are gnawing on a bone.

1: It was in Geiseltal ten years ago
  Or is it thirteen Who would still remember
  The year, the day, your stomach at your knees
  Surrounded. I was a Communist Ask me
  Why I have been cured of Communism
  Since I have seen their Soviet paradise.
2: Soon you'll see it from six feet below.
3: I say he'll get us out of here.
2:                          Heil Hitler!

(1 and 3 raise their right arm.)

2: Can you still raise your arm? Past the freezing point!
1: He was an unemployed guy, one of ours.
  Unemployed was our job description
  In Leuna 1928.
2: Now you're employed. To every dog his bone.
1: I don't recall his name. He was seventeen.
  And had slipped down the wrong way, robbery
  And murder. Great stuff for their propaganda
  Against us, three weeks till election day.
  That's what the Commies do, robbery and murder
  His wanted poster on each fence and wall
  He was hiding somewhere in Geiseltal
  We called a vote at our party meeting

And the majority agreed: We chase him
Doing the job the police couldn't do
And hand him over at the police precinct.
The honor of the party is at stake here
And someone rose and said If we must do this
And soil our fingers for the honor
Of the party What kind of honor is that
If we are dragging one of ours to the block.
Who are the judges Is this our state
Why don't we go and kill him ourselves
The hunt lasted three days His father had
Joined our posse fifty against one
And we turned three times over every bush
Until we found him Snot and tears were running
Down his face I never will forget that
And his father who hit him in the face
It was for our seats at city council.
We also took the price put on his head
Five hundred marks for the Red Welfare Fund.

2: (*Throws the bone over his shoulder.*)
That was the last bone. I don't want to know
If it came from a horse or if I HAD
A LOYAL COMRADE
(*1 vomits.*)   Go on, throw it up
Soon all of us will just be frozen meat.

(KRIEMHILD *and* HAGEN.)

KRIEMHILD: *There sits the murderer.*
HAGEN: *Whose murderer, Lady?*
KRIEMHILD: *The murderer of my husband.*
HAGEN: *Wake her up.*
She sleepwalks in a dream. Your husband lives
I have caroused with him this very night.
Yet, it is true, he is your second one.
When in his arms, do you think of the first?
Well, you are right, I killed him.
KRIEMHILD: *You hear this.*

HAGEN: *In Odenwald, there spouts a lively spring—*

KRIEMHILD: *Well, do then what you like.*

HAGEN: *To bed, to bed!*
You now have other duties.

KRIEMHILD: *Your derision*
I'll stifle right away in your black blood:
Go, Attila's butchers, go, and let him see
Why I have mounted a second husband's bed.
You may be sure, you won't escape me now
Ev'n if you will see one more morning sun.
I want to be back in my Siegfried's tomb.
But first I have to die my funeral gown
And that can only be done in your blood.

HAGEN: *I don't deny I threw the deadly spear*
With joy, and still enjoy the thought of it.
But your hand handed it to me. So you
Yourself atone if there's atonement due.

KRIEMHILD: *And do I not atone? What could befall you*
That could equal even half my pain.
Look at this crown and ask yourself.
It does remind you of a wedding like
None other that was celebrated on this earth
Of horrid kisses, between death and life
Which were exchanged on that most frightful night
And of a child whom I could never love.
Do you believe that I have saved my soul
When I after a fight that has no match
Mounted my second bridal bed with Attila?
Oh, be assured of it, in that brief moment
When I had to take off my woman's belt
But tied it ever tighter to my body
Until he, furious, cut it with his dagger,
That moment contained tortures worse than all
The horrors this great hall is holding for you
With smoke and fire, hunger, thirst, and death.
No, no, and if I bleed this whole world white,
Down to the youngest cooing dove
Who hasn't left her nest, weak as she is,

I wouldn't shrink back from it, not at all.
Bloodied comets are streaking through the skies
Instead of gentle, pious stars, and they
Blaze their dark tidings all over the world.
All good means are exhausted now, the bad ones
Assume their place, the way a poison does
When medicine won't offer any help.
And not till Siegfried's death has been revenged
Shall any deed on earth be called a crime.
Until that time justice shall be in hiding
And nature sunk into the deepest sleep.

HAGEN: *You're right. Why are we still pretending, Kriemhild?*
We know each other. Yet, be aware of this:
After the stag's first masterpiece has helped him
Escape the hunter, the second quickly follows
which pulls him downwards to destruction.

(Throws off his coat; underneath he wears a German general's uniform.)
Death now has risen, standing right behind us
I wrap around myself his darkest shadow
And only he catches the sunset's glow.

KRIEMHILD: (*Throws off her coat; underneath she wears the tunic of the Red
Army without any insignia; behind her the shadow of Stalin.*)
You ate my flesh and drank my blood
And chased me through ten countries
Into this wedding that's my other death
And stretched my skin across your drum
Now be my guests at the last supper
Eat your dead and quench your thirst with
Their blood The table will be richly decked
And celebrate your wedding with the naught
That's your abode in the realm of the dead.

(*Song:* A HUNTER BLEW INTO HIS HORN AND ALL THAT HE BLEW WAS MOST FORLORN.)

3: The Russians are attacking. The Volga's burning.

A Hunter Blew into His Horn

Bunker. Hitler's chancellory.

HITLER: (*Tears up a map.*)
  Poland a joke France a piece of cake
  The Balkans Greece Who counts my victories
  In Russia snow in Africa the sand
  The Jew was my undoing he drinks the
  Gasoline I need to win His ashes
  Are clogging the wheels of my tanks.

(*Enter* STALIN, *with an entourage of rats.*)

                                    Stalin
  The king of rats who has a giant's back
  He still savors Siberia Not for long
  Your back will be your hunchback when I'm gone
  When they will count the corpses, yours and mine
  Welcome to hell You Bolshevik
  They will know how good we were for them
  When everywhere humans devour humans
  Because there isn't land and food for all
  Nation without a space And they will jabber
  Of our butcheries day in day out
  While human blood is dripping from their teeth
  At every meal hypocrites and traitors
  I've wanted just the best A humankind
  Ready for pain and death and free of Jews
  The German shepherd is going to thank me.
  Rattenhuber.
(*Enter* RATTENHUBER.)
                  You've got the gasoline.
RATTENHUBER: Yes, my Führer.
HITLER: We will be needing it.
RATTENHUBER: Whereto, my Führer, will we travel.
HITLER: To
      Valhalla.

RATTENHUBER: That is far, my Führer.

HITLER: Yes.

(Pause.)

Ask the ladies to enter now.

(Enter GÖBBELS with dead children.)

GÖBBELS: These were my children They were my future
I've butchered them and they are yours now
We leave behind what will come after us
The future our enemy Victory is ours.

(Exit STALIN, waving. Enter LADIES, RATTENHUBER with containers of gasoline.)

HITLER: My ladies. I thank you for all the work you have done most loyally, what would life be without the loyalty of woman, I won't speak of death, in my service for Germany, which will perish with me. Well deserved, as I have to admit, treason and cowardice everywhere and at all our fronts. (Cannonade, detonations.) You hear the triumph of the subhuman who is assuming his rule. The subhuman has demonstrated that he is the stronger one. Humankind may perish. I am, you know it, the superhuman. I've done my part in the extermination of humankind that is flooding our planet. Others will come after me who shall continue my work. I shall leave this world since it has become too small for me, together with Miss Eva Braun whom I have married an hour ago, here you see the official document, signed by Mr. Richard Wagner, please, check his signature, so that neither hell nor high heaven will be able to separate us, because her hands are clean, and my hands are bloodied as the hands of all great men of history are bloodied, Alexander Caesar Frederick the Great Napolean (softly) Stalin. In the domain of history blood is a more efficient fuel than gasoline is, it leads you to eternity, and loyalty is the marrow of honor. I go back to the dead who have given birth to me. Jesus Christ was a son of man, I am the son of the dead. I've had my astrologer shot, Mister Friedrich Nietzsche, so that he shall precede me to the realm of death that is the only reality and whose deputy on earth I have been. Our grandchildren will understand me. Survive will my program: Against the lying babble of the priests LOVE YOUR ENEMIES the honest commandment of my German catechism DESTROY THEM WHEREVER YOU FIND THEM. Against the fundamental lie of Communism NO ONE OR EVERYONE the simple and popular truth THERE ISN'T ENOUGH FOR EVERYONE. I have elected Europe as my stake. Its flames shall relieve me of my duties as a statesman. I'm dying as a private person. (*Pause*) Yet the smoke of the burning cities will carry my glory all over the globe, and the ashes from the crematories will darken the skies and be my monument that the winds carry to the stars after I am gone. Because forever shall live the fame of the deeds of the dead, as the Edda said, the Holy Book the bible of the North. Long live the German shepherd. (*Shoots his dog.*)

LADIES: Heil Hitler.

(*Exit* HITLER. *Two shots, Dance of the ladies before the background of the burning German capital to the tune of Wagner's* GÖTTERDÄMMERUNG.)

The Guest Worker

Manor house near Parchim in Mecklenburg. The large main kitchen.
OLD WOMAN, MIDDLE-AGED WOMAN, YOUNG WOMAN. *They all are wearing widow's black.*

OLD WOMAN: The Russians have taken Parchim. The time has come.

YOUNG WOMAN: I don't want to die. I've still got a life to live.

MIDDLE-AGED WOMAN: What kind of life. Being the widow of a German officer.

YOUNG WOMAN: Widow. You've lived together for ten years, with you it's been forty. We had one day and one night.

OLD WOMAN: In Eastern Prussia they have nailed women to the barn doors—not to mention the raping—and children, with their bayonets. They're not human, that's Asia.

YOUNG WOMAN: Asia. In our concentration camps, I've been told, there are gas chambers where the Jews . . .

OLD WOMAN: A mere rumor.

YOUNG WOMAN: Ask your husband what it felt like to die in Plötzensee, hanging from a wire noose.

MIDDLE-AGED WOMAN: I'd be glad if at least we had a gas oven. It's supposed to be a beautiful death. I want a beautiful death.

YOUNG WOMAN: With vine leaves in your hair

(MIDDLE-AGED WOMAN *cries.*)

OLD WOMAN: What do you want. Ten stinking Asians who tear your clothes off your body and jump on top of you, one after another. Is that what you want, because you've had no more than one night with your husband. Our life is finished.

YOUNG WOMAN: I still could leave. Leave this ghost mansion with eighteen rooms for three widows in proud mourning.

MIDDLE-AGED WOMAN: We've always treated our Polish workers well.

OLD WOMAN: If you don't want to be one of us anymore, go but fast.

(YOUNG WOMAN *gets up, walks to the door.*)

MIDDLE-AGED WOMAN: And put on your bridal gown. Maybe you could use it again in the life that you've still got to live.

(YOUNG WOMAN *comes back and sits again.*)

OLD WOMAN: I knew you'd see reason.

YOUNG WOMAN: But how shall we kill ourselves. You'd want to eat rat poison. Or a kitchen knife in the breast, like Lucrezia Borgia. In ancient Rome they had their slaves for this. Our slaves were smarter than we are. They're long gone. Ah, I don't know either. (*Cries.*)

(*There is a knock at the door.* YOUNG WOMAN *and* MIDDLE-AGED WOMAN *jump up, screaming. In the door a Croatian* SS MAN *in only remnants of what used to be his uniform. He takes them off and stands naked before the women.*)

SS MAN: I need civvies. Excuse me for popping in here like this but I'm in a hurry, Waffen SS, if the Russians see my uniform I won't see my motherland ever again. My motherland is Croatia. In the buff I won't get far either. They'll know what I've taken off. And their tanks move faster than I can run. I've been running for thirty miles.

OLD WOMAN: Our husbands are dead. You can take your pick. The youngest one was your size. But you must do for us a job that has to be done. Do you have a weapon. We don't want to live anymore when the Russians put the torch to the mansion, (*to the* YOUNG WOMAN) our ghost mansion. And that will be soon.

SS MAN: The war's been lost. I don't carry a weapon anymore.

OLD WOMAN: Then go and look for one. For the act of kindness we've asked you to do for us. You're a soldier. Kill us. The widow of a German general is telling you so.

(*Exit the* SS MAN.)

YOUNG WOMAN: Act of kindness.

MIDDLE-AGED WOMAN: You'd rather sleep with him, wouldn't you. And feed his swine in Croatia. He looks like a peasant.

(*Enter* SS MAN.)

SS MAN: What do you have against peasants, lady. Peasants are useful animals. I've found an axe in the tool shed. The peasant has found an axe, a peasant's weapon. It'll do the job fast, you want it to be fast, won't you, and I'm in a hurry.
(THE WOMEN *are crowding together, horrified by the axe. The Croatian* SS MAN *slams the axe into the kitchen table.*)
I could do it with my hands, not without regrets where the young lady is concerned, you can trust in my hands, if you'd prefer that. I've wrung the chickens' necks on my father's farm in Croatia long before I learned the ABC.

YOUNG WOMAN: Don't you touch me. (*Exits into the house.*)

SS MAN: (*Pulls the axe from the table top.*) It'll be the axe, then.

OLD WOMAN: It's what we wanted. Let's go.

(OLD WOMAN *exits into the house, the* MIDDLE-AGED WOMAN *follows her somewhat hesitantly, then the* SS MAN *with the axe. Blackout.*)

(*When the lights come up again, the* THREE HUSBANDS *of the widows are seated at the table.* LIEUTENANT, CAPTAIN, GENERAL. *The* LIEUTENANT *and* CAPTAIN *have wounds from gunshots, the* GENERAL *is blue in the face, with the wire noose of Plötzensee around his neck.*)

CAPTAIN: You are my father but I cannot sit at the same table with a traitor. (*Gets up.*)

GENERAL: The flag means more than your death, is that it.

LIEUTENANT: (*Gets up and stands next to the* CAPTAIN.) Why have you broken people your oath.

GENERAL: Because we wanted to prevent what's coming now.

(CAPTAIN *and* LIEUTENANT *sit down again at the table, facing the traitor. Sounds of running steps and slamming doors from the house. In quick sequence, three screams stifled by three blows of the axe. The longest scream is the third one, accompanied by the sounds of a pursuit through several rooms. Silence. Blackout.)*

(The heavy steps of the CROATIAN *who is approaching. When the lights come up again, the kitchen is empty. The* CROATIAN *enters in a suit, shirt, and tie, the axe still in his hand. He slams the axe with its bloodied blade into the table top and leaves through the door to the outside. Blackout.*

When the lights come up again, the kitchen with its floor cracked and the furniture fallen apart, everything covered with a layer of dust. In the dust, that keeps drifting down from the ceiling, are seated at the kitchen table the THREE DEAD MEN *and facing them, decapitated, the* THREE WIDOWS.)*

CROATIAN: I am a farmer from Croatia. I work in Germany. After having worked for two years in Germany, I travel back to Croatia, to my village, to my family, my family is a wife and two children. I'm driving my own car that I've bought in Germany, I'm wearing a suit that I've bought in Germany, "off the rack" as they call it in Germany, with a shirt and tie because I need to look like a German. My farmer's clothes from Croatia are in the trunk of my car. The drive takes two days and two nights. I arrive during the second night. At the foot of the hill where my house sits, I step from my car and open the trunk. I take off the suit and my German shoes, rip the tie off my neck, the shirt off my breast, the buttons are popping, and throw the alien clothes into the trunk. I see the stars of my motherland, they are brighter than those in Germany, there's no smoke between me and the sky. The house is dark. I fold my suit in an orderly fashion, the way I learned in Germany, also the shirt. The tie will be rid of its creases by the time I need it again. I put on my farmer's clothes that I've worn two years ago when I traveled to Germany, for two days in an overcrowded train, smelling from the sweat of fear of lands foreign, my pants without creases, the coat of linen, the shoes made of bast. I walk through withered vines up the hill. The house is dark. I unlock the door with the key I carried with me for two years, in whatever clothes I was wearing, even in my overalls at the conveyer belt. I walk into the bedroom. I kiss my wife. She is naked under the blanket. I take off my farmer's clothes and lie down next to her. Her thighs have turned old, her breasts shriveled. I hear the children breathe in the other room. While I make love to my wife, I'm thinking of the brothels in Germany. My wife falls asleep, her head on my shoulder, my skin is wet from her tears. I lie awake until morning and stare at the cracked ceiling of the bedroom. When the children wake up, they recognize me, though they haven't seen me for two years, screaming PAPA; the wife gets up and prepares breakfast the way I was used to: eggs, tomatoes, peppers, bread. After breakfast I go to the tool shed, take the axe that's still hanging from the same hook, and slay my wife with it. With my hands that have worked for two years at the conveyor belt in Germany I kill my children. I leave the house. I lock the door and throw the key away, blindly somewhere between the withered vines. The next rain will sweep it into the soil. I walk through the withered vines down the hill to the car that I've bought in Germany, throw my farmer's clothes into the trunk, they were soiled when I hit my wife with the axe, I'll have to burn them; put on again my suit that I've bought off the rack in Germany, but first the shirt, the tie, and drive back to Germany.

(*Two* YOUNG MEN *stand in the kitchen and try to beat the dust from their custom-made suits of 1990 fashion.*)

YOUNG MAN 1: So, this is ours now. Restitution instead of recompense. (*Laughs.*) A ruin.

YOUNG MAN 2: A piece of real estate. You've got to be realistic. What counts is the price per square mile. We could create a golf course here, for instance, or start a riding school, RIDE AND RIDE AND RIDE (*laughs*), for the new aristocracy from Hamburg. From the nobility of blood to the nobility of money. That's progress for you.

YOUNG MAN 1: It's here where they died.

YOUNG MAN 2: An additional source of income. A tourist attraction. The Ghost Mansion of Parchim.

YOUNG MAN 1: If we're lucky, they are still haunting the place. Do you know the Grillparzer play THE FOREMOTHER.

> There my image in the mirror
> Raised its hands toward its head,
> And with wildly staring horror
> In the darkened glass I see
> How my features are distorted.
> They are still the selfsame features,
> Yet they're different, ghastly diff'rent,
> It looks no more like my face
> Than a corpse looks like a living.
> Wide it's opening its eyes,

Stares at me, and points its finger
Threatening and warning me.

YOUNG MAN 2: Kitty. Where is Kitty.

(*Enter* KITTY.)

Kitty!

KITTY: So this is your mansion. Yukkh!

The Second Epiphany

1 The Homecoming

Bedroom with double bed. A RUSSIAN SOLDIER *is raping a* GERMAN WOMAN.
*Enter a man in the striped outfit of the concentration camps, with the red
triangle of a political* PRISONER. *He watches a while, then slays the soldier.
The woman throws the corpse off, collects her torn clothes, stands with
her back against the wall.*

PRISONER: I ask you to forgive me, Comrade. I shouldn't have hit you as
hard as that, should I. We are Communists, you have liberated us, but
my wife is my wife. And maybe she even enjoyed it after all, twelve
years without a man. Property equals theft, doesn't it.

(*The* WOMAN *hits him, he pushes her away.*)

How long has it been that you had a woman. With me it is twelve
years. You don't know what it's like, twelve years in the camp, how
should you know that, you come from the Soviet Union, who would
believe the Nazi propaganda. The hunger and the bone-breaking work.
In the quarry, he who can't get up is dead. Or at the ovens. At the end
we ourselves had to write the lists of those who went into the oven, the
Jews were the first. I shouldn't have hit you as hard as that, should I.
The blood. Four days of walking through the battered countryside, rejoicing in your gut about each bombed building. They got what they
wanted, haven't they. Are you still listening. I felt sorry for the horses
in the Elbe River near Magdeburg where a column of refugees had been
shot to bits. A white arm that's reaching from the water for a dead baby
drifting by with the stream. He's dead, isn't he.

(*He falls asleep.* MILITARY POLICE PATROL. *The soldiers take one look at the
dead man and pull the* PRISONER *up from his sleep. Still half asleep, he sings
the International. The soldiers drive him from the room, hitting him with
the butts of their rifles.*)

KAPO: Hey German. Why didn't you win the war.
(*The* PRISONER *is silent.*)
You Fascist, lick my boots.
(*Pause.*)

Say Heil Hitler.

(*Pause. The* PRISONER *raises his fist for the Communist salute.* OTHER PRISONERS *beat him up and leave him on the ground.*)

KAPO: Welcome home, Bolshevik.

The Measures Taken 1956

Berliner Ensemble. Office of the Artistic Director. THREE WOMEN, *widows of Brecht. In the radio, news of the arrest of Wolfgang Harich as an enemy of the state.*

WOMAN 1: He said: if they send in the tanks
Because they haven't any new ideas, we must
Be on the barricades. With the people
Against the tanks.
WOMAN 2:   Did he really say that?
That wasn't smart, was it? After Budapest.
WOMAN 1: Yes, Brecht was smarter. He has doffed his cap
Before the tanks in nineteen fifty-three.
WOMAN 2: He didn't own a hat. And anyway
Who are the people. The people, if you asked them
Vote for Hitler.
WOMAN 1:   Maybe the people should
Be asked one more time. That was his opinion.
Maybe they wouldn't vote again for Hitler
But for Socialism. Without Ulbricht.
WOMAN 3: When he doffed his cap before the tanks
The rioters surrounded him; perhaps
It also wasn't smart. They could have killed him,
Couldn't they. and then his theater
That is in danger now because he died

Would have been finished three years earlier.
And now it's we who have to save this island
In a corrupted swamp of blood and money
With his disciples who don't understand him
And who believe they're smarter than he was
Maybe they are but what's the use of it
If being smart means be a weathercock.

WOMAN 1: Smart or not, he's been arrested and
He is my husband. I was in love with him.

WOMAN 2: That's on your mind again.

WOMAN 1:   And with your husband.
Forgive me, please, it just came over me.

WOMAN 2: It or him, where is the difference.
You're not the first one but the last one now.
I've gotten used to forgiving his women.
He should have known what he was doing, your
Husband. If you live in a glass house, don't
Throw stones

WOMAN 3:   He is a fool.

WOMAN 1:   He's a philosopher.

WOMAN 2: And he will find a way out of this mess,

WOMAN 3: He is too smart, he'll never find the hole.

WOMAN 2: How shall we help him.

WOMAN 3:   And why should we do that.
We save the theater or we save him.
The chasm is the same Man Equals Man
The prison or the coffin. Death was on time.
He died the moment it was time for him
To go unwashed into the realm of death.
Knowing when. He always was the smartest.
You don't step into the same river twice
You don't doff twice your cap before the tanks.

WOMAN 2: (*Turns on the intercom.*)
I've got to listen to rehearsal. It's important.
They're on break now.

WOMAN 3:   And they're in discussion.

WOMAN 1: That's what they've learned, yes. How to hold discussions.

VOICE OF PALITZSCH: Manfred, it won't work this way.

VOICE OF WEKWERTH: Peter, why.

VOICE OF PALITZSCH: The proletarians, Manfred.

VOICE OF WEKWERTH: The plebeians.

The action is in Rome.

VOICE OF PALITZSCH: We're in Berlin

The year is nineteen hundred fifty-six.

VOICE OF WEKWERTH: It's no contemporary drama, Peter

It is a parable. Stalin, if that's what

You mean, is marginal.

VOICE OF PALITZSCH: The margin's bloodied.

VOICE OF WEKWERTH: Well, if you think so. Fine, it's your opinion.

VOICE OF PALITZSCH: I speak of staging, not of politics.

The proletarians, or plebeians, if

You prefer that, Rome instead of Berlin,

Are different.

VOICE OF WEKWERTH: Well, what are they like. What do

You know of them.

VOICE OF PALITZSCH: They are polite, Manfred

They've learned to be polite. That is their cross.

Much pressure's needed till they throw it off.

VOICE OF WEKWERTH: You want more pressure.

VOICE OF PALITZSCH: That isn't what I've said.

(*Pause.*)

VOICE OF WEKWERTH: Well. Am I polite. I am a proletarian.

VOICE OF PALITZSCH: I don't know if the Party will believe you.

Your Party.

VOICE OF WEKWERTH: When will you be saying: ours.

VOICE OF PALITZSCH: I don't know, Manfred. Give me time.

VOICE OF WEKWERTH: Time, Time.

I don't know and I don't know and I don't know.

Knowledge is power

VOICE OF PALITZSCH: That was his childlike faith.

And what he has not written is now our

Tragedy: knowledge split from power.

VOICE OF WEKWERTH: Did you say our tragedy. But he

Has written it, his *Galileo.* The power

Of stupidity, stupidity in power.

VOICE OF PALITZSCH: Or just a different knowledge.

VOICE OF WEKWERTH: Don't be polite.

    You must be able to afford politeness.

    I can't afford it, your politeness.

VOICE OF PALITZSCH: As proletarian.

VOICE OF WEKWERTH: Now you're impolite.

VOICE OF PALITZSCH: I sometimes think, it's mostly late at night

    Or while I'm half asleep when morning dawns

    And the mushroom cloud splits my retina:

    The Little Monk is right, not Galileo

    (*He quotes from the speech of the Little Monk, who defends the wisdom of the Catholic Church;* Galileo, *scene 8.*)

VOICE OF WEKWERTH: That is treason.

VOICE OF PALITZSCH: Treason of whom?

VOICE OF WEKWERTH: Of reason.

VOICE OF PALITZSCH: Ah, Manfred, do you ever walk the streets.

VOICE OF WEKWERTH: Why should I. I know what is going on

    In our streets. And in the office buildings.

VOICE OF PALITZSCH: I see, you know. From your lips to God's ear.

VOICE OF WEKWERTH: That's far to go. Much too far for a voice.

    You see, there are things I do know which I

    Don't want to know, not anymore or not yet.

VOICE OF PALITZSCH: How long you'd like to wait for your knowledge.

WOMAN 2: Sometimes I'm really glad I am so old.

    Death's prime advantage is it lasts forever.

(*Rehearsal through the intercom. Marcus refuses the plebeians' demands for affordable corn;* Coriolanus; *Act I, scene 1.*)

VOICE OF WEKWERTH: Your cue: the price of grain. Reach for your sword.

    When you hear "price," you draw your sword.

    When someone wants to eat, you think of slaughter.

(*Rehearsal dialogue: Marcus conversing with Menenius; Act I, scene 1.*)

WOMAN 2: They're wet behind their ears, they know nothing.

    Children. Playing generals with cardboard

    Soldiers.

WOMAN 3:   They take what they can get.

    Horace is dead. He has worked in gold

    Or marble that his slaves hauled in for him.

We're working now, he knew it, with mere shit
And still need slaves to keep it moving.

WOMAN 2: I don't want to know this anymore.

WOMAN 3: Now he must go on living as two halves
The one of marble, and the other plaster.

WOMAN 2: Or quartered, like Orpheus by the plough.

WOMAN 1: Torn by the women.

WOMAN 3:   Those who've been rejected.

WOMAN 1: His head is swimming in the stream, though, and
Keeps singing.

WOMAN 3:   Who's still hearing him.

WOMAN 2:   The stream.

(*Rehearsal dialogue through intercom: Brutus and Sicinius discuss Marcus; Act I, scene 1.*)

VOICE OF PALITZSCH: Did he believe he was replaceable.

VOICE OF WEKWERTH: We wouldn't sit here, you, me, all of us
And do his work.

VOICE OF PALITZSCH: Are we doing it?

(*Enter the sculptor* FRITZ CREMER *with a trial cast of Brecht's steel coffin. Two* WORKERS *from the Hennigsdorf steel mill are carrying the coffin.*)

CREMER: I apologize, coffins aren't exactly my specialty. I'm a sculptor, and this is the first coffin I've done. I've forgotten to take the measurements. This is a trial cast. I need to know if the size is right.

WOMAN 2: (*Looks at the workers, points at one of them.*)
You.
(*The* WORKER *doesn't understand.*)
Could you, please, lie down and try it.
(*The* WORKER *doesn't understand.*)
In the coffin. To try it. It's only a trial. You've got the size.

WORKER 2: You couldn't afford a coffin like that.

WORKER 1: (*Lies down in the coffin.*)
I'm already in here.

WORKER 2:   Now you're distinguished.

WORKER 1: Your steel coffin is comfortable, poet.
What are you hiding from. Afraid of maggots.
Don't worry. At least they're not lying to you.

They do their work as we are doing ours.
Maybe you've loved yourself a bit too much
And your work. I do my work for money.
My fun starts after hours, beer and women.
It's time now to forget how they esteemed you,
This one or that one, poet. Death pays in cash.
(*He climbs out of the coffin.*)

WORKER 2: Are you drunk.

WORKER 1:   Am I? From what.

WORKER 2:   Did you
Talk in your sleep.

WORKER 1:   I didn't say a word.

WORKER 2: Who else?

WORKER 1:   The people's voice. Or the three witches.

(*Enter the* BURNING WOMAN.)

WORKER 2: A horse is kicking me.

WORKER 1:   Witch number four.
She burned to death in her hospital bed
Private insurance, at the Charité
She's got no lines. Singing is all she does now.

WORKER 2: Who told you that. How would you know about it.

WORKER 1: (*Sings with a foreign accent.*)
ROSE, OH ROSE, OH ROSE SO RED.

(BURNING WOMAN *laughs.* WOMAN 1 *cries.*)

WOMAN 2: Don't cry, you silly goose. I'm sorry. I know you loved him. At
least that's what you believe. Or his name that has befallen you like a
misfortune.
(WOMAN 1 *goes to the window.*)
But now he is dead and only a name written on a tombstone which was
a dog's piss-stone as he had wished it. Here, take a handkerchief. Wipe
the snot off, it'll cause wrinkles. The coffin fits.

(WOMAN 1 *hangs herself at the crossbeam of the window. No one takes notice except for the sculptor, who pulls a sketchbook from his coat and
starts to draw.*

Intercom: Rehearsal of Coriolanus. *Marcus, banished from Rome, curses the city and its people; he ends calling out for his mother; Act III, scene 2.)*

VOICE OF WEKWERTH: We'll cut the mother.

VOICE OF PALITZSCH: We can't pull that to
  An earlier spot.

VOICE OF SCHALL: Why not.

VOICES OF PALITZSCH AND WEKWERTH: It hurts the fable.

(*The three widows laugh.*)

WOMAN 2, WOMAN 3, BURNING WOMAN:
  When do we threesome meet again
  In lightning thunder, storm, and rain
  When the tumult has subsided
  Who's the winner was decided.

VOICE OF BRECHT: But they will say of me   He
  Has made proposals   We have not
  Adopted them   Why should we
  That shall be written on my tombstone and
  The birds shall shit on it and
  The grass shall grow over my name
  That is written on the tombstone   I want to be
  Forgotten by all a trace in the sand.

Party

An apartment in Frankenberg-in-Saxony. On the wall above the couch hangs a leather phallus.

ARCHITECT: My golden years, I won't spend them here in your workers' and
  farmers' state. I'm an architect. I want to build. I don't care about the
  What but I must determine the How, or I'm going to leave.

SCHUMANNGERHARD: You are going to build what we need. That's what we
  are paying you for. Our workers need housing. The right of housing is
  granted by the constitution.

ARCHITECT: Housing. Cement holes. Do you know what the people call
  your housing? P.O. boxes for workers. I could show you real housing.

SCHUMANNGERHARD: In the class enemy's papers.

ARCHITECT: Where else.

SCHUMANNGERHARD: P.O. boxes! With bathroom, hot water, and district heating. There wasn't anything like that before we came. Not for the worker. Not in Germany. We can't wait till we have the money to raise a palace for everyone. Or a house like yours here, Comrade architect.

MAYOR: Easy, easy. There's nothing we can't discuss.

SCHUMANNGERHARD: Not with me.

PROSSWIMMER: You can unpack your suitcases again. The beauty of Socialism is: What you build today, you can tear down tomorrow and build better.

MAYOR: A lot of water will have gone under the bridge before then.

SCHUMANNGERHARD: Not with us.

MAYOR: (*To the* ARCHITECT.) With us it's going upstream.

EBERTFRANZ: Communism will come, as surely as the amen in church.

MAYOR'S SON: Since you're into architecture right now: Do you know the story about building the tower. The Tower of Babylon. By Kafka. It's called *The City Coat of Arms*. It goes like this:

In the beginning, everything was quite in order during the building of the Tower of Babylon, yes, perhaps the order was too orderly, there was too much thought spent on guides, interpreters, housing for the workers, and a network of roadways, as if there were centuries of unlimited possibilities for work ahead. The opinion dominant at the time even went so far as to claim the work on the building could never proceed slowly enough; it wasn't necessary even to emphasize this opinion very much to prevent the putting down of foundations once and for all. The argument went like this The essential aspect of the whole enterprise is the idea of building a tower that would reach the heavens. Compared to this idea everything else is merely marginal. The idea once it is conceived in all its greatness, cannot disappear again; as long as there are human beings, there will be the strong desire to finish the building of the tower. In this regard there is no reason to worry about the future; on the contrary, the knowledge of humankind will increase, the art of architecture will have made considerable progress and will continue to make progress, a work detail we need a year to accomplish will a hundred years from now be done in maybe half a year, and better and more durable besides. Why then should we exhaust ourselves today, spending our strength to its limits? That would only make sense

if we could hope to complete the tower within the span of one gener-
ation. But that could no way be expected. It was rather conceivable
that the next generation with its much more sophisticated knowledge
would decide that the work of the preceding generation was bad and
tear down whatever had been built so far, as to begin it anew. Such
thinking paralyzed all energy, and there was more effort spent on the
building of the workers' housing than on that of the tower. Each group
from a specific region demanded the most beautiful quarter, which
caused quarrels that escalated into bloody skirmishes. These skir-
mishes never stopped; they provided a new argument for the leaders
that the tower, due to the lack of the necessary concentrated effort,
should be built very slowly or better yet, not at all, until a generally
accepted peace agreement existed. However, time wasn't simply spent
fighting; during the pauses the city was beautified, which in turn
caused new envy and new fighting. In this manner, the time of the first
generation passed, but those of the following generations were no dif-
ferent, only the sophistication of technology increased all the time and,
with it, the lust for fighting. In addition, by the second or third gener-
ation the lack of any reason whatsoever for building a tower that
would reach the heavens was recognized; but by now everyone had
become too closely connected to be able to leave the city. All the leg-
ends and songs created in this city are filled with a longing for a day
once prophesied, when the city shall be smashed with five blows in
quick succession by a giant fist. This is why the city chose a fist as its
coat of arms.

SCHUMANNGERHARD: You'd better keep an eye on your sonny there, Comrade Mayor, before his tongue gets burned. Or yours.

MAYOR: He reads a lot.

SCHUMANNGERHARD: Yes, the wrong books.

(*The* MAYOR'S SON *sits down on the couch, next to the* ARCHITECT'S WIFE.)

MAYOR'S SON: *My father is a burgher, my father is a burghermaster, my fa-*
ther is the master of a stool my father is the master of the stool of all the
burghers. That's by Klabund. You are beautiful, Mrs. Hickel. (*Puts his*
hand on her breast.)

MRS. HICKEL: (*Brushes his hand off.*) You're still too young for this. Call me
Erika.

MAYOR'S SON: Erika. (*Again puts his hand on her breast.*) You know this one
. . . (*Whispers.* MRS. HICKEL *laughs.*)

ARCHITECT: Now he's spoiling my wife. (*Without turning around.*) You're
alright, Erika.

MRS. HICKEL: Thanks, Hans Joachim. Things couldn't be better.

ARCHITECT: She's a minx.

SCHUMANNGERHARD: (*To the* MAYOR.) Upstream. One day you'll gag on your
jokes.

MAYOR: I'm convinced of it.

PROSSWIMMER: Why don't we stop quarreling. After all, we're in the same
boat and if it tips over we all get wet. You, too, artist, with your leather
cock above your couch. At your age, do you need that. They'd string
us up by our heels. By our heels.

EBERTFRANZ: Our workers are with us. I know them.

PROSSWIMMER: And they know you, too. Did you forget what the old lathe
operator told you yesterday, after your speech about the workers state
when you had to hold on to the lectern because you were pissed, I
don't blame you for it, you've suffered enough, why shouldn't you get
pissed. Shall I write down for you what he said: When we're ready to
string you all up, I'm going to cut you down, Franz. That's what I'd call
true love.

SCHUMANNGERHARD: (*To the* MAYOR.) Before I forget it: the young people
complained, Mayor, that there's no portrait of Stalin in your office.

MAYOR: Who are the young people.

SCHUMANNGERHARD: The secretary of their Party group. And that isn't funny.
He demands that we put the issue on the agenda for our meeting next
Tuesday. Why is there no portrait of Stalin above your desk, Mayor.
What is your position concerning Comrade Stalin.

MAYOR: I know I'm not stronger than the Soviet Union. That's my position
concerning Comrade Stalin.

ARCHITECT: You should take me as a model. In my house Comrade Stalin
is hanging in a place where I've got plenty of time to think about my
relation to him and no one is going to disturb me.

SCHUMANNGERHARD: In the toilet, well, that's really the limit.

PROSSWIMMER: We're a funny crowd, aren't we. (*Sits down on the couch
between the* ARCHITECT'S WIFE *and the* MAYOR'S SON.) The young know
nothing of danger, do they. But maturity has its advantages. With us, it's
taking longer. Women appreciate that.

MAYOR'S SON: Until it's over.

(MRS. HICKEL *laughs.*)

EBERTFRANZ: Yes, that's the limit. To whom do you owe the diploma you
flaunt while you're mocking our housing program.

ARCHITECT: Who else but Comrade Stalin.

SCHUMANNGERHARD: Good that you know it.

ARCHITECT: How could I ever forget it.

SCHUMANNGERHARD: But the toilet is the limit.

MRS. SCHUMANN: Do you always have to fight. And about your politics. Be
glad you're doing all right. Gerhard, I think we should go, the children.

SCHUMANNGERHARD: The children are asleep, and we'll go when I say
we'll go.

MRS. SCHUMANN: Later you'll be drunk again.

SCHUMANNGERHARD: I'll show you who's drunk. (*Chases the wife around
the table.*)

PROSSWIMMER: There we go again.

SCHUMANNGERHARD: I'll keep this up till the water boils in your asshole.

MAYOR'S SON: A penetrating glimpse into human sexuality. A Communist at
work on women's liberation.

(MRS. SCHUMANN, *bawling, runs from the room.* SCHUMANNGERHARD *sits
down.*)

EBERTFRANZ: Do you know the Ballad of the Red Blacksmith.

ARCHITECT: Maybe he had better lie down. You want to lie down, Franz.

EBERTFRANZ: (*To the* MAYOR'S SON.) You want to hear it, junior.

MAYOR'S SON: I can't wait.

PROSSWIMMER: It's forty-eight verses.

EBERTFRANZ: Twenty-four. (*Climbs with great effort onto the table and begins to recite the "Ballad of the Red Blacksmith" while he is precari-
ously balancing on the table top.*)

PROSSWIMMER: I can't stand this one more time. Not again. (*Goes to the
radio and turns it on. News of the Twentieth Party Congress of the
Communist Party of the Soviet Union. Khrushchev's speech about
Stalin's crimes.* EBERTFRANZ *is petrified on the table. Silence.*)

MAYOR: (*Laughs.*) Stalin, leader of nations.

MAYOR'S SON: *As morning dawned he saw himself with their eyes
Painted with cattle blood, meat in his hands
And still not quenched his thirst for other blood.*

He went to the seashore, alone with his
Red sword, 'round him the roaring laughter of
Both armies. Went, washed in the foreign surf,
Washed his sword, too, planted it hilt first,
The helper, firmly into alien soil, and
Soaking the shore with his own blood, he walked
Across his sword the long way into blackness.
(*Pause.*)
The Party, the Party, she's always right.

SCHUMANNGERHARD: (*Raising a threatening fist, walks toward the* MAYOR'S SON.) You want to prove the contrary to me. (*Goes back to the table and sits down.* EBERTFRANZ *climbs down and exits with a firm step.*)

ARCHITECT: (*Takes the leather phallus from the wall above the couch.*) Now I can hang him above the couch, my Stalin, where he belongs.

SCHUMANNGERHARD: All of you ought to be shot.

(*Silence.*)

MAYOR: HERE ON EARTH WE WANT TO BUILD
PARADISE ALREADY.

MAYOR'S SON: Without inferno no paradise. No heaven without hell. And Capitalism is the purgatory where the money is laundered.

SCHUMANNGERHARD: With blood.

MAYOR'S SON: Who cares. As long as it's clean. Except for the cattle in the stockyards, perhaps, with their last breath which feels shame facing the dead. The shame's name is solidarity.

PROSSWIMMER: (*To the* MAYOR.) Don't give your sonny any more booze. He's talking you out of house and home.

MAYOR'S SON: Out of louse and home.

MAYOR: What do you know.

(EBERTFRANZ *is heard screaming, stomping the floor, and tearing up paper. Then the toilet is flushed.*)

ARCHITECT: What's this now. He's gone crazy.

(ARCHITECT *and* MAYOR'S SON *exit.* SCHUMANNGERHARD *and the* MAYOR *get up and glare at each other.* ARCHITECT *and* MAYOR'S SON *return.*)

ARCHITECT: (*Throws shreds of torn paper on the table.*) That's what's left of Stalin. Comrade Ebert is hanging now in his place.

MAYOR'S SON: He has torn up the picture and flushed the shreds down the toilet. And hanged himself with his tie from the same hook. A miracle the tie didn't rip.

MAYOR: He's been skin and bones for some time now.

PROSSWIMMER: He always was against the mandatory necktie rule.

MAYOR'S SON: He's free of that rule now.

(SCHUMANNGERHARD *falls on his knees, puts his head on the table and cries.*)

MAYOR: Why are you bawling. His job will surely be yours now. You know why I envy him. He doesn't have to see you any longer, Comrade Schumann.

SCHUMANNGERHARD: I've lost two fathers.

MAYOR: Three, if I've been correctly informed about your C.V. The first was called Hitler, wasn't he.

MAYOR'S SON: Three fathers. No man could stand that. You'd like to hang yourself next to him. I'll get a rope for you. Your tie wouldn't hold your weight.

(SCHUMANNGERHARD *jumps to his feet, grabs a chair,* PROSSWIMMER *is holding him back. Curtain.*)

The Pink Giant

THE PINK GIANT: (*Masturbates at an oak tree, before him the corpses of a Russian officer's wife and her children.*)

Do you know me now? I am the Pink Giant, the Death of Brandenburg. That's what they call me in the papers. And nobody knows who I am. That is because I don't talk to anyone who isn't dead. AH HOW GOOD NOBODY KNOWS . . . My bride laughs at me when I'm standing before the mirror in a pink slip, and my father calls me a pervert. IF I HAD YOU I WOULD WANT YOU. In the army they were laughing about me when I couldn't make it over the top of the scaling wall. I'M SMELLING HUMAN FLESH SAID THE GIANT AND THE DAY AFTER TOMORROW I'LL FETCH THE QUEEN'S CHILD. The pink slip is my mother's. Mom is doing it now with the maggots. Forty-five the

Russians took her, twelve of them, my father stood by watching it. Now you know how it feels, Hail Stalin. Did you cry when he died, till your Young Pioneer's kerchief was dripping wet. Now it's your turn. BLOOD SAUSAGE SPOKE TO LIVER SAUSAGE. The coat is the army's, the army was my second mother. ROOKEDEGOOH THERE'S BLOOD IN YOUR SHOE. No one laughs about the Pink Giant.

(*He drags the corpses into the underbrush.*)

[DARK   COMRADES   IS   OUTER   SPACE
VERY DARK]

Sources Quoted
Heinrich von Kleist, *Prince Frederick of Homburg*
Friedrich Hölderlin, *Empedokles,* third version
Friedrich Hebbel, *The Nibelungs*
Franz Grillparzer, *The Foremother*
Bertolt Brecht, *The Life of Galileo*
Bertolt Brecht, *Coriolanus*
William Shakespeare/Heiner Müller, *Macbeth*
Franz Kafka, *The City Coat of Arms*
Heiner Müller, *Philoctetes*

Conversation in Brecht's Tower

A Dialogue

Conversation in Brecht's Tower (*Gespräch in Brecht's Turm*) is the edited transcript of a conversation which was videotaped on 16 October 1995. A slightly shortened version of the text was published in *Kalkfell / für Heiner Müller / Arbeitsbuch*, Berlin, 1996. The conversation between Heiner Müller and Ute Scharfenberg, a young dramaturge at the Berliner Ensemble, took place in the so-called tower room on the top floor of the Theater am Schiffbauerdamm's tower, a space quite separate from the theater's bustling offices of administration and dramaturgy and which Brecht used as a study.

In the fall of 1995, Heiner Müller had been invited to an international theater conference in Toronto, Why Theater, where he was going to appear in a public conversation with me. The recurrence of his cancer prevented his attendance, and he offered the video instead; it was shown at the conference with my translation and comments. Shortly after the taping, during which he suffered constant pain, Müller left for Munich to undergo chemotherapy. It was soon after his return to Berlin that he died, on 30 December 1995.

This text is the last of the many interviews and conversations Müller conducted and published. These dialogues stand in a tradition that began in classical Greece. It was revived during the Renaissance, adopted by the

European Enlightenment, and continued into the twentieth century when Brecht, among others, employed the form, for instance in his *Messingkauf* fragment. Müller liked the freedom to improvise and pursue a train of thought by way of spontaneous association, without being restricted through the discipline of writing. Most of all, he loved to talk and enjoyed the fun of intellectual sparring.

In *Conversation in Brecht's Tower* he constantly is shifting topics, sometimes returning to a previous argument, often veering off into the anecdotal or throwing in out-of-context quotations, which usually are paraphrased, in support of a particular argument. At times the reader may believe Müller is talking tongue-in-cheek, only to discover that his jokes have quite serious implications. In rambling fashion, he often raises issues he had discussed on previous occasions and contradicts or qualifies his earlier statements. But contradiction and provocation were part and parcel of the intellectual game he loved to play.

Two of the names mentioned are hardly familiar to non-German readers: Josef Szailer is an Austrian director who for many years headed an experimental theater company in Vienna, Angelus Novus, named after the hapless angel who appears in the writings of Benjamin and Müller. Szailer has staged texts by Müller and Brecht. Frank Castorf is the artistic director of the Volksbühne in what was East Berlin. His iconoclastic stagings of classic and contemporary works are very popular with young audiences while they tend to shock the more conservative spectators. He directed a number of Müller's plays, not each time to the author's liking, as we understand from the present text. Before Müller died, he had invited Castorf to stage a production of *The Task* at the Berliner Ensemble. The publishers of his writings in the USA to whom Müller refers in one of the anecdotes he used to illustrate a particular issue are Bonnie Marranca and Gautam Dasgupta of *Performing Arts Journal* and PAJ Books.

A final note: the transcript tries to preserve the informal quality of the exchange and Müller's often freewheeling ways with grammar and syntax.

C.W.

US: Mr. Müller, we are sitting in the tower room of the Berliner Ensemble. The tower room is famous; it was Bertolt Brecht's work place. —* Now you yourself are the artistic director of the BE. Do you have particular feelings about using this room?

HM: No, because you can't do your work in this theater. At any rate, you can't work here in peace and quite. Brecht could still do that since he had a separate entrance. It was, I believe, this door here. He could come and go without passing the doorman. It was a much better situation. — We should open that door again. As soon as you pass the stage door you won't be able to get your work done. But we are already deep into our topic, theater, now.

US: We have met here to make a contribution to the conference Why Theater in November of 1995, in Toronto. You were invited to speak at the conference. — What did you think when you heard the title "Why Theater?"

HM: I believe the only way to figure out what the answer could be would take a year — but it has to be year — when all the theaters in the world are closed. You could continue to pay the employees, here they are paid in any case. But there would be no theater for a whole year. Afterwards, maybe, we would know "why theater." We would see what had been missed and if it had been missed at all. It might happen that people would become used to it during that year, and could do very well without theater. I remember, for instance, a story the publisher of my American translations once told me. The couple owns a country house, somewhere north of New York City, and one day their neighbors asked what sort of work they did, she and her husband, who is her partner in the publishing house. She said they were involved in the theater, and the neighbors had no idea what theater was. They weren't illiterates but fairly well-off middle-class Americans, yet, they didn't know what that is. Then she tried to describe for them in quite simple terms what is theater. There is a stage and people enter and play other people, and they behave as if they were these others and play their story. And in front of the stage, there are people sitting who watch it all and like it or dislike it, and at the end they applaud or don't. Then the neighbor's wife had understood: "Oh yeah, TV!" She knew: it's

*Spaced dashes indicate pauses.

television — It may not be quite like that in Europe [*laughs*] but it is slowly moving in that direction.

US: Why is it that the arts of all things are always asked to justify their existence? And is there a hope expressed by it? Or which kind of a distrust?

[Pause. H.M. lights a cigar, dips it in whiskey, smokes.]

HM: If we take a very long view, we could talk about Bataille. There is a scheme that Bataille worked out, and it might be quite interesting as a point to start from. It differentiates two types of civilization. There is the civilization of economy, that is, for instance, the European and also the U.S. civilization. These are civilizations of economy, directed toward efficiency and defined through money or the value of money. And then there are civilizations of prodigality. Such as the old Indian cultures in Mexico and Peru. But also Egypt, Babylon, Assyria. And these civilizations of prodigality are, of course, also associated with certain rituals, there is human sacrifice, which also takes place in our civilization, however not as a ritual but by way of the increasing acceleration, traffic victims and so forth. And once in a while it needs a war. War functions like a safety valve; a mounting pressure is released. — But what I regard as interesting is the aspect of prodigality; and theater is prodigal. Theater is not cost-effective. If it is forced to become cost-effective, it has to sink beneath its standard and needs to direct itself toward the lowest standard of its audience. And it will arrive at a level where television simply functions more effectively, or the movies. If the theater can't remain something prodigal and luxurious, it cannot function anymore. But the civilization in which we are living is directed toward economy and not at all toward luxury or prodigality. Luxury is something that is rather concealed. There are a great many who live in luxury and others who live in the absolutely opposite condition. But luxury is rather hidden away. You don't flaunt it.

US: Yet, prodigality is also the Land of Cockaigne, is utopia. — You are now the director of a theater. Did this change your view of theater and of making theater? And your view of writing?

HM: I don't know. What has changed is perhaps merely that I have less time to think about it. That's the reason I can't honestly answer the question.

[Pause.]

US: Germany has been reunited for five years. You once said you are addressing your texts to an audience whose experience is articulated by these texts. On occasion of a production of *The Task* in West Germany, another country at the time, you wrote that you were struck by the fact that the West German audience dealt in a different way with the text, or had a different distance form the text, than the East German audience who had shared the experience of the socialist experiment. You said in this context, the texts are addressed at a specific audience. What kind of an experience do you have with your texts now? Are they tied to their own period and their own audience or will they still be understood? Do they still work?

[Pause. He smokes.]

HM: I believe that it's quite similar to the general evolution. World War II was a war fought for the work force, and the wars that are happening now—including those that are fought in a civilian, a peaceful or seemingly peaceful, fashion—these are wars for the workplace, for jobs. And whether a text can work depends on it's being able to find a workplace. Theaters are difficult workplaces these days, not only in Germany. There are enough workers, but the theater as a workplace has become problematic.

US: I often have been asked in Canada if we East Germans are happy now after having been reunited with West Germany. However, East Germany has been subjected to a radical provincialization in the way it is being deindustrialized. Many people experience a process of radical social decline in quite a precipitous fashion. People are living here under a powerful pressure of experience. It has been said that pressure of experience is the prerequisite for poetry and for the arts in general. — How can the theater deal with the pressure of experience felt by its audience?

HM: I don't actually believe in this pressure of experience. The pressure is caused instead by the media industry's massive efforts to prevent any experience. What is happening is more a process of erasing experience. It is basically like the phenomenon Walter Benjamin once described: The essential aspect of World War I was the battle of war materiel. That was the actual experience. And the remarkable aspect was that the survivors couldn't talk about it at all. It didn't become an experience because the pressure was so enormous that it couldn't be made into an experience. And quite a similar observation is what Ernst Jünger wrote, I believe in *Total Mobilization*: There is a dimension of pressure which is so over-powering that it isn't felt at all as pressure but creates a feeling of dizziness, and this dizziness is the illusion of freedom. For instance, the ever-increasing complexity and also the ubiquity, to use a polite expression, of bureaucracy is much more powerful, much more prominent in a democratic society than in any one of the former Eastern dictatorships. That is what we experience right now.

US: You once told me about an encounter in a bar, a young man who actually hated Germans, as he himself said, and whose precept was: "Anyway, I can't do a thing: I simply wriggle through life." He painted a world brimful of trip wires and traps, where he, the steadfast tin soldier afloat on his little barken raft, wiggles and waggles his way through the gutter. That is a world of total chaos. — You have claimed that the arts and the theater have to concern themselves with chaos, and you ask the question: How would the chaos function? "The efforts to impose an order have failed." That would also imply that an attitude such as Brecht's, namely that the world can be changed and that humans are capable of mastering history, has been refuted. — What sort of an attitude toward the world should the theater then assume?

[Pause.]

HM: Those are formulations that probably simplify the problem. "Mastering history"—that isn't quite what Brecht believed. It's not as simple as that. [Pauses. Smokes.] At bottom the issue is: Theater—if you regard the theater as one kind of media in a landscape of media—is the only site where things are still happening live. The spectator is physically present and the actor is physically present; it isn't a canned product. Every night it's different, though it is the same performance, the same staging, the same actors—even if it were the same audience: every night is different. There is one thing everybody could agree with in regard to the theater, whatever the differences in the audience may be, their different interests and different desires, there is one smallest common denominator, and that is actually the fear of dying, the fear of change, the final change is death, in the theater. — The basic element of theater is change and therefore theater is always dealing with death and is an exorcism, if it is good. And that's what people will never get from television or from movies. — Joseph Chaikin once put it this way: The specific essence of theater is not only the presence of the living actor and the living spectator but the presence of the dying actor and the dying spectator. Every moment you are alive is moving you toward death, you are living toward death; and at any time an actor on stage could die, through an accident or whatever, and a spectator, too, could die during a performance. When a television spectator dies, television won't notice it, the broadcast wouldn't be touched by it at all. That is something the theater cannot do. It is actually the advantage of the theater that it can't do this. In the theater, the human being isn't completely replaceable. If you have to recast a role you need to think carefully who might be right for it. You can't replace any actor with every other actor.

US: In Germany the dead are as numerous on stage as anywhere else. However, in the reality of history the dead were much more numerous here than in many other nations. Is the theater in Germany somehow special because of this? Is there something specifically different from, let's say, the theater in America or France?

HM: It's got nothing to do with that, if there is indeed a difference. What is different in the German theater has to do with German history. There never has been a completed revolution of the middle class in Germany. The surrogate for the French Revolution was the theater, beginning with Schiller. That is why the German theater system still is the most highly subsidized in the world. There is a larger density of theaters, that is, of theater buildings, in Germany than in any other European country, I believe, because it has been the surrogate for revolution. An emancipation in the spirit because it didn't happen in reality. It is [what has often been called] the "German Misery" but it's also an opportunity. In England the theater never played such a role; the Puritans closed the theaters. In Germany the theaters were necessary to channel revolutionary and criminal energies and to transform them into affirmative ones.

US: Is the theater a medium of enlightenment? Could it ever be such a medium and has it been effective as such? And if yes, if it has, is it still in the same position today? Or, which deficiencies did such a position incur?

HM: I think there isn't much to be gained anymore by using those terms. Enlightenment? That was always very debatable. For instance, I thought a recent polemic by Godard was very good. He was nominated for the New York Film Critics Circle Award and turned it down, among other reasons with the argument: he didn't succeed in preventing the reconstruction of Auschwitz by Steven Spielberg. Therefore he didn't deserve the prize [smiles], because he hadn't been capable of preventing that film. If a movie such as Spielberg's *Schindler's List* is considered to be enlightening, then enlightenment is rather a palliative or a falsification—whatever.

US: The film triggered a considerable euphoria in Germany. Classes of schoolchildren were taken by the busload to watch it.

HM: Schindler was a good German. That way it is possible to live with Auschwitz. "There were good Germans, too." It's boring. — But the idea itself, to reconstruct in a movie events like those, is obscene. And the theater's potential to remind us of such events is actually to be silent about them. Silence. There was an experiment once, I don't know by whom, that actors in the middle of their text, in the middle of a play, simply stopped, didn't move, and for five or ten minutes nothing happened. That should be tried again. What is going to happen in the audience, who is going to leave, who will protest, how will people respond if there is only silence? Actually, silence has always been the foundation of theater. Without silence you won't notice that people are talking. Without silence you won't hear a text at all. Whoever can't hear the silence, doesn't hear the text. That is why there isn't much gained by questions like: is there enlightenment or not? The theater is a conjuring of the dead rather than a medium of enlightenment.

US: What you are describing are perhaps two different ways of opening up an experience, a collective experience. Spielberg is doing it by way of a trivial description and this other experiment would rather be an effort— and this may be a far-fetched example—to let the myth speak as Attic tragedy did. Is the theater from the beginning present in the myth, as a germ if you will? And does it offer us therefore an occasion to make us comprehend an overwhelming experience first as a myth and then explore the experience further in the theater?

HM: Maybe it's quite a different problem. The trend is, in any case in the entertainment industry, in fashion, indeed in all of industry, to create novelty. The problem is always to manufacture something that is new, and this always implies displacing or forgetting or eliminating something old. This also means that the new is always the absolute present and there is no future. And when there is again something new, *this* will be the present, and there is again no future, and then there is again something new and again no future [laughs], only the present. If you apply this to the theater it would be the death of theater. Every innovation changes the way we look at everything, at every tradition. But every innovation also grows from tradition and can only be made and also be perceived in the context of tradition and, perhaps, of an expectation of something else. And in this respect the myth, or a specific myth, may be of interest. When you write or talk about Stalingrad, you think of the Nibelungs if you grew up in Germany; you think of Rosa Luxemburg if you grew up in the GDR—and all that belongs to this complex "Stalingrad." You also think of Stalin, of course, and everything connected with that. But it is interesting only in such a context, not as the isolated event.

[Pause.]

US: After all you have said about the theater, a question: Is its place on this time-arrow past-present-future, or does the theater belong to some other site?

[Pause. He smokes.]

HM: In the theater there is neither a past, nor a present, nor a future. It is a different time-space, and what is happening on stage always happens, if it's good, in the context of things which already have happened, which already have been made. And it also is never sufficient, you arrive at a border, at a point where you can think ahead if you are lucky, and it really works: where that which you have seen doesn't satisfy you anymore. At issue is actually how you are going to produce this dissatisfaction, this inadequacy. It is never fully achieved, because you never really get as far as you have imagined. There always remains a "rest to be carried," and it is this rest that enables you to continue with your work. There is no perfect theater, there is no perfect performance. And the idea of achieving a perfect performance, an effort at which people, like for instance, Peter Stein, failed—his idea to do Chekhov the way Stanislavsky would have done it under ideal conditions—that idea turns the theater into a mausoleum. It's dead.

US: So, the theater exists only as an enterprise of demolition, like a deserted building site, if you will. "Theater is a projection into the future or it won't amount to much." It is always unfinished.

HM: Something like that, yes, yes.

US: I have just read a conversation you conducted with [the Austrian director] Josef Szailer, in 1992, and what struck me as an important thought was: "Theater needs to be put in doubt." You argued like this: Theater won't be able to exist anymore if it claims a time that has nothing to do with the real time outside, and if it is a space that has nothing in common with the life outside.

HM: I could at any time state the opposite, too. I believe, the opposite is also true, that the theater has to maintain another kind of time, another concept of time. For instance, in the theater you can slow down actions, you can accelerate them — both ways offer an estranged view of the action. Insofar was my statement a bit misleading because I put it in such apodictic fashion.

[Pause.]

US: Theater understood as an autonomous space, which was the project of many theater concepts since the turn of the century, would then be the idea of treating events on stage by making them strange. Taking them out of their context and treating them as separate entities.

HM: Well, I would now say that the strangest things are actually the most beautiful ones. Theater needs to be beautiful. Even when you represent horror or atrocities, it has to be beautiful or it won't be strange. [Smiles.] The strangest thing in our reality is beauty. And it is the greatest provocation. That may sound very odd but I think it has to be added here. After all, you won't create anything if you don't have a desire for beauty. Dissatisfaction with the world, dissatisfaction with reality is the source of all inspiration, be it in the theater or the fine arts or literature. If you are pleased with the world as it is, you don't need to create anything, you can lean back and rest. If you would like to see another world, you would like something different; you'd like everything to simply exist according to the golden mean. That is interesting with Castorf's work: all his good productions are staged completely according to the golden mean. [Smiles.] If it's potato salad or shit that is thrown across stage, if they dance on broken eggs, it is done according to the golden mean, and that is the power of his work if it is good.

US: That is the "principle of hope," . . .

HM: Well, what do I know. [Pauses. Smokes. Drinks.] But there is also— you know this line by Rilke that has been quoted ad nauseam: "The beautiful is the beginning of the horror we can barely suffer." But that is also the power of the beautiful, that the horror is hiding behind it, that it will end — at least for the individual. And the more beautiful something is, or the more you think something is beautiful or see its beauty, the harder it is to take leave of it. And that is the real provocation.

US: That dispenses with my last question: Is the theater dying, and how long will it be doing so? Well, the theater has already died. — It is dying all the time, it's always in the process of dying and then in one of reconstruction again.

HM: Well, the only real question, the one behind all of this . . . For instance, there was a production of *Mauser,* which unfortunately I didn't see but read reports about, in a penitentiary in Bogota, I believe, or maybe in Argentina, I'm not quite sure. It was a penitentiary mainly for murderers who had been sentenced to death. Some social worker staged and performed *Mauser* with them. And it was an extraordinary experience for all of them, since the play is about killing, and it became absolutely clear to me, the essential borderline. — You have to think about it: What does it mean if you cross that border. — in the play someone is executed—fictitiously of course, theater is fiction—and afterwards he can step to the footlights and accept the applause. Let's assume you would make such a performance into a ritual: There is someone who has been sentenced to death, and he plays the person who is killed at the end, and he is really killed — What would that mean, such a crossing of the borderline? It's the same problem you have with the sexual act on stage. It is faked, it's indicated, and everyone is greatly amused. It's a kind of macho amusement, most of the time. This became especially evident in Castorf's production [of Müller's play *The Battle,* which Castorf coupled with a German farce of the '30s, *Pension Schoeller*]. People laughed like a bunch of drunken soldiers—deeply disgusting. But let's assume this would actually be done for real. Something quite peculiar is created then. I don't know if this is correct, but it is a central question we have to put to the theater: There will be gladiator games again in the not too distant future. There will be performances where people will be actually killed. There is already an indication of this in television, everything is moving in that direction: reality TV. What will that mean for the theater? Will the theater become part of it, will it be integrated or will it find another route and remain symbolic? That is the essential question. [Smokes.]

And the other question is — there is this crazy Californian with a kind of surfer philosophy, who figured out that in the year 2012 all the laws of physics will be suspended, that is, the space-time continuum won't exist anymore, only virtual reality and only spiritual communication. That will make art dispensable; that is, everyone will be an artist. [Laughs.] A technological variant of Marx's utopia that everyone will become, among other things, an artist in a communist society, only this won't be a communist society but one defined by robots. Yet, this is a problem the theater should already pay attention to right now. For instance, it is thinkable that there will be plays — I became aware of this with *Hamletmachine.* When I wrote the text, I had for the first time — no, it wasn't the first time, that was with *Mauser* — I had no idea whatsoever how it could be realized on stage, not the slightest idea. There was a text, and there was no space in my imagination for the text, no stage, no actors, nothing. It was written in a kind of soundproof zone, and that has been happening with me increasingly. It was the same with *Hamletmachine;* there are those desperate stage directions that are impossible to realize, a symptom of my inability to imagine ways to realize them and see the space where these events could happen. That means these are at bottom plays or texts whose only place of action is my brain or my head. They are performed here, within this skull. How do you do that on a theater stage? That is at the core of Artaud's theater provocation, which is hardly a theory and has simply become a method. A theater made of brain currents, of nerves in your skull. But, as I have said, this remains an open question for me, I don't know where it will lead to. You can only discover the answers when you are grounding the work strictly in the text and insist on the text; then certain constraints will appear which may lead to new forms of theater or a new way to manipulate a theater space. — But without this step into an absolute darkness, the absolutely unfamiliar, the theater cannot continue. The worst aspect of theater is the pressure which is, of course, economic pressure that forces people . . . For instance, in quite primitive terms, if you are a stage director and somewhat prominent, that is, you make a lot of money with each of your productions, you need to make much more money to be able to pay your taxes. And so you make one production, two, three, four, five, six, or even eight a year. No person can do that without losing creativity and the potential for innovation. After a time it will become merely a routine, that is to say, everyone does what he does well. Theater won't be interesting at all unless you do what you cannot do. That is the only way something new can be created. But the whole system is structured to prevent that. The system forces people to stick with what they do well and do what they can do well. That means they'll do it increasingly less well and their work will get weaker every time around. The only way out is that you create situations for yourself. — For instance, I have read this today and found it quite appealing that Thomas Bernhard intentionally incurred enormous debts to be motivated to write. You need such kind of an enforcement. You always need pressures which push you to enter the unfamiliar, the darkness, without a torchlight. That is still possible in the theater. It isn't possible at all anymore in the technological media because of the huge amount of money involved and the huge apparatus; nothing really innovative can be created anymore there. [Pause.] But since the theater is essentially based on its dealing with living human beings, it is still possible there. "Of all there is the most unfamiliar one is the human being." [Pause. Drinks. Laughs.] One of those unfathomable dicta.

us: This theater that happens only within the head is, of course, removed from the market in a most radical manner. — But there is still, on the other side, what Brecht once signified as the natural theater in his essay *Street Scene*. That is, the theater which is happening every day between people, since people are social beings and are only able to live by living with each other and communicating with each other. What about that? That could never disappear in virtual reality, could it?

HM: I believe that is changing. I recall, for instance, the first time I was in New York. To begin with the first impression of New York: "You already know all this from the movies." And then you go to a coffee house or a bar, and the people who are sitting there, drinking and talking, you know them all, too, from the movies. I believe one thing that Brecht always very much fought against: the theater deriving its direction from theater instead of from reality, isn't going to work anymore; because reality derives its direction increasingly from virtual reality, that is from movies and television. When I think of children, of my little daughter, for instance, they sit several hours each day before the TV or watch videos. How shall they differentiate between this virtual reality and reality? It becomes at a very early age for them the real thing, and they will behave like Happy Max, or whoever these characters are, and reality is directed by its representation instead of the other way around. And eventually the reality will disappear in the representation; you have to think of it as its extension. That is what this crazy Californian meant with the disappearance of reality in virtual reality when everything has become nothing but art.

US: But reality has the advantage that it offers also what I would call the dwarf-like. You really enjoy it when you see people who are hunchbacked or toothless or cross-eyed, and you are tempted to treat them in a voyeuristic manner. You don't have that in virtual reality, there are only plastic faces that look as if they were made in a test tube. It' s all the same and you get simply tired of it. I don't believe this temptation is going to die out, namely to enjoy the spectacular, the spooky and the dwarf-like.

HM: I think the trend of television is to depict ever more reality, and ever more of it in its totality. That is quite inevitable. And it will replace the voyeuristic view at reality. I find it interesting that in Japan it is still outlawed to show the handicapped on television. There are no blind people on Japanese TV, no deaf-mutes, no cripples. It is forbidden. It is an effort to prevent something [Laughs] that can't be prevented at all. [Laughs.] Exactly in the sense you just mentioned, voyeurism will be introduced at some point, and then you'll watch those cripples much better on TV, and seeing them on TV provides a much greater satisfaction to the voyeur. The camera can move around and show the feet in close-up, one at a time . . .

US: . . . and they let them speak on command . . .

HM: . . . and let them speak on command. It is much more impressive; you can't escape it.

US: And yet, I still believe that the desire to tell fables and experience stories will always remain. That has also been shown in experiments where fragments were produced, in a most radical fashion, and then the spectators were asked what they had seen. Everyone created for himself a story from what he had watched. I don't believe this is going to disappear. I believe it is an essential human desire or a means of survival.

HM: [Nods.] Mmh. From your lips to God's ear. [Laughs.] By the way, a nice story. I have forgotten the name of the author, some science fiction writer. He describes a scene where a space ship, having lost its way on a long journey, discovers somewhere in outer space an enormous skeleton. It is thirty miles long and fifteen miles wide, and it is God. That is the conclusive proof that God is dead. It's very silly [laughs], but I think it is a good yarn.

US: Is there anything you haven't been asked? Or that I haven't asked but you'd like to say?

[Pause.]

HM: Difficult, difficult. [Pauses. Smokes. Smiles.] Actually, no, I've been asked just about everything. — One thing might still be important. I'm just reading this peculiar book. It's based on a philosophy of management, an effort to create an orderly system and to derive some rules from it for management. It is quite cynical and quite intelligent, and it presents a thesis I found very interesting: In every institution people are in pursuit of solutions, solutions to problems. But that is a completely unrealistic approach, because the problem really is that there are many available solutions but not enough problems. [Laughs.] The issue is rather to create problems, to find problems and then enlarge them out of proportion; then you'll find the solutions automatically, they are waiting in any trash bin. What is missing are the problems. This means, of course, that you also need an awareness of problems. I believe this is quite correct, especially for the theater. The people in a theater system like Germany's receive their regular salary, are permanently employed and have no money problems. — It is, of course, never enough but you get your money every month. There is no danger, no existential threat anymore, and consequently there are no problems. The issue is to confront these people with problems, to make their work a problem for them, so that they'll become interested in solutions after all. I think this is important. — There is also the story of the boiled frog. I don't know if you know it. It is used [laughs] as a parable for management philosophy. If you throw a frog into hot water—and this is true, it has been proved—he tries, of course, to get out as quickly as possible. If you place a frog into lukewarm water and raise the temperature gradually, then he happily boils to death. He is being cooked while feeling enormously well and won't even notice it. He simply doesn't get it. [Laughs.] That is a parable for the life in our contemporary societies [laughs] and, of course, also for the theater, being a little model of our society. [Laughs.] The frog that has been cooked.

US: To turn the conclusion around: Nothing is as deadly as a theater that functions to perfection.

HM: Yes, exactly. All this clamor about "the crisis of the theater," over and over again; these great debates: "the theater in crisis." Theater *is* crisis. It is the definition of theater—or should be. It can only function as crisis and in a crisis, or it has no relation whatsoever to the society outside the theater walls.

Late Poems
1992–1995

These poems were published posthumously in *Kalkfell / für Heiner Müller / Arbeitsbuch,* Berlin, 1996; some of the poems had appeared in various books, playbills, and journals; and they all were included in *Heiner Müller: Die Gedichte,* Frankfurt am Main, 1998. Frank Hörnigk, the editor of the forthcoming complete edition of Müller's writings, observed that Müller "found his own language almost exclusively in poems during the last decade of his life." The author dated nearly every poem during those years, a change from his previous habit of rarely if ever dating his texts.

As the first poem's title, *Coronary Vessel,* indicates, most of them explore the many faces of a death Heiner Müller knew he had to confront in the near future. Only a few of the poems respond directly to historical events during the time Müller was slowly dying of cancer, and these events also revealed faces of death, be it the genocide of Bosnia's civil war or the *fin de partie* of socialism.

In many of his writings Müller referred to the image he saw in the mirror—an image we all are seeing in our mirrors. He felt it is the face of the enemy. Now, there was no face looking back anymore: "The glass stays empty." Death wiped the mirror blank.

C.W.

Coronary Vessel

The doctor shows me the x-ray THAT'S THE SPOT
SEE FOR YOURSELF now you know where God lives
Ashes the dream of seven masterpieces
Climb three flights and the Sphinx bares her claw
Be glad if the cardiac arrest strikes you unawares
So there won't be one more cripple cruising the landscape
Blizzard in the brain Lead in the veins
What you wanted to ignore TIME IS A DEADLINE
On the ride home the trees: a shameless green

Birth of a Soldier*

On the TV screen a soldier from England
Counting the corpses in a Bosnian village
He cries beneath the blue helmet. With the next glance
I see how his jaws are grinding
A wolf who bares the teeth
The grimace his last salute to humanity

Vampire

The masks are worn out fin de partie
Proletarian and killer Farmer and soldier
No sound escapes from borrowed mouths
Dispersed the power against which my verse once
Crashed like the surf in rainbow colors
In the teeth's fence the final scream has died
WELCOME TO WORKUTA COM(M)MISSAR
Where walls stood mirrors now surround me
My gaze is searching for my face The glass stays empty

*Asterisks indicate lines written in English in the original.

Thinking about Michelangelo

He who couldn't find his way out of the stone
                              Seized by
The Borgias
                    Plagued by parasites
On the flayed man's skin askew his face
He loved other matter than the stone
The sex in the marble

Blackfilm

The visible
Can be photographed
O PARADISE
OF BLINDNESS
What still can be heard
Is canned
PLUG UP YOUR EARS SON
The feelings
Are of yesterday Nothing new
Is being thought The world
Evades its description
All things human
become alien

Showdown*

In a cage of glass we saw them stand
The killer and the victim unbeknownst
To each other and still unaware of who
Would kill whom caged in glass they stood
With others we stared greedy to behold
The victim's neck gripped by the killer's hand
Death is the stuff we build our cities from

That only fear of dying holds together
And hope that we still breathe when morning dawns
No one can rise if no one else will fall
The places marked the Where the When
The shore won't worry if the boat is smashed
Inside the glass the war starts Man against man
The rent is paid with the last choking hold
Better for cash than wild in the darkest woods
Man—and be it on the ghostly boat
That's rocking deep down in his breast—
As killer only he achieves the final luster
The voyeur's fear To die and not to know
Which hand did break like glass whose neck
The rest is called Abyss Horror or Lust
In this or in another land

Theaterdeath

An empty theater. On stage is dying
A player according to his art's demands
The dagger in his neck. His lust exhausted
A final solo courting the applause.
And not one hand. In a box, as empty
As the theater, a forgotten robe
The silk is whispering what the player screams.
The silk turns red, the robe grows heavy
From the player's blood that pours out while he dies
In the chandelier's luster that blanches the scene
The forgotten robe drinks empty the veins of
The dying man who now resembles no one but himself
Neither lust nor terror of transfiguration left
His blood a colored stain of no return.

Empty Time

My shadow of yesterday
Has been burnt by the sun
In a tiresome April

Dust on the books

At night
The clocks run faster

No wind from the sea

Waiting for nothing

CHRONOLOGY

1929   Heiner Müller is born 9 January in Eppendorf, Saxony. His father was a low-level Social-Democrat Party functionary, his mother a factory worker.

1933   Hitler appointed chancellor 30 January. Heiner's father arrested and interned in a concentration camp. Released after a year, he is for a long time without employment. Mother works in a textile factory. After being banned from Eppendorf, the family lives with the father's parents in Bräunsdorf.

1938   The Müllers move to the town of Waren in Mecklenburg, northern Germany, where the father is hired as an accountant.

1939   World War II begins. Heiner enters high school and also has to join the Jungvolk, a branch of Hitler Youth. He tries his hand at writing ballads.

1940   Father briefly under arrest again.

1944   Heiner is drafted into the paramilitary Labor Service but sees little military action.

1945   Hitler commits suicide 30 April. Germany capitulates. After briefly being a POW of the U.S. army, Heiner walks home to Waren. His father is appointed deputy county administrator. Heiner works at the county office.

1947   Father appointed mayor of Frankenberg in Saxony. Heiner continues high school.

1948   After finishing high school, Heiner works as a librarian; he submits a radio play for a playwriting contest.

1949   Germany is divided into Federal Republic of Germany and German Democratic Republic. Bertolt Brecht returns to Berlin and founds Berliner Ensemble. Heiner continues working at the Frankenberg city library. He attends a writers workshop.

1951   Parents defect to West Germany after the father suffered in-
        creasing pressure from the Soviet authorities, among other
        things for the collapse of a new building in Frankenberg.
        Heiner stays in the GDR and moves to Berlin, where he ekes
        out a meager living as a journalist and literary critic. He mar-
        ries a young nurse, who is pregnant with his child; the mar-
        riage ends in divorce after a few years.

1953   Stalin dies 5 March. 17 June: Workers rise against the govern-
        ment in East Berlin, the uprising spreads quickly across the
        GDR but is quickly crushed. Heiner is employed by the Writers
        Association; he meets Inge Schwenker, a writer. They marry in
        1955.

1956   In February, Khrushchev denounces Stalin's crimes; officially
        Stalinism ends. Brecht dies 14 August. In October, a Hungarian
        revolution first succeeds but then is defeated by the Red Army.
        Heiner becomes a staff writer with a cultural journal.

1957   The play *Ten Days That Shook the World* (after John Reed), by
        Heiner Müller and Hagen Müller-Stahl (not a relative), opens at
        Berlin Volkbühne.

1958   *The Scab* and *The Correction* premiere. Heiner is appointed
        dramaturge at Maxim Gorky Theater, Berlin.

1959   Heiner and Inge Müller receive Heinrich-Mann-Prize for *Scab*
        and *Correction.*

1961   The Berlin Wall is erected in August. In October Müller's
        play *The Resettled Woman* is closed after one preview for
        "counter-revolutionary tendencies." Heiner is expelled from
        the Writers Association. His work can be neither published
        nor performed. For several years he has to live on royalties for
        a radio play (a detective story) he wrote under an assumed
        name.

1965   The play *The Construction Site* can be published but is sharply
        attacked for ideological deviance at a plenum of the Socialist
        Unity Party's Central Committee.

1966   Inge Müller commits suicide.

1967   Müller's Sophocles adaptation *Oedipus Tyrant* opens at Berlin
        Deutsches Theater. During rehearsals he meets Ginka Tschola-
        kova, a Bulgarian theater student whom he marries in 1970.

1968   The Sophocles adaptation *Philoctetes* premieres with great suc-
        cess in Munich. It will become one of Müller's most performed

plays. In August, the armed forces of the Soviet bloc invade Czechoslavakia; its reformist government is deposed.

1969   *Lanzelot,* an opera by Paul Dressau with Müller's libretto, opens at Berlin State Opera. His translation of Aeschylus's *Prometheus* premiers in Zürich.

During the 1960s Müller completed also the plays *Heracles 5, The Horatian, Women's Comedy* (based on a radio play by Inge), and *Horizons.*

1970   Heiner is appointed dramaturge at the Berliner Ensemble; he writes *Mauser.*

1971   *Germania Death in Berlin,* a play Müller began in the '50s, is completed. He adapts *Macbeth,* it is performed in the GDR, West Germany, and Switzerland. Honecker becomes head of party and state in the GDR.

1972   *Macbeth* triggers the first heated discussion of Müller's "nihilistic pessimism." The same year he writes *Zement* for the Berliner Ensemble.

1973   *The Horatian* opens in West Berlin, *Zement* at the Berliner Ensemble in East Berlin.

1974   Heiner revises two texts from the '50s: *Traktor* and *The Battle.* They are performed the following year.

1975   Müller is a writer-in-residence at the University of Texas, Austin, where he collaborates on the first production of *Mauser* with a student theater group. He travels widely in the U.S.

During subsequent years, he will pay several visits to the States and travel also to Mexico and the Caribbean.

1976   He is appointed dramaturge at the East Berlin Volksbühne, where *The Farmers* is staged. He writes *Gundling's Life Frederick of Prussia Lessing's Sleep Dream Scream.*

1977   Müller completes *Hamletmachine.*

1978   *Germania Death in Berlin* premiers in Munich.

1979   Heiner writes *The Task. Gundling . . .* premieres in Frankfurt, *Hamletmachine* in Saint Denis, France. The West German Mülheim Dramatists Prize is awarded to Müller.

1980   *The Construction Site* opens at the Volksbühne, where Heiner also directs for the first time himself, a staging of *The Task,* in collaboration with his wife, Ginka Tscholakova.

1981   *Quartet* is completed during an extended stay in Italy. Heiner and Ginka have been divorced.

1982	Premiere of *Quartet* at the Bochum Theater, staged by B. K. Tragelehn (who had directed, in 1961, the banned production of *The Resettled Woman*). Müller himself stages his *Macbeth* adaptation at the Volksbühne, in collaboration with Ginka. He also directs *The Task* at Bochum. *Despoiled Shore Medeamaterial Landscape with Argonauts* is completed.
1983	Premiere of *Despoiled Shore . . .* at Bochum Theater.
1984	Müller contributes text to Robert Wilson's production of *CIVIL warS* at the Cologne Theater. It marks the beginning of a close friendship and many collaborative efforts. He writes *Explosion of a Memory* (it is used by Wilson in his production of *Alcestis* at the American Repertory Theatre, Cambridge, Massachusetts, in 1986).

The first volume of Müller's writings in English, *Hamletmachine,* is published by Performing Arts Journal Publications, New York.

1985	The Shakespeare adaptation *Anatomy Titus Fall of Rome A Shakespeare Commentary* is premiered at the Bochum Theater. Heiner completes the first two segments of *Volokolamsk Highway,* one of which opens the same year at the Potsdam Theater. Robert Wilson stages *Hamletmachine* in New York and, a year later, in Hamburg. Müller receives the prestigious Georg Büchner Prize of the [West] German Academy for Language and Poetry, in Darmstadt.

Gorbachev becomes general secretary of the Soviet Communist Party; he soon begins to initiate reforms.

1986	Müller completes two more parts of *Volokolamsk Highway.* He receives the National Prize of the GDR.
1987	Müller contributes text for Wilson's production *Death Destruction & Detroit II* at the West Berlin Schaubühne. He becomes a resident director at Deutsches Theater.
1988	He stages *The Scab* at Deutsches Theater, inserting into the performance his texts *The Horatian* and *Centaurs* (part 4 of *Volokolamsk Highway*). The complete text of *Volokolamsk Highway* is premiered in Paris (as *La Route des Chars*) and, later, in Cologne.
1989	Heiner begins rehearsal for *Hamlet/Machine,* a combination of Shakespeare's play translated by Müller and his own 1977 text *Hamletmachine.* The GDR celebrates its fortieth anniversary in

October, while thousands have left the country for the West via Hungary and Czechoslavakia. In late October and early November, East Germans in many cities demonstrate for democracy and civil liberties. Honecker is deposed by his own Party. On 4 November, half a million Berliners attend a demonstration of artists and intellectuals at Berlin's Alexander Platz. Müller reads to the rally a "Call for Free Trade Unions" and is booed by many in the crowd. A few days later, the East German authorities open the Berlin Wall. Müller continues rehearsal for *Hamlet/Machine.*

1990   *Hamlet/Machine,* an eight-hour performance, opens at Deutsches Theater. Free elections in the GDR bring a multiparty government to power. In May, the Frankfurt Theater Festival "experimenta 6" is exclusively devoted to Müller's work; more than thirty different productions and concerts are presented. He is elected president of the Academy of the Arts in East Berlin. In October, Germany is reunited. Müller receives the Kleist Prize.

1991   He stages *Mauser* at Deutsches Theater, collaging the text with *Quartet* and the final segment of *Volokolamsk Highway, The Foundling.* Gives numerous interviews and tries to mediate the problems of unification of the East and West German Academies of the Arts. At the end of the year, the Soviet Union is dissolved. The Cold War ends with the triumph of capitalism and the establishment of a global market economy. Müller is awarded the European Theater Prize.

1992   Müller is invited to join the new directorate of the Berliner Ensemble as one of its five members. He publishes an autobiography, *War without Battle,* and writes *Mommsen's Block.* Heiner marries Brigitte Maria Mayer, an artist and photographer. Their daughter Anna is born in November.

1993   Müller stages *Quartet* and a collage of Brecht's *Fatzer* with his own texts *The Duel* and *Traktor* at the Ensemble. At the Bayreuth Wagner Festival, he directs *Tristan und Isolde.* He is accused of Stasi contacts but no proof of any denunciatory actions is found.

1994   The Berliner Ensemble suffers from frequent disagreements among its directors. Müller writes *The Night of the Directors* and works on the project of *Ajax. Mommsen's Block* premieres at Stanford University's Drama Department. Heiner is diagnosed with cancer; his esophagus is removed at a Munich hospital.

1995   Heiner recuperates during January and February as a guest of the Getty Foundation, in Los Angeles, where he completes a draft of *Germania 3*. After his return to Berlin, he is appointed artistic director of the Berliner Ensemble and directs Brecht's *The Resistible Rise of Arturo Ui*. He re-stages *Tristan* at Bayreuth. In November he undergoes chemotherapy in Munich for the cancer's recurrence.

Shortly after his return to Berlin, he succumbs to an attack of pneumonia, 30 December.

1996   First week of January, the Ensemble conducts seven days of readings from Müller's works. He is buried in the same cemetery as Brecht and Hegel. *Germania 3,* whose premiere he had planned to direct, opens at the Bochum Theater in May and at the Berliner Ensemble in June.

Library of Congress Cataloging-in-Publication Data

Müller, Heiner, 1929–1995
    [Selections. English. 2001]
    A Heiner Müller reader ; plays, poetry, prose / edited and
translated by Carl Weber.
        p.   cm.—(PAJ books)
    ISBN 0-8018-6577-8 (alk. paper)—ISBN 0-8018-6578-6
(pbk. : alk. paper)
    1. Müller, Heiner, 1929–1995—Translations into English.
I. Weber, Carl, 1925– II. Title.   III. Series.

PT2673.U29 A282 2001
823'.914—dc21   00-062732